SHERLOCK HOLMES

& THE TWELVE THEFTS OF CHRISTMAS

ALSO AVAILABLE FROM TIM MAJOR
AND TITAN BOOKS

Sherlock Holmes: The Back to Front Murder
Sherlock Holmes: The Defaced Men
Snakeskins
Hope Island

THE NEW ADVENTURES OF SHERLOCK HOLMES

Sherlock Holmes:
Cry of the Innocents
Cavan Scott

Sherlock Holmes:
The Breath of God
Guy Adams

Sherlock Holmes:
The Patchwork Devil
Cavan Scott

Sherlock Homes:
The Army of Dr Moreau
Guy Adams

Sherlock Holmes:
The Labyrinth of Death
James Lovegrove

Sherlock Holmes:
A Betrayal in Blood
Mark A. Latham

Sherlock Holmes:
The Thinking Engine
James Lovegrove

Sherlock Holmes:
The Legacy of Deeds
Nick Kyme

Sherlock Holmes:
Gods of War
James Lovegrove

Sherlock Holmes:
The Red Tower
Mark A. Latham

Sherlock Holmes:
The Stuff of Nightmares
James Lovegrove

Sherlock Holmes:
The Vanishing Man
Philip Purser-Hallard

Sherlock Holmes:
The Spirit Box
George Mann

Sherlock Holmes:
The Spider's Web
Philip Purser-Hallard

Sherlock Holmes:
The Will of the Dead
George Mann

Sherlock Holmes:
The Monster of the Mere
Philip Purser-Hallard

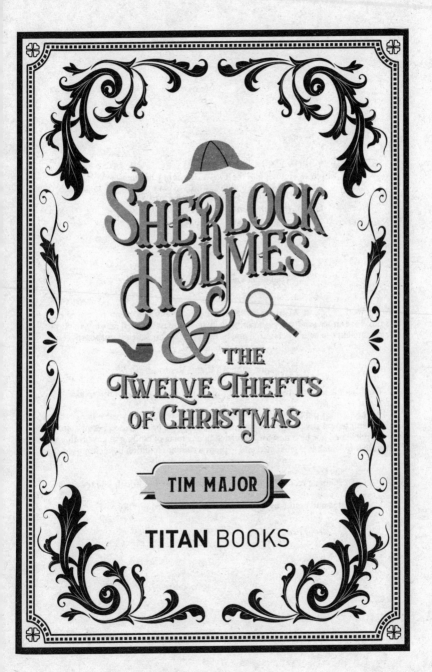

SHERLOCK HOLMES & THE TWELVE THEFTS OF CHRISTMAS

TIM MAJOR

TITAN BOOKS

Sherlock Holmes and the Twelve Thefts of Christmas
Print edition ISBN: 9781803361949
E-book edition ISBN: 9781803361932

Published by Titan Books
A division of Titan Publishing Group Ltd
144 Southwark Street, London SE1 0UP
www.titanbooks.com

First paperback edition: October 2023
10 9 8 7 6 5 4 3 2 1

A CIP catalogue record for this title is available from the British Library.

Printed and bound by CPI Group (UK) Ltd, Croydon, CR0 4YY.

For Rose

CHAPTER ONE

December 15th, 1890

The first flakes of snow had begun to fall, glowing under the lamps that had only recently been lit. By the time I rang upon the bell of No. 221b Baker Street they had become a flurry, and my shoulders were dusted with white.

The door was answered immediately by Mrs. Hudson, the steadfast landlady of the house. A rather sparse-looking wreath that hung from the door knocker rocked with the motion, and a sprig or two fell free.

"Dr. Watson!" she exclaimed, taking my gloved hand and kneading it. "I'm ever so glad you're here."

"Why?" I asked in alarm. The previous occasion she had expressed a need for me to come to Baker Street was at a time that Holmes had appeared fatally ill. Though his state had turned out to be a ruse related to a case, he had fooled not only his housekeeper, but myself to boot. At this moment I was singularly unprepared for any similar shock.

Mrs. Hudson's face fell. "Because it is Christmastime."

"Oh." Feeling rather foolish, I entered the hallway and made a show of knocking the snow from my jacket.

Mrs. Hudson remained at the doorway, gazing out at the street. I watched her from behind as she leaned on the door frame, her face tilting up to look at the meandering snowflakes.

"If I may say, you appear somewhat preoccupied," I said. During the years I had lived in these premises I had become fond of the landlady, and I was somewhat attuned to her behaviour. "Are you at all unwell at present, Mrs. Hudson?"

She stepped back, pushed the door closed gently, then turned to face me. Her expression was inscrutable. I saw that she was clutching some slips of paper to her chest, and wondered whether they might not be the cause of her malaise.

"Quite well," she said. "How is Mrs. Watson, may I ask?"

"Quite well," I said, then realised I had parroted her own words. I added, "She is very much looking forward to Christmas. The decorations have been hung, the lighted candles are placed in the windows daily, and any carollers are rewarded most generously. Mary adores the Yuletide season."

Mrs. Hudson nodded thoughtfully.

I could not think what to add. I glanced again at the emaciated wreath, then turned to the stairs that led up to Holmes's rooms. Uncertain whether Mrs. Hudson required more from our awkward conversation, I said, "Well, then. I had better..." and cleared my throat.

I retreated up the staircase, but Mrs. Hudson closed the door and followed me – quite unnecessarily given that I could hardly have forgotten the way, and there could be no reason that Holmes might require any announcement of my presence by a third party. So, it was I who knocked on his door, pushed it open and entered, and it was Mrs. Hudson who lingered behind me on the threshold as if she were the visitor and not I.

Sherlock Holmes was sitting in almost darkness. Though he was upon the sofa by the fireplace, the fire was not lit and the air within the sitting-room was decidedly colder than downstairs. Holmes's knees were drawn up to his chin and his arms wrapped around them, and he stared directly ahead at the empty chair opposite, his pipe protruding from his mouth like a sharp beak. He did not look at me and only seemed to register that he was not alone in the room when Mrs. Hudson tutted and began to clear breakfast dishes from the table. Even then, he only turned his head and watched me with a single raised eyebrow.

"How are you, Holmes?" I asked.

His only response was a shrug. He chewed on the stem of his pipe for several more seconds.

Then, most abruptly, a transformation overtook him. His limbs unfolded and he leapt from his seat. His eyes became alert and glistening.

"My good Watson!" he cried, taking my hand and shaking it rapidly. "What brings you to my door? I hope that you have something for me?"

"As a matter of fact, that is precisely the reason for my coming," I said, reaching into the inner pocket of my jacket to retrieve an envelope, which I offered to him.

Holmes tore open the envelope and unfolded the card within. His lips moved as he read the words: *Our Yuletide best wishes, with all love and friendship, Mary and John Watson.*

"It is a Christmas card," Holmes said blankly.

I laughed. "My word, Holmes! Your deductive facilities have no bounds." Then, noticing his crestfallen state, I said, "It is the done thing, to send Christmas wishes to one's friends, is it not?"

Once again, Holmes shrugged his shoulders. "I had hoped—" he began, then stopped.

Now I realised what he had meant by 'I hope you have something for me'. He had hoped not for a friendly gesture, but something to occupy his mind. I had witnessed his lethargy many times in between cases; his ability to all but shut down his bodily processes while waiting for something new to inspire his imagination. I wondered how long he had been sitting on the sofa, smoking and staring at the empty chairs which would be occupied by myself and by new clients.

He placed the card on the table in the centre of the room and wandered to the window. Outside, the snowfall was becoming ever denser.

"I suppose that you consider festive traditions to be meaningless, or even nonsensical," I said.

Without turning, Holmes said, "I have little stake in others' behaviour when it comes to such things. I appreciate that there are a good many rehearsed actions which provide great delight to the public at large but which, as you rightly suggest, rather baffle me. They may do as they please. But what irks me is the consequence of this preoccupation: the coming to a halt of every other activity. Can Christmastime really be so absorbing that the thief prefers to put off his plans until the new year, the murderer to enjoy the seasonal company of the man or woman who will soon become his prey?"

"You would prefer that crimes were committed than not, then? That heinous behaviour was manifested on Christmas Day itself?"

Holmes turned, and the gleam in his eyes was answer enough. Then his attention moved to a point over my shoulder. I looked around to see Mrs. Hudson lifting my Christmas card from the table and nodding slowly as she read its contents. It was with a rush of guilt that I realised I ought to have brought a second card to give to her.

"Well, I won't bother you any longer," she murmured, and left by the door.

I glanced at Holmes.

"She has been behaving in this unhappy manner since the beginning of December," Holmes remarked in answer to my unspoken question.

"Is it loneliness, pure and simple?" I asked.

"How could I possibly know?" Holmes snapped. Then his manner softened. "But I am glad you are here, Watson. Perhaps when you are done you might call in on her, spend a little time downstairs in her rooms. She has always enjoyed your company."

I nodded. "Very well. I suppose a doctor's bedside manner can be deployed in a variety of situations."

We both turned sharply as the door crashed open. Mrs. Hudson was framed in the doorway once more. She glanced apologetically at Holmes's chemistry bench which had been struck violently, then she reached for the handle, testing the swing of the door and frowning at its brass hinges.

"Yes, Mrs. Hudson?" Holmes said with infinite weariness.

"Oh!" she exclaimed, remembering her original intent. "I have something for you! I ought to have given it to you earlier, which was my reason for coming up here in the first place. I'd been on my way upstairs to see you, you see, when Dr. Watson called. And then it quite went out of my head." She glanced at the unlit fire and tutted. "Lord, it's still so cold in here. It won't do you any good at all, Mr. Holmes."

Both Holmes and I looked at the slips of paper that she held before her.

Warily, Holmes asked, "Are they Christmas cards, too?"

"No."

"A gift from you to demonstrate your festive good wishes, then?"

"No. Not my own good wishes, at least." She held out the items to Holmes. "It's two tickets to the Theatre Royal – and box seats at that!"

Holmes's eyes raised to the ceiling.

Having handed over the tickets, Mrs. Hudson bustled to the fireplace and set to lighting the woodpile already prepared in the grate.

"But that is a wonderful gift!" I remarked, hoping to rouse Holmes from his ungrateful response. "Who has sent them, Mrs. Hudson?"

"A Mr. Jacchus," she said brightly. "I *knew* I didn't know any Mr. Jacchus, but there the envelope was, mixed in with my own post, with my own name at the top. I'd opened the envelope a moment before I registered that it was a 'care of' address, and that alongside it was Mr. Holmes's name. And then I came rushing up here. Or rather, I came rushing out of my kitchen, and then the bell rang – that was you, Dr. Watson. And then we both—"

"Thank you," I said, interrupting her. "We were all present for the remainder of the story."

I turned to Holmes. With a conscious attempt to prevent any hint of petulance in my tone, I said, "This Mr. Jacchus is certainly a generous friend. Box seats, indeed! Might I ask who he is, Holmes?"

"Matthew Jacchus," Holmes replied. "A jeweller with premises in Hatton Garden. He is no friend of mine, but a former client."

I suspected I was unable to hide my satisfaction. "A successful case, I presume, to warrant such a show of gratefulness?"

Holmes nodded. He turned the tickets over in his hands.

"Was there no note?" he asked.

"None," the landlady replied from beside the fireplace, within which was now a lively flame.

Holmes put out his hand again. "Then the envelope, if you please."

Mrs. Hudson turned around on her knees. She looked down at her hands, her brow creasing as she registered that they were now empty. Next, she patted the pockets of her housecoat. Then, slowly, her gaze went back to the fire, which now blazed merrily.

Holmes groaned.

"I was distracted," Mrs. Hudson began, gabbling in her haste, "and it was so *cold* in here – you oughtn't to let it get like that, Mr. Holmes. There's no kindling in the basket – that's my fault, of course – and in that case the only way to bring a fire out quickly is with paper spills, and I suppose it's an automatic thing for me to use whatever's to hand. And the *tickets* are the gift, aren't they? The envelope was right there in my hand – you see that it was a natural enough—"

Holmes raised a hand and she stopped speaking immediately, blinking rapidly.

I went to the fire and bent to look into the grate. I could make out black specks in the embers that might once have been paper, but nothing more. I shook my head.

With a show of great patience that must have cost him a great deal, Holmes asked, "Can you recall what was written on the envelope, Mrs. Hudson?"

"Certainly," she replied instantly. "There was my name, and the address—"

"I meant on its rear."

"Ah. Yes. It read: 'To Holmes. With compliments. M. Jacchus.'"

"Nothing more than that?"

"I don't think so."

Holmes's lips pursed, and I knew he was stifling an urge to berate her.

Partly to distract him from his ire, I said, "But what is the great mystery, Holmes? A gift from a grateful client may be somewhat unexpected, but it is hardly to be treated with suspicion."

"Quite the contrary, in this case," Holmes retorted. "Everything related to Matthew Jacchus is to be treated with the utmost suspicion."

As he had spoken he had returned to the sofa to perch there as before. I went to my usual chair, and Mrs. Hudson drifted to the less comfortable cane-backed chair and sat, all the while glancing at each of us in turn as though she expected at any moment to be told to leave. We waited for Holmes to continue.

"Jacchus came to me in February this year hoping to clear his name," Holmes said. "He had been tasked with repairing a brooch of considerable value, on behalf of a member of the Norfolk Lennoxes, whose shrewd investments have increased the fortune of that family threefold in recent years. The brooch was of a particularly distinct design, a stunted cross with emeralds embedded in each of the four limbs, a sapphire in the centre, and pearls set between the limbs. I may be no great authority on matters of taste, but I suspect it is rather a crass demonstrator of sheer wealth, as opposed to an altogether successful scheme.

What is important is that it was still in Jacchus's possession when a story came to light that some unknown operator had attempted to sell a brooch of the very same description to a prospective buyer in Worthing, who – unfortunately for the seller – happened to have a close connection to the Lennox family."

"Then had it been stolen from Jacchus's premises?" I asked. "Or are you going to tell us that he was guilty of attempting to sell it after all?"

"Neither," Holmes replied, and a sly smile grew on his face; it was the first time he had displayed any enthusiasm since my arrival. "He still had the brooch, but when it was inspected by an expert, it was proven to be a forgery."

Mrs. Hudson leaned forward in her chair. "And so he came to you because he was suspected of being a forger himself?"

"Indeed."

"And you proved that he was not?"

"I did nothing of the sort," Holmes replied in a scandalised tone.

"Whyever not?" I asked. "And furthermore, why would Jacchus now be grateful if he remained accused of forgery despite your efforts?"

Holmes tapped his index fingers together. "Because he *is* a forger."

He watched us both, appearing to enjoy our confusion immensely.

"Matthew Jacchus has routinely dabbled in forgery, usually of artefacts of middling value. I have known of his activities for many years, but they did not concern me until he requested my services."

"But why did he—" I began.

"Because he was innocent."

I let out a groan of dismay.

"Allow me to explain," Holmes said. "Jacchus was, and remains, a forger. However, I was able to prove that he did not forge this particular item. If nothing else, his skills were not up to the job. I will not bore you with the details of a drawn-out procedure, but it was the case that the true brooch had been exchanged for a copy several days *before* it was entrusted to Jacchus – that is, it was the forgery that was entrusted to him – and he worked diligently upon its repair, never suspecting that it was not the real item."

"Then did you recover the real brooch?" Mrs. Hudson asked breathlessly.

"No," Holmes replied, with no hint of regret. "I traced it as far as Vilnius, where it was sold in secrecy to a minor member of the Hapsburg royal family – in whose possession, I presume, it remains."

"Then what of Matthew Jacchus?" I asked.

"His innocence was proven by a process by which I proved to the police that he was not equal to the task of its forgery. You may consider my method rather a roundabout way of concluding a case, but it provided a useful diversion during a period of little else to interest me. I simply made contact with an artisan, learned the trade and created my own copy of the brooch."

"What?" I exploded.

Holmes waved a hand. "It was no particular challenge, merely a dedicated application of the training I had received in so short a time. Furthermore, the jewels were real, though far from as high quality as those in the original piece. All the same, it was enough to trick Jacchus into believing the real brooch had been retrieved, during an assessment he performed under the watchful eye of Inspector Lestrade of Scotland Yard. That assessment in turn was enough to persuade the police that Jacchus was a relative amateur of his criminal craft, and on this occasion at least, entirely innocent."

I stared at my friend in amazement. More than his claim to have learned to create fine – albeit forged – jewellery, what astounded me was his casual dismissal of that same ability.

Mrs. Hudson fidgeted in her seat, clearly less impressed than I. "What about the Lennoxes?" she asked. "You might have concluded your case, but they didn't get their brooch."

Holmes smiled. "It is hardly my concern, unless a member of that family happens to request my services. But as it was, they were entirely satisfied with the outcome, though it is Lestrade who must claim credit for it. What occurred next was an accident, or rather a series of accidents, the likes of which are something of a speciality of Scotland Yard. Somehow or other, my own forgery made its way into the hands of the Lennoxes. A mix-up with the boxes of evidence, perhaps, or some headstrong junior officer making a wrong assumption and wishing to close a case. Would you have me resent the fact that my humble copy of that fine yet ugly brooch was equal to the scrutiny of its owner? For I find that I harbour no regrets whatsoever."

I shook my head and laughed. "Holmes, you are a true wonder."

Holmes nodded, as though this were simply a statement of fact. "While Jacchus's innocence had been proved, and therefore my obligation to my client fulfilled, he was hardly grateful. His standing among the criminal underworld was much reduced when word got out about the trick I had played on him. For the rest of the year to date, he has been reduced to legitimate work buying, selling and repairing jewellery. In short, his preferred career has been cut short." Holmes paused, then added, "Now that I think of it, he has failed to pay me for my services. So you see why I am sceptical that he might send me a Christmas gift of tickets to the opera. Now, Mrs. Hudson, tell me more about this envelope."

His landlady frowned and looked again at the roaring fire. "What more is there to tell?"

"The handwriting, for a start. What were its distinguishing features?"

"I don't remember."

I saw my friend's clasped fingers tighten upon one another. "Was the name a signature?"

Mrs. Hudson considered this. "No."

"Then was it printed neatly, or in a more flowing hand?"

Mrs. Hudson scratched her forehead. "How can I be expected to recall that?"

The veins stood out on Holmes's temple. It occurred to me that it must be unbearable for him to hold such a conversation with somebody unversed in the business of close observation.

"Was the J larger than its neighbours, for example?" he asked with affected patience.

She shook her head slowly. "It was the same size." Then she clapped a hand to her cheek. "Oh! It was printed!"

"You already stated that it was not a flowing style."

"No, no – I mean it was typewritten."

My friend's head jerked up immediately. "Good. Now, the characters themselves. Were they all upper case, or a mixture?"

I pitied poor Mrs. Hudson, whose mind was surely unused to such intense deployment. Her nose wrinkled and her eyes closed in deep thought. Finally, she pronounced, "A mixture. I'm certain of it."

"And the size of the envelope?"

Her hands lifted and she made two 'L' shapes to describe an oblong that was long and narrow.

"And were there any sharp creases or furrows along its length?"

"I don't think so."

"Then the machine was almost certainly a Remington No. 5," Holmes muttered.

"How can you possibly determine that?" I demanded.

"Some of the earlier models can be eliminated due to the lack of a shift key which triggers a change of letter case," Holmes began in a matter-of-fact tone, "and the narrow carriage of the popular No. 2 model would not allow the insertion of an envelope so large. The No. 3 might be a contender if it had ever been put onto the market, though its far *wider* carriage would have introduced creases in the length of the envelope. What is important is that the machine used is the most up-to-date model, and therefore far more expensive than the economical No. 4. May I examine your fingers, Mrs. Hudson?"

As if it were an automatic response, the housekeeper held out her hands. Holmes jumped up, took a magnifying glass from his bench, then returned to kneel before her, scrutinising the tips of her fingers. Presently he nodded in satisfaction and rocked back on his haunches, then sat cross-legged on the rug, looking for all the world like a well-behaved child at the feet of his mother.

"Well?" I asked.

"Underwood," Holmes replied quietly.

"I beg your pardon?"

"There are faint traces of blue ink, which is evidently from an Underwood ribbon."

I almost challenged him on the point, but then decided against it. I could have no hope of contesting Holmes in such areas of expertise.

"Is that uncommon?" I asked. "Underwood is a perfectly usual brand, I believe."

Holmes nodded. "But not of this rich pigment." He offered the magnifying glass to me, but I declined with a shake of my head. "The variety sold in Europe is distinctly paler, to trained eyes. The ribbon used in this case is direct from New York City, whereas the Remington No. 5 was designed specifically to meet the needs of the European market. We have learned much about the sender of these tickets, in addition to the high value of the box seats themselves."

We all looked at the tickets, which were still on the table.

"I confess I'd almost forgotten about them," I said. "So, Holmes, what do you make of them?"

"Evidently, they represent a trap," Holmes replied.

Mrs. Hudson's hand went to her mouth. "Then you must not go to the opera!"

"On the contrary," Holmes retorted.

"But you have just stated that somebody hopes to ensnare you when you are there!" I exclaimed.

Holmes rose to his feet. "Quite. I have longed for a diversion such as this." He went to the table and examined the tickets once again. Then, in as casual tone as could be imagined, he asked, "Will you stay for dinner and then join me at the theatre tonight, Watson?"

I thought of my wife, Mary, who was at home waiting for me. Given the manner of our meeting in the very room in which I now stood, she had always been resolute in understanding the need to indulge Holmes in his whims, even when they promised to be dangerous.

"I would be glad to."

CHAPTER TWO

Though it took no little amount of convincing by Holmes, the front-of-house staff at the Theatre Royal in Drury Lane were persuaded to allow us to enter the building fifteen minutes before the doors were opened to the public at large. Holmes moved around the periphery of the lobby – though what he was searching for, I had no idea – and then strode in the direction of the auditorium, sweeping past the unfortunate fellow whose task it was to check tickets and who had not been alerted to our early presence. I proffered our tickets and reassured the man that all was well, then hurried after my friend.

I had spent evenings at this very theatre on many occasions, but I had never seen it in want of an audience. When I had ascended the stairs and entered the auditorium by a door to the upper circle, I was immediately gripped by a sense of vertigo that I had never experienced before, which seemed inspired as much by the emptiness of the vast space as my altitude above the stalls and stage. The giant lamps that hung from the ceiling were all lit, and in the absence of human bodies this light turned every part of the auditorium – seats, panelling, gilt decoration and all – a bright and somewhat sickly amber colour.

I gathered my wits and cast around for any sign of Holmes, then, realising that I held the clue in my own hand, checked our tickets to determine which box was ours. It was the rightmost of the row, and sure enough I found Holmes within it, standing in its direct centre, his arms folded and regarding the part of the stage visible in front of the lowered curtain in a fixed manner, as if it were an enemy fortification that he intended to capture.

"Rather a good view, isn't it?" I said, peering over the low wall of the box.

"Do you mean a good view of the stage, or a good view of us sitting within this cage?" Holmes retorted.

"The former," I replied. Then I added, "Are you suggesting that we may be attacked from without?"

Holmes shook his head. "It is only clear that somebody wishes me to be installed here this evening. I do not fear an attack."

"That doesn't quite answer my question, Holmes. When you say you do not fear an attack, do you mean that you think there will be no attack, or simply that you are not fearful?"

Holmes behaved as if he had not heard me. He leaned so far over the wall of the box that I darted forward to grasp the tails of his coat, but he waved me away. First he bowed his head to look directly below our box, then to the left and, finally, he examined the column between our position and the stage. Then he backed away from the precipice and sat upon one of the seats and then the other, all the time gazing at the stage, raising his right arm along his line of sight and then sweeping it from side to side as if to determine his field of vision.

"What is your conclusion?" I asked.

"I have none as yet. Perhaps we are to rendezvous with somebody who is yet to arrive. Possibly, it is the performance itself that we are expected to witness."

I laughed, despite his concern. The idea that when attending the theatre the performance might merely be an afterthought seemed particularly droll.

"It appears that it will be a sort of variety presentation," I said, having pulled from my jacket pocket a programme hastily bought from the ticket-checker, and now beginning to leaf through it. "I confess I recognise few of the works."

Holmes snatched the paper from me eagerly and set to examining its contents. After some minutes he set it aside.

I heard the duplicated sighs of more than one door opening at once, and then I saw the first audience members entering the stalls and dress circle below. This sight seemed to reinvigorate Holmes, and he watched the increasing activity with interest, like a lookout in the crow's nest of a ship.

However, I saw nothing of note as the attendees found their seats and settled, and while Holmes's close attention never wavered, neither did he seem to see anything that aroused his suspicions.

Presently the lights dimmed, the murmur within the auditorium became gradually muted and I settled into my seat in somewhat nervous anticipation of the performance.

The orchestra launched into a piece that began calmly but soon became frantic, the conductor's head oscillating violently and the violinists striking at their instruments as though they hoped to saw through them. Then the curtain raised to reveal two men dressed in extravagant robes who, upon inspection of the programme, I determined to be King Philip II of Spain and the Grand Inquisitor, from Verdi's *Don Carlo*. After exchanged barbs, King Philip proceeded to deliver a bombastic monologue, none of which I could make out, and instead of attempting to decipher it I soon became distracted by trivial details: his waving of his arms, the slight bowing of the boards beneath his feet, the vast expanse of his mouth as he bellowed his lines.

Next came more familiar fare. The first pair of actors was replaced with a younger couple, and while the unfortunate woman was forced to simply watch on in mock fascination, the male performed a lusty rendition of 'La Donna è Mobile' from *Rigoletto*. I glanced at Holmes, whose fingers were rapping on the wall of the box, entirely out of sequence with the music played by the orchestra. It was clear to me that his impatience was already reaching its limit.

After the Duke of Mantua reached his inevitable conclusion, a troop of actors emerged from the wings and onto the stage, all dressed in drab garments, and proceeded to embark upon the prisoners' chorus from Beethoven's *Fidelio*. I saw Holmes lean forward and grip the rail, his eyes fixing on each of the prisoners in turn. Then his head bowed in what I interpreted as disappointment.

To my surprise, Holmes rose to his feet.

"Where are you going?" I asked in astonishment.

"I find that I cannot simply wait for whatever is coming my way," he replied. "I must seek it out."

"Shall I come, too?"

"Better that you remain here, to observe."

I was tempted to add that if an attack were to be launched, I might find myself in the firing line in his place. However, I did not voice this objection – the principal reason being that, had he requested I perform precisely that role of dummy target, I would have volunteered gladly.

The prisoners' complaint seemed interminable, and in Holmes's absence I found my mind wandering to thoughts of what he might be doing at this moment. Finally, the actors shuffled off stage, with exaggerated simulations of chained feet. Then came a lull. After some seconds had passed in silence, I put my head over the rail to look down at the orchestra pit. The conductor's neck was twisted to look over his shoulder, perhaps waiting for a signal from the direction of the stage.

Then I saw him sigh with relief as a single figure emerged from the wings – that is, from almost directly beneath my position. It was a woman wearing a hooded cloak, the cowl hiding the upper part of her face. Her skin was very pale in the limelight and her lips were dark.

The orchestra struck up a mournful prelude, but the singer did not yet sing. The conductor's neck twisted once again, conveying his confusion. Then he signalled to his orchestra, who repeated the introductory phrase. I saw a pair of violinists exchange uncertain glances at this error.

Still the woman did not sing. Finally, the conductor seemed to conclude that there could be no winning this contest, and he lowered his hands gradually, his musicians taking his lead and coming to a halt.

I watched the actress carefully. She appeared as motionless as a statue. I noticed that nobody in the audience had emitted so much as a murmur since the disruption had begun. Perhaps they were all equally transfixed.

My eyes strayed to the rest of the empty stage, then to the opposite wing of the backstage area which must only have been visible from the box in which I sat, as it was situated at the end of its row. I gasped – I had made out a pair of gleaming eyes! Yet my heartbeat slowed a little as the figure edged forward a fraction, and I recognised Sherlock Holmes pressed against the wall that divided the backstage area from the auditorium. He, too, was intently watching the silent woman who stood on the stage.

When she began to sing, the relief in the auditorium was palpable. I glanced again at the conductor, who had by now turned fully to watch the stage, and who seemed to have no intention of urging his orchestra to play along.

The melody was very beautiful: it rose in gradual increments, playful but with urgency, falling back at times as though indicating bashfulness. When the singer reached the highest point, she paused and commenced again from the lowest note. I could determine none of the words – perhaps there were none? I looked down at the programme which was now clenched tightly in my right hand. The intended piece was listed as the Demogorgon's epilogue from Percy Bysshe Shelley's *Prometheus Unbound*, but despite my imperfect knowledge of such things, I understood that this music had no relation to that drama.

Yet the song clearly fascinated the audience, despite its wordlessness and its circular nature, which perhaps ought to have been maddening. Each time the singer reached the apex of the melody, she began again. I saw Holmes in the wings, one hand over his mouth, appearing consumed by his thoughts.

After perhaps ten or a dozen iterations of the ascent, the singer stopped without warning. As before, silence fell across the auditorium. Thankfully, it did not last nearly so long this time. The woman's dark lips parted and, still staring directly ahead, she began to speak.

"Man, who wert once a despot and a slave,

A dupe and a deceiver! a decay,

A traveller from the cradle to the grave

Through the dim night of this immortal day:"

Then I was startled by voices coming from the wing beneath me, crying out, "Speak: thy strong words may never pass away." Clearly, this was now the performance that had been anticipated by the other members of the cast.

The woman continued, "This is the day which down the void abysm," and then I gasped as her head lifted for the first time, her hood slipped back enough to reveal her dark eyes – and she looked directly up at me. Our eyes met, and I found that I could not so much as blink. Then, to my even greater amazement, her dark lips curled into a wry smile before she intoned the words:

"Love, from its awful throne of patient power

In the wise heart, from the last giddy hour

Of dread endurance…"

As she continued to speak, she turned slowly, surveying the auditorium.

"Gentleness, Virtue, Wisdom and Endurance –

These are the seals of that most firm assurance."

She displayed no sense of dismay at not finding Holmes in our box – for I was now certain that was her ambition. If anything, her delivery now became more strident.

"To suffer woes which Hope thinks infinite;

To forgive wrongs darker than death or night;

To defy Power, which seems omnipotent."

Her slow revolution came to a halt when she was facing directly away from me – that is, she was now looking directly into the wings where Holmes stood. He made no attempt to hide from her gaze. His hand had dropped from his mouth and now clasped his other hand, completing a posture which might have suggested either gleeful anticipation or pleading.

"To love, and bear; to hope till Hope creates

From its own wreck the thing it contemplates"

I fancied that I saw Holmes smile faintly.

"Neither to change, nor falter, nor repent;

This, like thy glory, Titan, is to be

Good, great and joyous, beautiful and free;

This is alone Life, Joy, Empire and Victory."

This last word was denied its full impact, as no sooner had she had intoned it the stage filled with new bodies. These actors were all dressed in gaily coloured outfits of the Renaissance period, and they spoke to one another in that garbled nonsense which is supposed to evoke chatter upon the stage. I glimpsed Holmes for a moment more before he became obscured by the crowd pushing onto the stage. Then I searched for the woman who had been singing, but she had already retreated and been swallowed up in the confusion of bodies.

I watched the new proceedings vacantly for several seconds before telling myself that the signal for which we had been waiting had evidently been given, and there was no need to subject myself to any more of the dreary programme. I dashed from the box and along the rear of the other balcony boxes, seeing little need to attempt to move quietly due to the commotion and cacophony on the stage. I clattered down the stairs and then, instead of entering the lobby, I made my way through a narrow corridor which I judged must lead in the direction of the backstage area. The label on the next door I came to read *No admittance to the public*, which only made me more certain. I pushed through it without a second thought.

Despite my situation, I found myself distracted by the hubbub behind the scenes. Everybody I saw spoke in hushed voices or even deployed hand gestures to convey their meaning, but nevertheless there seemed constant activity even in the corridors. The true back part of the stage was presumably now to my left, judging by the rumble of voices and the squeaking of shoe soles on wood that echoed from that direction. I pressed onwards to a row of doors which I took to be the dressing rooms, on the assumption that Holmes would have attempted to pursue the singer here after her retreat from the stage.

Sure enough, I found him in the third small chamber along this corridor, the door of which was ajar. He was sitting on a stool before a mirror framed by lamps, though he was not looking into it but at the counter before him.

"Holmes?" I said quietly.

He raised his head.

"The woman," I said. "Who is she?"

Holmes only nodded. He stood slowly, and now I saw that he held in his hands a mass of fabric. Only when it billowed out did I realise that it was the very cloak that the singer had worn on the stage.

"She was too quick for me," Holmes said, though I detected no trace of dismay in his tone.

"Might she reappear in one of the later pieces?" I asked, though I was still entirely unclear of the significance of her first performance, a confusion only exacerbated by my friend's odd response to it. "Perhaps if we returned to our box…"

"She is gone," Holmes said simply. "But she has left something behind."

He laid the cloak on the counter, then picked up a piece of paper, which must have been what he had been studying when I entered the room. It featured musical notation, and while I was a novice at interpreting such things, I nevertheless recognised the music at once. The notes rose from the lower part of the bar to well above its upper extent until, after two lines of this behaviour, they began again from the bottom, the sequence repeating again and again.

"Then this is what she sang," I said.

"And it is the message which I was summoned here to receive," Holmes said. "It is not a threat, but a challenge."

"But from whom?" I demanded, now utterly exasperated. "I ask you again: who is she?"

A smile spread slowly on Holmes's face. "You have already provided the answer yourself. She is *the woman*."

CHAPTER THREE

The next morning I arrived at Baker Street at nine o'clock sharp, having once again made my excuses for failing to attend my practice, a habit that always became more frequent whenever one of Sherlock Holmes's adventures captured my imagination. Once again, Mrs. Hudson answered the door, and once again her expression was one of distracted melancholy. From beyond her came the sounds of a violin played with excessive force. However, I assumed that she was well used to such things and that this was not the cause of her mood. Indeed, when not in the company of others Holmes tended to produce only careless scraping sounds rather than anything close to the melody I could hear at this moment.

"My dear lady," I began, with forced merriness to my tone. "I do wish you'd gather your wits."

The housekeeper nodded solemnly. "I've been telling myself that very thing, just this minute." Then she added, "You see, it was only recently that I lost them."

I nodded encouragingly, despite my confusion. Remembering my pledge to Holmes, I said, "I had hoped to spend a little time with you, yesterday, before the distraction of the opera tickets.

Perhaps we might share a drink and some stories after I've called on Holmes?"

She frowned. "But that wouldn't help find them, would it?"

"I'm sorry—" I halted, my head tilting. "Are we still speaking of your wits?"

"No! My wool."

"Your—" I cleared my throat. "I think we may be at cross-purposes. You have lost your wool?"

"Two skeins, and big ones at that. One's crimson, the other pine green – ever so festive, and I'd promised them both to the maid before she leaves to-day to be at home with her elderly parents over Christmas. Those skeins must be around here. They can't just up and leave, can they?" She eyed me suspiciously. "What were you talking about, then?"

I shook my head. "Yesterday I could not help but notice that you were dejected. Regarding your being alone at Christmastime, or so I thought."

"Ah. Yes," she replied, and became immediately pensive. "I am that, a little. And now to add to it all, I've lost my wool."

I opened my mouth to speak, but had no idea how to proceed. It appeared that, far from reviving her spirits, I'd sunk her further into gloom.

"Well," I said, clapping my hands together in a pantomime of jollity. "Perhaps later, then."

I did not look back as I climbed the stairs, and it was with a keen sense of gratefulness that I entered Holmes's sitting-room.

He did not notice me at first, as he was standing by the window, gazing down at the snow-covered street even as he attacked his Stradivarius with great fervour. Every so often he glanced at the lower part of the pane, where I saw that he had fixed the sheet music he had acquired the previous day. Now that I paid full attention, I recognised that not only were the sounds from the violin decidedly more pleasant than those that they ordinarily produced, I detected the same rising melody that I had heard the day before. Each time he reached the pinnacle of this melodic summit, Holmes referred to the notation again, exhaled thoughtfully, and began anew.

The previous evening, Holmes had made his excuses shortly after I had found him in the backstage dressing-room, and then had insisted that he preferred to walk home. Though I had called after him to assure him that I would call again very soon, he had not responded. Now I hoped that catching him unawares might provide me with an answer.

So, without announcing myself, I said, "For how long have you been in correspondence with Irene Norton, née Adler?"

Holmes stopped playing immediately. Without turning, he said, "She does not refer to herself by her husband's name. And I do not correspond with her."

His careful choice of words struck me. "Indirectly, then? Or is it only she who has made contact with you before now?"

At first he didn't reply. Then he turned and, with the care of a mother with her infant child, he placed the violin gently into its case.

"In a manner of speaking."

"When? And by what means?" Then I checked myself. This was his private affair, after all, and though my curiosity may have been understandable, I ought not to feel entitled to its satiation. Hurriedly, I added, "If you don't mind my asking."

"In December of 1888 – that is, the December after you and I made her acquaintance – I discovered an advertisement in the back pages of the *Times*, which, as you know, I check habitually as it provides a barometer of the concerns of the public."

"And what did this advertisement say?"

Did Holmes's pale cheeks really colour at this moment? Perhaps not, but his hesitation spoke volumes.

"It does not matter," he said quickly.

This, too, was an uncharacteristic response. I knew that in the mind of Sherlock Holmes *nothing* was trivial. All the same, I moved on swiftly.

"And what was the outcome?" I asked.

"A series of challenges – or puzzles, if you prefer. All were provided by the same means, and all were..." He trailed off and seemed lost in thought for a while. "They required some amount of consideration."

I could not prevent myself from beaming at the thought of Holmes being bested, even for a moment, in any game. "And at the end? Presumably you did succeed in solving the puzzles."

Holmes hesitated, then shook his head. It struck me that it might have meant one of two things: that he did not care to divulge this information to me, or that he had failed to complete Irene Adler's challenges.

I had a keen sense that our discussion may be brought to a close at any moment, so I asked, "And last year – did she pose another challenge?"

Holmes went to his chemistry bench and made a show of inspecting bottles. "I had the idea of returning the favour," he said in a quieter voice.

"And how did she get along with your own puzzles?"

"So far as I know, she made no attempt. As a consequence, I had thought—" He stopped himself.

"You had thought the arrangement was over," I said. "And now you find that it is not."

Holmes turned. "Quite so. I understand your temptation to attribute meaning to these circumstances, but I urge you not to do so. However, I will concede that I am grateful. I have been lethargic and idle, and now I hope to be neither of those things."

Glancing at the violin, I asked, "Then what is the significance of the music?"

"I do not know. I have made no progress whatsoever. The Adler Variations remain a total mystery."

I smiled again at the indulgent, rather grandiloquent, term he had coined. "Are they variations? I had not noticed."

Immediately, Holmes darted to the window and pulled the sheet music from the pane. Now I saw that the notation continued onto the rear of the paper – there were a greater number of instances of the repeating melody than I had realised. Offering it to me, Holmes said, "Look, here – the rising melody begins and ends at the same pitch in each case, but the plateaus and partial descents vary a little with each of the twelve repetitions. What it means, I cannot say, but my hope is that this challenge will provide complexity, with variations upon a common formula."

"Perhaps the composer's own history may provide useful background."

"Indeed, but we know little enough of that. I will point out, though, my correct deduction about the typewriter ribbon. Her pretence of sending the tickets from Matthew Jacchus was evidently not intended to dupe me for a moment, especially if I had had the opportunity to examine the envelope before it was burned in the fire. I have no doubt that the usage of a New York Underwood ribbon was intended as a signal to me. The facts could not have been clearer. She is American, and now moves within Europe, and though she may no longer be particularly wealthy, in her years as an adventuress she has certainly known wealth enough to have purchased or been given a modern typewriter."

"Moves within Europe?" I repeated blankly. "Where does she live nowadays, if not in London, along with her husband – Geoffrey Norton, was that his name?"

"Godfrey Norton," Holmes corrected. "As for her usual location, I do not know."

I gaped at him. "You *never* say 'I do not know'. Or at least if you do say it, you know something far more pertinent and you are saying it only for theatrical effect. Yet this morning you have already used the phrase twice."

"I do not care to find out her current arrangement," Holmes insisted. "And I am convinced that it would not be pertinent to solving her challenge. There are rules to all games, are there not?"

I had to concede this point, but my amazement was undimmed.

"Then what will be your approach to unravelling the Adler Variations, in the first instance?" I asked.

Holmes went to pick up his Stradivarius from its case. "I will devote my time to it, by means of playing it unceasingly until an idea strikes me."

The thought of being trapped in the room for long with Holmes playing his violin in full flow did not appeal to me. As I edged towards the door, I made one final appeal. "What of your other cases?"

"There are none."

"I mean, if one should present itself."

Holmes scoffed. "That is hardly likely. December is a fallow time for my profession, Watson, which is precisely why I welcome this great game so heartily."

I had just reached the door when it swung open, and I was forced to duck away from it to avoid being struck.

"Mrs. Hudson, you might have knocked!" I exclaimed – but the housekeeper only nodded vaguely in my direction, her neck craning as she looked at Holmes's chemistry bench and the nearby bookshelves, no doubt still searching for her missing wool.

The sound of a throat being cleared came from the corridor behind her, and the landlady said perfunctorily, "Inspector Lestrade to see you, Mr. Holmes," and then retreated from the room, bumping into the selfsame policeman on her way out.

Lestrade strode into the room, taking the hat from his head as he entered and pressing it to his lean body. "Ah, Holmes—" Then he noticed me cowering behind the door and reached forward to help me to a standing position. "And Dr. Watson – are you ill, sir?"

I grunted a wordless reply as I recovered myself.

"You have come with a case for Holmes?" I asked.

Lestrade raised an eyebrow. "One hardly requires his skills of deduction to make that assertion."

"Yet I find great satisfaction in it all the same," I countered. "Holmes insists that there are no cases to be had in mid-December."

Holmes was still holding up his bow, ready to strike the strings. "I was referring to cases worth my time. Is this one worth my time, Lestrade?"

Lestrade placed his hat on the table and tapped it twice before answering. "Frankly, no."

Contrary creature that he was, I saw that Holmes's interest was piqued by this blunt admission. The Stradivarius went once more into its case. "Please explain," he said.

"On the face of it, the fact is that yesterday afternoon a statue was stolen from the British Museum."

"Very well. In what circumstances?"

"A rush job, an opportunist. It was chiselled at the base and wrenched off its stand so inexpertly that the feet were left behind."

Holmes sighed. "You are quite right; that hardly seems in my field. You know that I have certain criteria—"

"Yes, though I have yet to understand them," Lestrade said.

Holmes bowed subtly. "Nevertheless, they exist, and this theft appears to fulfil none of them." Then he paused. "But you stated yourself that it was not worth my time. Why is that?"

"Because the statue is utterly worthless."

Once again, Holmes's response might have been unexpected in any other person. His manner became immediately more alert, his chin jutting forward. "Was any other statue damaged?"

"None. Only this one, of—" Lestrade pulled out a scrap of paper from his jacket pocket and read, "Veritas, one of those Roman goddesses. And the peculiarity – or the simple misfortune, perhaps, from the point of view of the thief – is that this statue is the only plaster copy in the entire building. A copy was made for reasons of weight distribution, I am told. The original stone version was judged too fragile and has long been hidden away. The fragility is all in the ankles, apparently, which explains the snapping."

Holmes's eyes gleamed. "Indeed? And what of the original?"

"Still in its right place, under lock and key."

Holmes went to the coat-stand and began to pull on his overcoat.

"Then you intend to assist me after all?" Lestrade asked. "Does my description match one of your mysterious criteria after all?"

Holmes only replied with a vague humming noise.

I pointed to the violin. "And what of the composition to which you intended to dedicate your time, Holmes?"

Holmes hesitated, then plucked up the sheet music, folded it carefully and slipped it into his inner pocket.

"All in good time," he replied. "Let us go."

CHAPTER FOUR

Lestrade let us into the building by the western of the two officer's houses on Great Russell Street, presumably to avoid any interest that might accompany the arrival of the great detective by the colonnaded front entrance. From here we were taken quickly through studies and clerks' rooms until we emerged into the museum proper.

"If I may play the part of tourist guide for a moment," Lestrade began. He pointed along the corridor to the right, which led along the front part of the building towards the main entrance. At its far end I saw that a barrier had been erected to prevent visitors from coming this way. "The chamber you see there is the Roman gallery, whereas everything to the left of this point, all the way to the corner of the building, are known as the Greco-Roman saloons. I was told of the distinction earlier, but it seems to me a frustratingly fine one. The missing goddess is of the Greco-Roman sort."

As he moved away, I glanced into a transept opposite the door through which we had passed. Again, barriers had been placed on its far side to prevent entry; it seemed that Scotland

Yard had cordoned off this entire corner of the ground floor of the building.

The inspector's voice echoed from the next chamber. "The greater part of the collection is through the next doorway, in the long room. But our thief or thieves set to work here."

Holmes and I followed him. At first I was distracted by that more distant long saloon to which he had referred, the walls of which were positively thronging with pedestals and mounted shelves containing figures from myth and antiquity. Not for the first time during a visit to a museum, I wondered whether cramming such things all together was wise; even the merest glance into that space made me decidedly dizzy and overwhelmed. Finally, my attention shifted to what was directly before me in the much smaller, square chamber we had entered. It was no great wonder that I had initially looked directly over the pedestal that stood in the centre of the square area, as it was only waist-height and empty. Now that I looked closer, though, I saw that upon it, among a landscape of sculpted foliage, was a pair of slender, bare feet.

"These, then, are the feet of our unfortunate goddess," Lestrade announced, pointing.

"Indeed?" Holmes asked politely.

Lestrade appeared about to confirm this, but then seemed to realise that Holmes was mocking him. He cleared his throat loudly. "As you may imagine, the superintendents of the museum have no desire to reveal that a theft has been committed so easily, no matter that the statue is of no value. Their prime interest, and the interest of Scotland Yard, come to that, is how a statue of moderate size might have been removed and then smuggled out without attracting any notice. Our thief may have bungled the operation this time, but on the next occasion his spoils may represent far greater a loss."

Holmes nodded vaguely, then began to examine the bare feet. While I knew that they were plaster, it was only at their truncated upper part where this was evident; the substance crumbled where the thief had snapped the ankles, whereas otherwise the smooth surface appeared as much like stone as any other statue in the gallery. I saw chisel marks below the toes and also digging into the arch of the foot – between the heel and the position of the lateral plantar ligament, if the appendage had belonged to a person of flesh and blood. Clearly the thief had initially intended to free the statue in its entirety, but had been desperate, no doubt conscious of limited available time to effect the theft.

"Are these galleries well monitored, then?" I asked Lestrade.

He nodded, then led me once again through the doorway by which we had entered the chamber. He pointed to a connecting area to the left, which lacked any museum objects. "There is always a guard stationed out in that transept – the poor fellow must have been only a matter of feet away when the crime was committed. His placement is over there, in the diagonally opposite corner."

Holmes moved past us to stand in that very location.

"As you can see, Holmes," Lestrade said, "there are doors to each chamber from this point. Furthermore, there are lines of sight into both routes by which one may leave the chamber that contained our luckless goddess; the second exit is at the corner of the building, at the end of the long gallery. In addition, the most direct escape would be directly towards the main entrance, which would provide our guard with by far the better view. I should add that nothing raising any suspicion was noted by guards anywhere else in the building, nor at the cloakrooms or at the front desk before the main entrance."

"Could it have been smuggled under clothes, perhaps?" I ventured. "A long cloak, for instance?"

"It'd have to be a *very* big cloak," Lestrade replied. "The statue is not as substantial as many of the others here, but the description provided by the curator raises a clear opposing argument to your suggestion: the arms of Veritas are raised above her head. From fingertip to toe – or rather, ankle – she is fully five feet tall. My own supposition is that the upper limbs were snapped, just as the feet were. Our man is evidently no great lover of art."

Holmes made a scoffing noise. "Is the guard who was on duty here to-day?"

"Yes, and I have told him to make himself available for a second round of questioning. Wait just one moment, if you please."

Lestrade left, and Holmes and I returned to the square chamber containing the feet of the goddess. Other than the central pedestal, this room was little more than a conduit to the much larger gallery containing Greco-Roman statues, and its bare walls left one with the sensation of being outdoors rather than in. There were tall, empty vases in the two corners of the inner walls, and a large urn placed on the floor in the centre of a wide, dim alcove on the outer.

"Well, Holmes?" I said.

My friend interrupted his inspection of the feet to look up at me. He did not reply.

"Are your criteria satisfied?" I went on.

"Most certainly," he replied. "I have often maintained that the greatest interest may be found in the smallest of crimes. This theft is superficially a shambles, but unless the selection of the only plaster copy in the building is simple bad luck, its involvement raises the significance of the act in my estimation."

"And yet, as you say, it *could* be simple bad luck."

The disdainful curl of Holmes's lips told me not to pursue this line of reasoning.

He glanced over my shoulder, and I turned to see Lestrade accompanied by a man who was clearly the guard who had been on duty the previous day. His hands kneaded together continually, and he sucked at the ends of his long, nicotine-stained moustache – a most distasteful tic that betrayed his anxiety.

Over the course of a few minutes Holmes questioned the man – whose name was Morris – comprehensively. His answers provided little information that Lestrade had not already supplied, adding merely the fact that there had been an intermittent flow of visitors the previous afternoon, most of them appearing to have arrived alone. None of them had carried anything large that might arouse suspicion – the largest items being a case held by a businessman and a slender portfolio carried by an amateur artist, presumably with the intent of sitting and sketching one or more of the statues. As far as I could determine, Holmes appeared satisfied as to the guard's diligence, who had last performed his round of the galleries at one o'clock. The theft had first been remarked upon by a gentleman visitor entering the chamber at ten minutes to two, at which point Morris had hurried in, seen the mutilated feet, and raised the alarm.

When he had concluded his questioning, Holmes remarked, "In future I would suggest you make your rounds on the half-hour mark rather than on the hour. I presume there were more visitors before one o'clock, and fewer directly afterwards?"

The guard nodded. "How could you know that?"

Lestrade grunted and shook his head. "There's no need for genius on that score. One o'clock is the usual end of the lunch hour, so visitors from nearby workplaces will have hurried away. It stands to reason that the time directly after that would be the least popular, and therefore the ideal moment to effect a crime." Despite the certainty in his tone, he nevertheless glanced at Holmes, who nodded approval. Lestrade attempted to disguise a smile of satisfaction.

"Nevertheless," Holmes said, "I accept that there could be little hope of anybody passing your post while making off with a sizeable statue with raised arms."

Morris exhaled with obvious relief. Then he frowned. "But then where is it?"

Holmes turned to me. "Would you like to speculate, Watson?"

Against my better judgement, I did exactly that. "There is one means of escape that we have not considered." I turned to point at a small doorway marked *Staff only*. "The route through the officer's houses, by which we ourselves came here this morning."

"It is always locked, sir," Morris said immediately, "and as you see, it is within my range of sight from the transept."

I sighed. "Then I am at a loss, Holmes. So far as I can see, if we are to accept that the guard here was watching throughout" – I registered the man's suddenly erect posture, and added hastily – "which is clearly the case... then there is no earthly way that the statue could have been smuggled away between one and two o'clock yesterday."

To my surprise, Holmes nodded.

"Then you are giving up?" I asked incredulously.

Holmes responded with a barking laugh. "Quite the opposite. I have solved the mystery."

Presumably it was his intent that the three of us stared at him in utter incomprehension.

"And might you care to let us in on the answer?" Lestrade asked irritably.

"Certainly," Holmes said. "The statue is plaster, so its removal from the base is itself no particular puzzle. It was only unfortunate that the ankles are so slender, and that the thief was in such a great hurry, taking not enough time to prise it away intact. The question remains why this action was not heard." Turning to the guard, he asked, "Is it your custom to eat hardboiled eggs every day as part of your luncheon?"

Morris blinked. "However could you—"

"There are traces of broken shell in your corner of the transept, along with scattered breadcrumbs."

The guard's cheeks glowed red. "I'd be grateful if you didn't tell my superiors, sir. In truth, my lunch is supposed to be eaten after my shift ends, at three. To tell the truth, though, I'm usually ravenous even before it arrives. I mean, who eats their lunch at *three*, sir?"

Holmes waved away the question. "Then the food is not kept at your station before you consume it?"

"My pal Robert brings it at one," Morris replied in a morose tone. "I do the same for him when he takes the middle shift." He looked up. "But surely you're not suggesting that the cracking of an egg could have masked the sounds of somebody hacking away at a statue? I keep my eyes on each of the doorways in turn throughout, sir." He paused. "Which I suppose explains my untidiness as regards the eggshell."

Holmes shook his head. "The arrangement of the plaster dust upon the pedestal is close to the feet, rather than the chips being propelled further away. That indicates that the chisel was covered by a cloth, which would have muted the sound to a large degree – and which also explains the imprecision of the chisel strikes. I am convinced of your diligence in executing your role, so I am sure that even when you are accustomed to having a brief conversation with your colleague, your eyes never stray from the doorways you are required to oversee. And yet, that brief conversation would provide the ideal moment to create a sound that somebody might prefer to remain unnoticed."

It seemed to me that the crimson hue of the guard's cheeks might never abate.

"Nevertheless," I said, partly to distract the unfortunate fellow from his guilt, "the issue remains about how the statue could have been stolen."

Holmes replied immediately, "You said it yourself: the statue was not smuggled away between one o'clock and ten minutes to two, as it would have been impossible to do so."

"Ah!" I exclaimed. "It was somehow taken later, then." I frowned. "That gentleman who first attracted Mr. Morris's notice to the statue being missing... might he have been causing a deliberate distraction, allowing an accomplice to make an exit in the opposite direction?"

"I ought to remind you that such a plan would still involve carrying a five-foot tall, exceedingly fragile statue under cover," Holmes said. "In turn, that would mean taking the long way around in order to circumnavigate the guard's position, and then somehow avoiding even greater scrutiny at the main entrance."

"Then... what?" I asked helplessly. "No. I mean to say: when?"

"Never."

With an exaggerated show of patience, Lestrade said, "*Please*, Holmes. Just tell us the answer."

"Very well," Holmes replied. "When I say that the statue was never taken, I mean that it is still here."

In what seemed an involuntary movement, Lestrade turned to look at the empty space above the pedestal. He stared at it for a second, then whirled around.

"Are you hoping to make fools of us?" he demanded.

Without answer, Holmes pointed to the large urn in the shadowed alcove of the chamber.

At first Lestrade didn't react, but then in a single abrupt movement he leapt to the urn and stared into it from above.

"It's empty," he said, with the simple disappointment of a child.

"And it would hardly serve our thief's purposes," I said, "if he had simply broken up the statue and jammed the pieces into a vase."

"Ah. Remind me, then," Holmes said, his tone of self-satisfaction unchanged, "what are our thief's purposes?"

"To steal the statue, of course."

"I think not."

We watched on as Holmes bent to the urn, lifted it and placed it aside. Then he pointed at the place where it had stood. I moved closer to examine the faint marks on the floorboards which showed where it had been positioned, presumably for some time, as the circular area of the wooden boards was a deeper hue than the surrounding parts which had been exposed to light and the tread of visitors.

I bent to the ground, puzzled by the shape on the floor. Then I looked back to the urn itself to reassure myself that its base formed a complete circle.

"It doesn't make sense," I said slowly.

"What doesn't?" Holmes asked casually.

I pointed at the mark on the floorboards. "It's clear to see where the urn has been placed, and yet before you moved it just now, it occupied a place some distance away from this mark. And more to the point, there is no earthly way that the urn *could* be placed where this marking appears to indicate, because the bowl of the urn bows out well beyond the dimensions of the base, which in the marking appears semi-circular as well as being flush against the wall."

Holmes folded his arms over his chest, waiting for me to continue.

"What the devil are we to conclude, then?" Lestrade asked.

I gazed at him blankly. "I suppose… that the urn at one time projected into the wall, for some reason."

Holmes chuckled. "Close enough, Watson."

Then he brushed past me and knocked sharply on the wall of the alcove, producing a distinctly hollow sound.

"Good lord," Lestrade muttered under his breath.

I rose and stood back to better observe the wall within the alcove. The fact that it was unlit and featureless had meant that I had given it no more than a cursory inspection earlier. Now that I examined it more closely, I saw that upon its surface were horizontal and vertical lines at two-feet intervals.

"This is no wall. It has been unfolded and placed here…" I said in wonder. Then, in triumph, I cried, "The artist's portfolio!"

Holmes regarded me with something close to admiration. "Capital, Watson! An ingenious concept, is it not? Presumably the false wall was capable of being unfolded and put in place in a matter of moments, once the statue was removed." His fingers began to trace along the edges of the wall.

"Then the statue," Lestrade said haltingly, "is behind this wall?"

"This *appearance* of a wall," Holmes corrected him. "Here, Inspector, do lend a hand."

Despite the assertion that the wall had been simple to put up, it took all three of us working together (the guard having stood back to watch us in abject amazement) in order to free it from its tight fit. When we did so, it crumpled along its folds, and I saw that it was made of very fine plasterboard, barely thicker than card. Once it had dropped to the floor, I saw that the alcove was rather more than a foot deeper than it had first appeared. However, that revelation was secondary to a far more immediate one. Tucked into this hidden space was a figure of a woman – Veritas herself – with her arms raised above her head in a playful posture as though she were mocking us.

Holmes made a strange sound that was part exhalation, part thoughtful hum, but at first I did not see what had caused it. Then I looked up at the face of the goddess jammed into the narrow space, and saw that something covered her left eye: a square of paper upon which was drawn a large circle, fixed in place as though intended to represent a crude monocle.

"What do you make of that?" I asked.

Holmes did not deign to answer. With great care he felt around the scrap of paper, then peeled it intact from its position.

For his part, Lestrade ignored the mysterious circle, his attention remaining focused entirely on the statue. "What earthly reason could the beggar have had for hiding the statue here, merely six feet from its original place?" he demanded. "The job of recovering the thing at a later date has scarcely been made any easier, particularly with a false wall with which the thief would have to wrestle before he might even retrieve it."

A faint smile appeared on Holmes's thin face. "You continue to use the word 'thief', Lestrade, and yet nothing is missing."

"Yes, but—" Lestrade hesitated. "It's an act of preparation for a later theft."

"Perhaps. Perhaps not. Nevertheless, we have our Veritas." Holmes turned to the astonished Morris. "Might you be so good as to inform the superintendent of the successful recovery?"

Lestrade watched the guard scurry away, then said, "I suppose you've earned the right to be pleased with yourself, Holmes – but the fact remains that we must protect this institution against future crimes. Even if this statue can be made safe, what of every other artefact in the building? You will remember that they are valuable, whereas this one is not. Any one of them might be snapped at the ankles and carted off."

"And yet I feel confident that they will not."

I said to Holmes, "It seems to me that you know more than you are letting on."

With an indulgent smile, he replied, "You may take it that I *always* know more than I let on."

Lestrade made a harrumphing sound. "Don't know how you can bear to spend so much time with him, Watson. I never could stomach smugness in others. All the same, I'm glad to have your guarantee of no further thefts, which will certainly improve my festive mood these coming days. We'll end up putting this statue business down to a joke in poor taste, I'd imagine. Now, perhaps you might both prefer to leave me to dispense with the formalities—"

"Of course," Holmes said with a bow, "it would be simpler if you explained the matter to the superintendent yourself. We will bid you farewell and take an early luncheon."

Lestrade flashed a grateful smile – which was extinguished immediately as shouts of alarm rang out, echoing along the flagstones of the wide corridor from the direction of the main entrance.

CHAPTER FIVE

The next several minutes were total confusion. We hared to the main entrance, where we found a clerk gabbling to the superintendent, who was already in conversation with our friend Morris and who looked from one to the other of his employees with a wide-mouthed expression of utter incomprehension. When the clerk finally made clear that the superintendent ought to follow him at once, he did so trailed by not only Morris but the trio of myself, Holmes and Lestrade. We trooped through a narrow corridor and then into the vast internal space of the circular reading room, where we each performed individual navigations of desks, chairs and labyrinthine concentric circles of counters, watched on in amazement by scholars with reading-glasses still nipping the ends of their noses. Without acknowledging the confusion and chaos we left in our wake, we plunged through the doorway opposite and then came to a halt in a chamber situated between two long libraries.

The poor clerk, having performed this sprint twice, bent double, clutching his thighs as he gasped for breath.

Yet the superintendent was in no mood to indulge. "Where, man? Which painting?"

The clerk pointed to the rear part of the room, and we all turned to look in that direction – including those of us who had accompanied him here, and also the dozen or so men who perched on stools or paused their browsing of the shelves.

We moved as a shoal to the rear of the chamber and finally I saw what had caused the raising of the alarm. The central part of this connecting room between libraries was filled with low, glass-topped cases displaying coins and fragments of ceramics, but the rear was dedicated to a rather hotch-potch collection of framed paintings. Amid the paintings on the right wall, hanging at head height, was a thick gilt frame like any of the others, two feet in height and one wide – but unlike the others it was entirely empty, its central part revealing only the navy wallpaper behind it.

There was a brief lull as we all digested what had occurred – and then pandemonium erupted. Everybody who had been watching from the twin libraries to either side swept into the middle chamber. The superintendent demanded that the police be sent for immediately, then whirled around only to find himself face to face with Inspector Lestrade. Then followed a disjointed conversation in which the superintendent attempted to explain the situation and Lestrade in turn insisted that he was already well aware of it.

Amid all of this, Holmes remained impassive. He had somehow placed himself directly before the empty frame despite the pushing and shoving from all sides, and now he stood with his head tilted to one side, his hand cupping his chin as though he were studying a true artwork rather than its absence.

I managed to collar the unhappy clerk who had first discovered the theft, and asked him, "Which painting has been taken?"

"I don't know," he replied.

The superintendent spun around. "Don't know? Then find out, man! Fetch the catalogue!"

The clerk's head bobbed and he darted away. When he returned, nobody in the now-cramped chamber had satisfied their thirst for knowledge by any means, except perhaps Holmes, who stood very close to the empty frame, his fingers running lightly over its surface. I saw the superintendent look in that direction and then open his mouth as if to rebuke Holmes, but then he seemed to recall that the painting could hardly now be further damaged, and he refrained from speaking. He resumed looking over the clerk's shoulder as the younger man rifled through the pages of the large catalogue placed on one of the glass display cases.

I, too, watched with interest, along with Lestrade, as the clerk's motions slowed and he turned overleaf and then ran his finger down the page. With narrowed eyes he turned to look at the empty frame, then back at the catalogue.

"Well?" the superintendent barked. "Do you have the name?"

"No, sir," the clerk replied.

"But this is a detailed record of every piece held in the museum. Explain yourself!"

"It… has no name, sir."

The superintendent's head bowed. For the first time he seemed aware of the crowd of people around him. With a forced display of patience, he said slowly, "Of course it has a name. I ask you to look again."

Lestrade moved to stand beside Holmes, who was now examining the inside of the frame, where a few threads were all that were left where the canvas had been cut away.

"Can you determine anything about this mysterious painting from these scraps that remain?" he asked.

"I shouldn't imagine so," Holmes replied casually.

Lestrade stared at him. "You seem decidedly unconcerned about this crime that has taken place."

At the same time, the clerk raised his voice above the general chatter. "I tell you that I cannot find its catalogue entry, and yet every other painting is present and correct in the list."

Holmes turned to face the chamber at large, and he cleared his throat. Somehow, the sound cut through all of the muttered conversation, and everybody fell silent.

"You will find no record in that catalogue," Holmes announced, "because no painting ever hung here, and no painting has been stolen."

At first only Lestrade reacted, emitting a deep groan and pinching the bridge of his nose. Then the chamber became alive with questions, all addressed to Holmes.

Like a fairground showman, Holmes held up his hands for silence, and the crowd obliged.

"I will prove it," he said, then turned to the frame once again. "Observe these protruding lines that appear in quarter-intervals along the sides, and halfway along the base and head. Combine this with the straightforward observation that the frame is distinctly lighter than it appears – in fact it is cunningly disguised balsawood – their purpose is soon revealed."

To the accompaniment of a collective gasp from the crowd, Holmes, in a single fluid motion, reached up to the upper part of the frame and deftly unhooked it from the wall. The superintendent, the clerk and Morris the guard all moved forward instinctively, but then stopped immediately as Holmes shifted his grip to one corner of the frame – a position that would have been impossible had it been made of mahogany as it appeared. Its long sides buckled, each becoming irregular zigzags, and likewise the top and bottom struts began to fold and contract. Now I saw that the depth profile of the frame would allow two opposite sides to nest one within the other when they were folded flush.

"I will not collapse it fully," Holmes said, "as I do not wish to disturb its inner elements which would necessarily brush against one another when closed. But I trust that my demonstration illustrates the operation of the device."

In a tone of wonderment, the superintendent said, "Then the frame was in fact brought here to the museum and hung, and it truly never contained an artwork?"

"Quite so," Holmes replied.

Examining the half-collapsed contraption, I said, "It appears to reduce to, what, ten inches in length? It would be very easily concealed under a jacket in that form, despite its bulkiness. But the question remains as to why."

"Yes," Lestrade added. "You may have cottoned on to its design quickly enough, Holmes, but I'm confident that I or one of my colleagues, or any of the staff here, might have determined the truth readily enough."

To my surprise, Holmes nodded in agreement. "Quite so. It is simply another playful trick, no doubt perpetrated by our artist visitor who, during an earlier appearance at the museum, carried a portfolio. Given that this ruse would inevitably be revealed, and far more readily than the hidden statue, the only question relates to its purpose."

He replaced the frame on the wall, and now I saw that its lightness allowed it to hang from nothing more than a pin.

The mystery having been revealed, several of the scholars shuffled closer to the frame in turn to inspect the marvel. One of them jarred my elbow sharply on the way past, making me turn around ready to accuse the perpetrator only to meet the myopic, bespectacled eyes and doe-like expression of a young man accustomed to the close scrutiny of books, and my resolve faltered. Each of the scholars peered at the frame first from the front and then from the side to see its hinges, and then they moved away to return to their stools and books, their curiosity satiated.

"I do wonder if the trick might have gone unnoticed for longer if not for your presence, Holmes," I said thoughtfully. I pointed at the threads that hung at various points around its inner part.

"These fragments of canvas are most persuasive, as if something really has been cut away—" I stopped, peering at the right-hand strut, halfway between two of its hinges, where some solid object protruded very slightly. "But there is something else here."

Holmes gestured for me to move aside so that he might take my place. Then, with surprising speed, he produced from his pocket a pair of tweezers. Though by now I ought to have been accustomed to Holmes's preparedness, I still marvelled at his tendency to carry so many of the tools of his profession at all times. With great care, he bent to the frame and eased out the object: a half-inch-square shard of glass with a metallic coating on its rear surface.

"But this undermines the ruse entirely!" I exclaimed. "What could be the thought behind inserting a piece of mirrored glass, which has no place in a framed painting?"

Holmes turned the glass over several times, then, finding nothing notable in the object itself, slipped it into a handkerchief and then into his pocket.

"It is a message," he said.

By now the superintendent had ushered away the last of the onlookers, and he was in deep discussion with the clerk who had discovered the painting, and Morris, the guard to whom we had first spoken. It was with some relief that I found myself able to move around the rear of the chamber with greater ease.

"But the only message that a mirror can provide is one's own visage," I said.

Holmes did not reply.

"Or backwards writing," Lestrade said. When we both looked at him askance, he added, "That's the sort of thing you're always discovering, Holmes. Backwards writing, revealing something or other."

Holmes tutted and resumed his examination of the frame.

"It *is* a good idea," I said quietly to Lestrade, "but without any writing to hand, I fear it may be unsupported by the circumstances."

Lestrade shrugged his shoulders with affected nonchalance. "Then what else is there? Any mirror would show only us and this collection of ugly paintings."

Holmes spun around instantly and clasped the inspector's arms. "What did you say?"

Lestrade blinked. "I said it would show us—"

Eagerly, Holmes concluded, "And the paintings!" Then he shoved Lestrade to one side and darted across the length of the room.

"*Ugly* paintings is what I said," Lestrade muttered in a wounded tone.

I watched Holmes inspect each of the pictures that hung on the wall opposite the empty frame. He turned repeatedly, and when I ventured too close he waved an arm, bidding me to retreat.

"What is it that you are looking for?" I asked.

"Be so good as to stand before the empty frame," Holmes responded, perhaps not having even registered my question.

I did as he asked, though I felt a fool looking at the framed expanse of blank wallpaper. I tried to ignore Lestrade's chuckle.

"Good," came Holmes's voice from behind me. "So if I situate myself directly behind you... Ah, this is it."

"May I turn around?" I asked.

When Holmes didn't reply, I turned to see him in contemplation of a small picture that did indeed appear to be located directly opposite the trick frame. If the frame had been filled not with a canvas but a mirrored glass, this would certainly be the most visible of the reflected collection.

Lestrade and I approached the picture. It was a scene featuring many figures arranged in a murky street, all contained within an inscribed circular framing device which was itself centred within the physical square wooden frame. The gap between these two outlines was filled with gruesome beasts and twisted, almost nightmarish, foliage. The main tableau depicted some ten people gathered before an eleventh who stood apart from them and behind a heavy-looking table. This person who commanded so much attention held up a small ball between thumb and index finger – I realised that others were placed upon the table along with a series of cups, and concluded that this was a magician or street charlatan about to perform a cup-and-ball trick.

I went to the catalogue which still lay open on the glass counter and spent some little time reading the descriptions of each of the paintings in this part of the room. Then I concluded, "This must be *The Conjurer*. It is by an unknown copyist, after Hieronymus Bosch, the Dutchman."

"And what of its significance?" Holmes murmured.

I considered this, then replied, "The crowd depicted is not unlike the gathering that was in this very room only minutes ago. And when you revealed the folding hinges of the empty frame, you were perhaps similar to that gentleman on the right of the picture – who must be the conjurer."

Holmes gave a non-committal grunt. "Either that, or I am the figure bent *before* the conjurer, at the forefront of the onlookers, who is engrossed in watching the game."

I moved closer to look at the old man in the painting who stood directly before the conjurer as he performed his patter. While most of the members of the crowd watched on with merely casual interest, this person was entirely intent on watching the conjurer – so much so that he paid no notice to a clerical-looking figure behind him, whose eyes were raised even as his hand strayed to the game-player's purse that hung at his waist.

In a flurry, Holmes produced his own pocketbook from his jacket. Lestrade and I glanced at one another and performed the same action, then each breathed a sigh of relief as the items were discovered in their proper places.

"It seems this trickster of ours is rather inconsistent," Lestrade said with finality.

Holmes shook his head. "Quite the opposite. It is only that we are a step behind. If I am correct in my interpretation of this message, all we have succeeded in achieving is to faithfully play the part of these unsuspecting onlookers. We have allowed ourselves to be detained in exactly the manner that was intended, and my own presence here at this moment is no accident. The same person who performed the trick of the statue and the false wall is intent on leading me in a particular direction – or rather, of making a fool of me."

Lestrade offered a wan smile, and I imagined that at this moment he sympathised strongly with Holmes.

"Then what are we to do now?" I asked.

"What is of most importance is that we cut this charade short, and return to whatever it is that we are being distracted *from*."

Without another word, Holmes strode out of the chamber in the direction of the exit.

CHAPTER SIX

M y sense of disorientation was in no way improved upon
our return to Baker Street. As we entered the front door
and shook the snow from our shoes, the sound of voices was
audible from upstairs. Holmes and I looked at one another, and
then Holmes sprang up the steps two at a time and threw open
the door to his rooms. I stumbled in his wake to see two people
standing beside the fireplace, and another passing through the
doorway that led to the bedroom that I had once called my own,
gabbling loudly. This third person was in the room for only a
matter of moments before she called out, "Not here either!" and
then emerged, revealing herself to be Mrs. Hudson.

"What is the meaning of this?" Holmes demanded.

Only now did the trio turn to look at him, Mrs. Hudson
having previously made such a disturbance that his opening of
the door had gone unnoticed.

"Mr. *Holmes!*" Mrs. Hudson cried out, and rushed to him.
"However did you do that?"

"Do what, my good woman?" Holmes demanded.

Mrs. Hudson turned to look around the room, then back to

her lodger. "Oh! I'd thought you were here. Though of course you *are* here. But I mean earlier."

"Upon what evidence did you base your assumption?" Holmes asked. His eyes darted around the room, alighting on a dozen unknown points.

"Evidence?" Mrs. Hudson contemplated this for several seconds. "No evidence. I just tend to know whether you're home or not, that's all." Then she frowned. "I must be losing my touch."

Afraid that she was about to launch into one of her soul-searching episodes, I said hurriedly, "And you came up here to show in these guests, I suppose. We had better make our introductions."

To my relief, Mrs. Hudson backed away, perhaps remembering only now that there were two others in the room. She bobbed her head and left by the door.

The two guests watched us warily, clearly embarrassed by this confusion. The lean young man wore a dull grey suit of a peculiar style which revealed no collar, and which appeared almost like a military uniform. His hair was exceedingly fair, and the shock of it atop his head was complemented by his rather wild whiskers. The woman beside him was dark-haired, and her complexion ruddier than her companion's pale skin. Her skirt was plain but she wore a blouse that was as startlingly white as the snow outside the window, and I saw her pull at the cuffs as though the item were unfamiliar to her, or at least that it was causing her discomfort.

I gestured for the couple to sit in the seats opposite Holmes's armchair. Holmes himself remained in the doorway, his eyes still darting. I pictured him as a watchdog, all but sniffing the air.

"Holmes," I said, "won't you join us?"

My friend blinked and then nodded. He launched himself towards his armchair and sank into it, watching his two guests with suspicion.

I realised that there was no place for me to sit before the fireplace, so I retreated to the hard chair at my former desk.

"Well then, who are you?" Holmes asked.

To his credit, the young man appeared not at all put off by this brusque manner. "My name is Fridtjof Nansen," he replied. Then he bowed his head as his companion said something under her breath, and then corrected himself. "*Dr.* Fridtjof Nansen. This is my wife, Eva. We come to you to ask for your help."

Instantly, Holmes's attitude changed. His eyes darted, and he muttered to himself rapidly – I caught the words 'squint' and 'effect of frostbite' but could make out nothing else. Then he leapt from the seat and shook his guest's hand warmly, and went on to extend the same cordiality to the young man's wife.

"I should have deduced as much in normal circumstances," Holmes said somewhat defensively. "I find that I am distractable this morning. Do not suppose that I am usually so sluggish."

I could not help but approach the young man, too. "Nansen, is it really you?" I said excitedly, taking my turn to shake him by the hand. "I have read at length of your travels. For how long have you been in the country?"

Nansen frowned. In his halting, imperfect English he said, "I return to Norway in May last year. Is that the country you mean?"

"Actually, I meant—" I stopped and shook my head. "It does not matter. I'm very happy to make your acquaintance. Your crossing of Greenland was a tremendous feat which has no doubt inspired the schoolboys of England just as much as those in your own country. I, too, am fascinated by the idea of exploration in such extreme conditions. May I ask why you are here in London?"

"I meet with many different people," Nansen said. "To-morrow I speak to your own explorers and learned men. I am very happy to share the knowledge I have got."

Holmes sat down once again, but now his posture was transformed: he perched on the very edge of his seat, all of his attention directed towards his guests.

"However," he said, "it is not your schedule of public engagements that brings you to my rooms. Pray, describe your plight and your need for my help."

Nansen nodded, appearing satisfied at having reached the matter at hand so quickly. "It is a simple thing. I would not come to you if it is only myself who sees it. But it troubles my wife. When she sees these things it sets her mind working, and she cannot sleep."

Holmes's eyes shifted briefly to Eva Nansen. Her rounded features were attractive, and I could see that she was most intelligent though the hesitancy in her eyes contrasted with her upright Scandinavian bearing.

"What is it that you have both witnessed?" Holmes urged gently.

"Gifts," Nansen replied.

His wife exhaled sharply. "You should not describe them in that way."

The explorer shrugged his shoulders. To Holmes, he said, "It is a joke I make. I call them gifts to make them not so frightening. It is Christmas, and gifts are good."

"And what are these gifts?" Holmes asked.

"Animals. Dead animals." Nansen stretched his legs, affecting nonchalance. "They appear on our doorstep overnight. Not every night, but sometimes. Perhaps one time every month."

"Do you mean like the offerings of a house cat?" I asked. "Are these simply small animals, like mice?"

Nansen laughed. "We get those as well – we have cats and a dog, too. But the cats and dog cannot carry a wolverine. And they cannot take meat from the bone and prepare it. Those first animals are whole, but some later ones are not. We are given meat that is ready for the pan, if only it has not been on the ground overnight."

Suddenly, Eva Nansen cried, "They are threats, pure and simple!"

Holmes was unperturbed by her outburst. "What nature of threat, Mrs. Nansen? How do you interpret their appearance at your door?"

Her expression clouded. "I do not know."

Her husband raised both of his large hands in a dismissive gesture. "They are jokes. Bad jokes, yes, but they should not be taken as serious."

"Then how do you explain—" his wife began. Then she seemed to remember where they were, and instead she turned to Holmes. "I allowed my husband to dismiss these threats for a long time. We have found them at our door one dozen times, over a period of a little over eight months. I should have acted sooner, and now I find that I have no alternative."

Holmes watched her intently, his eyes shining.

"When we came here to England," Mrs. Nansen continued, "I hoped at least to have some time away from this trouble. But it has followed us here."

Holmes's hands clasped together. "Then more threats have been made during your visit?"

"Only two," Nansen said quickly. "We have been loaned a cottage in which we stay while we are here. It is very nice. This morning we find on the doorstep a rabbit. The morning before, a… what is it called? A field vole, very small."

"But mightn't there be a less sensational explanation?" I asked. "We have a great deal of predatory wildlife in rural parts of our country, Dr. Nansen."

It was Eva Nansen who replied. "The rabbit, at least, was skinned and boned. It was spread upon the step most carefully."

"Is your suspicion that these offerings relate to the crossing of Greenland?" Holmes asked. I noted that his eyes rested upon both man and wife, indicating that he was equally interested in their differing views.

"No," Nansen replied immediately.

At the same moment, his wife nodded firmly and supplied a prompt, "Yes."

Holmes smiled warmly, as though this discrepancy were entirely understandable.

"We will return to Norway on Christmas Eve," Mrs. Nansen said. "I cannot bear the thought that we might live in fear at Christmastime, and Fridtjof agrees that this situation must be resolved before then." She paused, biting her lip. "But in truth, it is a period further ahead that troubles me. My husband intends to go away again in the future, this time in an attempt to reach the pole, and yet I cannot allow it if his life is in danger."

Holmes nodded. Once again appearing to address both of his guests at once, he asked, "And do you have suspicions about who might be responsible?"

This time, the couple exchanged glances. Fridtjof Nansen's head bowed in deference to his wife.

"My husband believes that it is merely somebody from our town who wishes him ill because of his success," she began, and now that she spoke at length I realised that her grasp of English grammatical rules was far more exact than her husband's. "But the idea that they might follow him on a boat from Norway to England cannot be entertained. It is my opinion that the meat is put there by somebody who knows my husband closely, and whose objection to him is far more profound."

"A fellow Arctic explorer, perhaps?" I ventured. Then I saw Holmes's eyes flash, and I told myself not to supply our clients' answers.

"We are all gentlemen," Nansen said. "There is contest, of course—" He bowed his head once again as his wife murmured in his ear. "Competition. Friendly competition. But these pieces of meat, they are like games in the school playground. No Norwegian man of science would do this."

"What of your relations with the other members of your expedition team, who accompanied you during your crossing of Greenland?" Holmes asked. Now his gaze was on Nansen's wife alone.

I saw Nansen's posture stiffen. "This is something I will not hear."

Holmes did not respond, still watching Eva Nansen. Eventually, she said, "The members of that team all enjoy my husband's full confidence."

Holmes nodded. "Please, Dr. Nansen, describe these men."

Nansen's spine straightened. "They are three Norwegians and two Mountain-Lapps. First there is Einar Hagen, a first lieutenant in the Trondhjem brigade and perhaps soon a captain. He is a good sportsman and a first-rate skier. Then Henrik Gylling, himself a captain of another sort: of schooners and steamers. Martin Johannessen Dahl is the youngest, a forester of only twenty-five years. These three men I know for a long time and trust fully before our expedition. You can imagine that months in the ice only makes such a bond stronger. The two Mountain-Lapps are Hassi, who is the older, and Schal, the younger, both reindeer farmers who join the team for money rather than a spirit of adventure, though they each serve our cause honourably. I will have no doubt put on any member of my team."

"You appreciate that I must begin my work with my mind open to all possibilities," Holmes replied.

Mrs. Nansen leaned forward sharply. "Then you will help us?"

Holmes did not reply at first. He looked around the room, appearing as close to uncertainty as I had ever seen him.

Finally, he replied, "Yes."

She reached out to clasp his hands, and though Holmes did not pull away, he became completely immobile. Then, addressing her, he asked, "Am I correct that you live in Christiania?"

She shook her head. "We lived for a time in the western district of that city, in an apartment. But my husband dreamed of living in a farming town called Lysaker—"

"I shoot duck there as a child," Nansen interjected.

His wife continued, "And he had a fine log house built for us there."

"It is distant," Nansen said. "Far from everywhere."

Eva Nansen's eyelids flickered, and I detected in this response that, despite her pride in her new home, she had not shared her husband's impulse to leave the city behind. I could imagine few women in her place – that is, those accustomed to urban life and high society, and then taken away from it all – who might have welcomed such a decision.

"And is it your habit to entertain visitors there?" Holmes asked.

"Rarely," Mrs. Nansen said quickly. "Only those people who assist my husband in his future plans."

"Then surely that includes the members of the original expedition team?" I asked.

Mrs. Nansen bowed her head in assent.

"Furthermore," Holmes added, "if the house is remote, is it the case that they are obliged to stay at the house rather than return immediately?"

Nansen rose from his seat. "I do not like these questions. In truth, the only people who stay with us are members of our own family and a single member of my team."

"Who is that?" Holmes asked plainly.

Reluctantly, Nansen replied, "Henrik Gylling."

Mrs. Nansen's eyes rose to the ceiling.

"I presume that all of those people are in your home country," I said. "So we are far from reaching an understanding of how these unusual threats might continue while you are here in London."

The husband and wife exchanged glances.

"Has anybody accompanied you on your visit?" Holmes asked.

"Only one person," Mrs. Nansen said. She still gazed up at her husband, as if forcing him to be the one to provide the answer.

With a tightly set jaw, Nansen said again, "Henrik Gylling." Then he spun to face Holmes. "I tell you I will not have a moment's doubt about him. He is as fine a man as I ever met, and we are close as brothers."

Holmes nodded acquiescence. "It may be instructive to speak with him, all the same."

With narrowed eyes, Nansen said, "You will not accuse him?"

"Not if he has done nothing to warrant it."

Nansen's shoulders slackened visibly. "My lecture to the men of the Royal Geographical Society is to-morrow afternoon.

If you both come there as my guests, we will dine together with Gylling afterwards."

"Very well," Holmes replied, with no trace of satisfaction.

I, on the other hand, was elated at the idea of spending an afternoon in that illustrious place, hearing tales of exploration and adventure. I was still lost in my thoughts when Nansen and his wife rose and left, though I noted that Eva Nansen lingered in the doorway, glancing back at Holmes and I as if she might speak, before she hurried away.

CHAPTER SEVEN

"Well, Holmes!" I exclaimed when we had heard the outer door open and shut. "An illustrious client indeed!"

Holmes did not respond. He had already risen from his chair and was pacing around the room once again. He continued glancing out of the window even after the sound of the carriage wheels crunching through snow had faded away.

Only now did I recall our reason for hurrying back to Baker Street this morning.

"Do you still fear that a trick has been played on us?" I asked. Then, with a start, I added, "Surely Fridtjof Nansen cannot be a part of it!"

Holmes only puffed out his cheeks in response.

In a wondering tone, I continued, "His arrival was most conveniently timed…" I shook my head. "But he is a figure of international renown. I am being absurd. Unless… that *was* the explorer Nansen, wasn't it?"

Holmes approached me and put a hand on my shoulder. "Calm your mind, Watson. Your ideas are running away with you. Yes, that was the real Nansen, and while the tale he told may have been far-fetched, I am convinced that it was sincere."

"But… might there yet be a connection with the events at the British Museum?"

"That is yet to be determined."

He resumed stalking around the room, then stopped abruptly in its centre, once again staring at the window. No – not the window, but the cupboard beneath it, upon which lay his violin case.

"What is the matter, Holmes?" I asked.

"When we left this morning, I left the case containing my violin open."

He sprang across the room and threw open the case lid. Then he stood staring at its contents. I hurried over to look.

The Stradivarius was in its correct place, but it was far from intact. At first I could not think what was so clearly wrong about its appearance, until I registered that its neck was a plain black shape, uninterrupted by strings.

"Who would take violin strings?" I asked. Then I added, "Or rather, perhaps the question is: *why* would they? No – it is: *how*?"

A strange sound halted my gabbling. I turned to my friend in astonishment to see that he was chuckling.

"What is this?" I exploded. "Holmes, you have been robbed!"

Holmes shook his head helplessly as if his mirth was too much to bear. I watched as he took from his pocket a piece of paper, and as he unfolded it I saw that it was the manuscript upon which was written the strange composition that he had dubbed the Adler Variations.

"Then…" I began wonderingly, "am I to take it that all of these tricks were perpetrated by Irene Adler?"

"Naturally," Holmes replied.

"Both the statue and the painting?"

"Yes. She was our artist with the portfolio, and the mysterious visitor who hung an empty frame in the library chamber."

"And now she has stolen your violin strings?"

"Quite so. She has made clear that we have been allowing ourselves to be distracted by a previous ploy even as she has effected another." He smiled reflectively. "Or perhaps this third theft had already been performed at the moment we discovered the empty picture frame, in the certain knowledge that I would reach the correct conclusion."

"Three thefts in a single morning," I said in wonder. Then I said sharply, "But the threats against Nansen: they are real and unconnected?"

Holmes waved a hand. "As I have already said: that is yet to be determined."

Still I felt I had not yet caught up. "What of my other questions, though? Firstly, how might Irene Adler have entered your rooms to perpetrate this theft of your personal property?"

"That would have presented no trouble at all. I rarely lock the door these days."

"Good lord!" I cried. "Whyever not?"

"Everything of importance is held within my safe, which is impregnable. And I find a locked door an unnecessary bother when I am safe in the knowledge that nobody would dare attempt to enter."

"Though this morning somebody has done precisely that, of course."

"Yes. Even so, I stand by my assumption regarding any other person." Holmes's fingers touched the bare neck of the violin lightly.

"I suppose it would have been a simple matter to evade Mrs. Hudson, who—" I broke off, then added, "If you recall, she told us that she heard noises from upstairs and assumed you were home."

"As you say, Mrs. Hudson is no sort of guard," Holmes said. "She has been known to allow tradesmen to roam freely throughout the building, and ever more so recently. Pray do not tell anybody about these habits of hers. It is only that she craves company."

I sat down heavily in my seat, amazed at my friend's nonchalance. At length, I said, "Very well. Now, to return to my questions. We have dispensed most unsatisfactorily with the 'how'. But what of the 'why'?"

Holmes held up the sheet music. "It is a variation on a theme."

"This again! What theme?"

He pursed his lips, tapping the paper rhythmically as he gazed at it. Then he lifted the violin from its case and nodded with satisfaction as he looked into the now empty space. Carefully, he plucked something from within the case and held it up, turning it for me to see.

It was a square of paper equal in size to the one we had found placed on the eye of Veritas. Rather than a circle, it comprised of two perpendicular lines drawn thickly in ink.

"What the devil can she mean by these signs?" I asked. But then, as Holmes produced from his pocket the first piece of paper he had discovered at the British Museum, I cried, "They are numbers! A nought and a seven!"

"Perhaps so." Holmes placed both squares onto the cupboard top and rotated the newer clue. "Or they may be letters: an O and an L. Or any number of other things: a circumference and a segment of a circle, for example."

"You do not seem the least irked at not knowing the answer," I noted.

"One must learn to recognise when one lacks the entirety of the necessary data. I trust that it will be supplied in due course, if only we follow the trail doggedly."

"Then you are content to traipse around in Adler's wake, going only where she leads you?"

"Indeed. That is the nature of the game."

It occurred to me that he was describing not only the challenge that his correspondent had set. Perhaps he might have happily followed in Irene Adler's footsteps for other reasons, too.

"You have not yet identified Adler's theme," I said, unable to disguise my irritation.

For several seconds Holmes gazed at the naked Stradivarius. Presently, he held up the sheet music again and I saw his eyes widen with some revelation.

Without warning, he pushed items aside on the cupboard top, then went to his desk and began to dig through the mess of scientific instruments.

"What on earth are you looking for now?" I asked.

"Check your desk!" Holmes snapped.

"For what?"

But he did not reply. Now he turned his attention to the bookcase, pulling out volumes and rifling through their pages, then casting them aside carelessly. Obediently, I unlocked and opened the drawers of my writing-desk, but found everything as it should be. By the time I had completed this appraisal, Holmes had entered his bedroom and sounds of falling objects came from within.

"What are you doing?" I cried.

When Holmes emerged from his room, his hair was mussed and his cheeks pink with exertion.

"I apologise," he said. "I am allowing my eagerness to get the better of me. She would never require such bluntness in solving the riddle."

"What riddle?"

"The riddle of the Adler Variations, of course. I have an idea, but I must prove that…" He trailed off, then once again he darted away, this time to the coat-stand, muttering, "Yes, she would have great satisfaction in making me complicit." He proceeded to yank his overcoat from the stand and then plunge his hand into each of its pockets in turn. Then, with a look of acute disappointment on his face, he repeated the action with my own coat.

"You ought to know better than to go through a man's pockets," I protested, but then my curiosity overwhelmed me. "What are you searching for?"

Holmes threw my coat upon his own, which was already on the floor. He patted his jacket and then his trouser pockets. He looked up expectantly and then moved towards me.

"I'll check for myself," I assured him. Like him, I checked my trouser pockets and found nothing. Then I thrust my hands into my jacket pockets. Instantly my top lip curled as my fingers touched a coil of wire in the left pocket, which put me in mind of poachers' snares. I thought of the carcasses left upon the doorstep of the Nansens' home and bile rose immediately in my throat.

Holmes watched me intently as I drew the mysterious item from my pocket and held it before me.

I cannot with any accuracy describe my relief when I saw that what I held was a neatly looped and tied set of violin strings.

Holmes snatched the strings from me, crying, "Just as I had hoped!"

I stared at him in amazement. "How has this new trick been effected? I have been wearing my jacket all morning."

Holmes beamed at me.

Slowly, I said, "Then she was there, at the museum?"

"It appears so," Holmes replied, his eyes gleaming. "Do you recall coming into close contact with anybody during our visit?"

I thought back to the episode in the library chamber of the museum. "I was shoved to one side by one of those scholars. He was a bookish type, short-sighted, unassuming..." I groaned. "I see now why you so respect her, Holmes. You and she have much in common, down to your fascination with play-acting at different roles. Even so, if her intention was to return the strings, albeit by such circuitous means, what was the purpose of stealing them in the first place?"

Holmes brandished the sheet music again. "I was blind, Watson. The melody that repeats with slight differences twelve times is not the only theme with variations."

He laid the paper on the table to allow me to examine it. I could make out the changes in the increments of rising pitch, but no more than that.

"I'm sorry," I said, "I have no great facility for music. You'll have to interpret for me."

He jabbed a finger at the end of the first passage. "There."

"I see nothing."

Holmes laughed softly. He lowered his finger to the end of the second passage. "And here."

"But you are indicating the point where the melody has already been completed."

"And yet there is a variation at that very point."

I stared blankly at the paper. "I still do not see it."

"That is because there is nothing to see."

"Holmes, you know that I dislike this sort of riddle."

"What is this?" He stabbed at the paper again, at a point directly after the third variation of the melody. Here I saw a bar featuring no notes, before the melody began afresh from its lowest pitch.

When Holmes moved his index finger away, I looked at the character drawn directly where he had indicated, which was nothing more than a black oblong.

"I believe it is called a rest," I said. "It simply means that the player ought to silent for a time, does it not? I am not so uncultured as you might suppose."

"Good. Now, what of these?" His finger rose to indicate the other positions. After the first melody were two characters: another black oblong, then a curled figure rather like a stylised letter Z.

"Silence, again," I replied. "Or rather, two silences."

Even as I said this, the words sounded wrong to my ears. Two silences?

"And this?" Holmes asked, indicating the end of the second passage.

Here there were three figures: one black oblong upon the staff line, following by one of the curled characters and then a figure formed from a diagonal and two attached dots, like berries upon a bough of holly.

"Surely each of these represents a silence of differing length," I said hesitantly.

"That is so."

I turned the sheet of paper over to see that, as Holmes had suggested, the notation for each period of silence was slightly different in each instance of the twelve rising melodies, with permutations of the characters I had already seen, plus others of a similar nature.

"As far as I can tell," I began without a great deal of confidence, "they all represent the same thing. That is, they are confined to a single bar following the conclusion of the melody, before it begins again. It is certainly idiosyncratic to vary the notation when they translate only to silence, but is there anything more interesting to it than that?"

"What is interesting is that they do not add up."

I frowned at this uncharacteristic admission of ignorance, before realising his meaning. "Oh. You mean in literal terms?"

Holmes pointed again. "Here, the rests total three-quarters of a measure. In this next instance, the sum is missing an eighth note. In each case, some amount, whether small or large, is lacking."

"I suppose you will tell me that it is no error, though."

Holmes bowed his head.

"Then…" I paused to consider the puzzle. "Then what do the omissions in these variations represent?"

"Nothing."

"Holmes, I beg you, let us have no more of this opaqueness."

Holmes nodded. "My reasoning is as follows: Irene Adler's intent is to provide a series of challenges with variations on a common theme. We have already witnessed three of them. What do they have in common?"

"A statue, a painting and a set of violin strings," I said slowly. "They are all related to the arts."

"True, but that is not the striking commonality." He gestured at the violin strings which I still held in my hand. "What is it that might be considered unusual or surprising about them, each case taken in isolation?"

"Well, the fact that I hold the stolen item at this moment. That is hardly usual after a theft, given that we have as yet made no effort to catch the perpetrator."

"Good. Go on."

"And the statue... that was not taken either. It was merely hidden, close to its original position. If there was a crime it was the damage done to it, which I suppose is itself diminished due to the fact that it was a plaster copy. I should note that Lestrade would point out the waste of the police's time and attention, mind you." I looked up at Holmes. "But the picture frame is another matter. As you demonstrated so promptly and convincingly, there had never been a painting inside it."

"Yet all observers were convinced that there had been a theft, were they not?"

"True. So..." My breath caught. "Then the theme is that nothing has been stolen in each case, despite all appearances!"

Holmes indicated the silences in the music notation. "I am convinced that is the message. In this musical notation, something is evidently missing – or, if you prefer, something has been removed from its rightful place – but on closer inspection it is nothing at all. Applying this to the disappearances we have investigated, one might summarise the theme as 'theft without theft'."

Though I marvelled at his ability to entertain such a nonsensical concept so readily, all I could think to say was, "So then you expect more such instances?"

"Naturally." He pointed at the squares of paper placed on the cupboard top, upon which were written the letters O and L. "Our efforts have been rewarded with these two clues, but they cannot be the only ones we will come by, if we are diligent."

"You speak of diligence, Holmes... but it strikes me that you intend to stand watch for more 'thefts without theft' at the very moment that you have engaged a new client. Will you help Fridtjof Nansen and his wife, as you have promised?"

"Certainly."

"But do you do so only on the chance that their case may be connected somehow to the Adler Variations?"

Holmes raised both eyebrows haughtily. "My reasons are

immaterial. Now, if you will excuse me, I will retire to the sofa to read the newspapers that have so far gone ignored."

His phrase echoed in my thoughts: *My reasons are immaterial.* As Holmes leafed through the *Times*, I watched his darting eyes and wondered whether he was skimming articles with the sole intent of discovering further 'thefts without theft' – that is, whether his focus had narrowed solely to watching for flags put up by Irene Adler.

CHAPTER EIGHT

I emerged from the cab to stand alongside Holmes, gazing up at number 1, Savile Row, the four-storey building within which so much adventure had been plotted and initiated. I may be a medical man, but the brand of scientific ideas debated in this esteemed location are of almost equal interest to me, and the thrill of exploration that I found in childhood books has not abandoned me in adulthood.

After indulging my awe for a time, Holmes strode to the door and announced us as Nansen's guests. We were promptly shown through to the map room in the courtyard, a large space with light provided by means of a towering, curved-glass roof, and lined on all sides with wide counters containing shallow drawers which I presumed must hold the maps that gave the room its name. Above the main space, accessed by a twisting iron staircase, was a mezzanine library crammed with bookshelves.

I assumed that in ordinary circumstances the main part of the chamber would have contained tables to allow members to lay out and scrutinise the maps. In contrast, this afternoon several dozen chairs had been arranged in rows, facing the rear of the room where Fridtjof Nansen already stood upon a low dais. A large group of men were in the process of taking their seats, their muttering a pleasing hubbub. I looked around the crowd, hoping to see adventurers about whom I had read, but to my disappointment most of the attendees were well advanced in years. I consoled myself with the thought that some of them must once have been great men.

When Nansen saw us over the heads of the crowd, he made to move in our direction – but then Holmes shook his head firmly and Nansen stopped short.

"Do you not desire to speak with Nansen before he begins?" I asked.

"It is not he that I wish to avoid," Holmes replied. With an unobtrusive gesture, he indicated the dais.

Another man sat on a chair at its rear, almost in darkness, his hands jammed into the pockets of his trousers. He appeared a decade or so older than Nansen, and unlike Nansen his hair was dark, with little in its shade, or that of his skin, that suggested that he was a Norwegian. His beard was a single sharp spike and his eyes had a searching, perhaps even hunted, quality. He wore a bulky woollen jersey and his scowling lips gripped the stem of a short pipe at which he puffed inexorably.

"Gylling appears decidedly unhappy about being here to-night," I murmured as we took our seats.

"No less than Nansen himself," Holmes replied.

I saw that it was true. Having retaken his place upon the dais, Nansen observed the crowd with a weary expression. The thought struck me that a *true* adventurer, an explorer and a pioneer, must find such spaces confining. I asked myself why Nansen had agreed to come to London at all, if this event was its central purpose.

When all of the attendees had found seats, an elderly, straw-whiskered gentleman climbed with Nansen's assistance onto the dais. He spread his arms and began to speak.

"Gentlemen, the northernmost reaches of the globe present a perpetual challenge. The considerations for any journey in that region are great, the hardships greater. Of course, many of you may consider any exploration of the frozen north as a simple rehearsal of the ultimate prize: to reach the pole—"

Here, I saw both Nansen and Gylling flinch visibly.

"—but I beg you to consider each achievement in isolation," the speaker continued. Then he beamed. "And isolation is another thing that we may expect our guest to speak about this afternoon. Without further delay, join me in welcoming to our society Dr. Fridtjof Nansen, leader of the first successful crossing of Greenland!"

His mangling of 'Fridtjof', with the 'd' and 'j' enunciated slowly and unnecessarily, elicited another wince from the owner of that name. Nevertheless, Nansen adopted a forced smile and stepped forward to address the room.

"I will be frank," he began, bowing to the speaker who had introduced him, and who had only barely succeeded in leaving the stage without toppling from it to the floor below. "I am of such a mind, too. All exploration of Arctic regions *is* only practice for a trek to the North Pole. And more frankness: that is my ambition, and my reason for coming here. Within the next two, maybe three, years I hope to mount an expedition to the pole. To-day I hope to entertain, but I also hope to inspire. That inspiration must be expressed as investment. I hope to enable my plans to become real."

There was no response to his words from the room at large. Perhaps these men were unused to such plain speaking. Suddenly Nansen's presence here made absolute sense. Any expedition leader was obliged to establish his profile as a means of securing funding, and so this afternoon's event represented work; an aspect of Nansen's vocation about which he was clearly less than enthusiastic. Nevertheless, I found that I admired his refusal to dress up his motivations as anything other than unavoidable necessity.

As if to acknowledge the tension that he had created, Nansen clapped his hands together, startling some of the old gentlemen sitting in the front row of seats. "But the entertainment must come first, yes?"

A murmur of uncertain agreement came from his audience.

Nansen began what was evidently a well-repeated account of the expedition, beginning in June of 1888 as he and his men were picked up by the sealer ship *Jason* at the Icelandic port of Ísafjörður. After more than a month of travel and assisting the captain of that vessel in his hunting of seals for their skins and blubber, the true adventure commenced. As the sealer could only come within twelve miles of the east coast of Greenland due to the terrific amount of thick ice floes, Nansen's team were obliged to set off in rowing boats, attempting to pick their way through gaps in the ice or, frequently, dragging their boats over the pack ice instead. Increasingly, though, their inability to find an unobstructed course reduced them to camping on the floes, watching helplessly as they drifted further and further south from their intended point of arrival on land, the terrified Lapps who comprised one-third of the expedition team praying and huddling beneath their upturned boat.

At this point in the narrative I found myself leaning forward in my seat, oblivious to all but Nansen's words and the startling pictures they painted in my mind. Nansen's adventure seemed a Jules Verne tale brought to life. At several points I shivered in sympathy for the plight of his team.

I turned to look at Holmes, whose eyes shifted from Nansen to the still-silent Gylling sitting at the rear of the dais. Chastened, I reminded myself of our reason for coming here.

The audience gasped or made muttered exclamations at each of Nansen's pronouncements about the hopping between floes in the direction of land, the continual flow of ice that only ever left them further from their destination each day, the ever-present threat of being pushed fully out to sea on a mobile island of ice and with only ineffective rowing boats as an alternative. Yet a combination of luck – in the form of a change of direction of the travelling floes – and sheer determination allowed them to push relentlessly northwards and to finally reach land, two hundred and forty miles south of their intended destination and having spent more than three weeks in agonised resentment at having failed to complete their initial twelve-mile trek in a direct line across the ice.

I dabbed at my forehead with my handkerchief, perspiring as if I had performed an equal share of the physical efforts of these admirable men.

"My word, Holmes," I murmured. "Is this not a marvellous tale!"

Holmes nodded curtly. I stifled my annoyance that he was not more affected. In many ways, Holmes was as remarkable a man as Fridtjof Nansen, and as tenacious. Indeed, if he found himself in a rowing boat far from the eastern coast of a frozen land, it was perfectly imaginable that he might simply bow his head and set to work stoically and without complaint in order to achieve his goal. Briefly I entertained the idea of Holmes accompanying Nansen on his proposed journey to the North Pole, and I could not help but smile.

"So," Nansen said from the dais, interrupting my fanciful thoughts, "now we find ourselves at Umivik Bay. It is the middle of August, far more late in the year than I would like. Our plan is to go to Christianshaab in Disko Bay, three hundred and seventy miles north and west of our starting place, but before that we must climb the mountains of inland ice to reach the level we will walk on. It is hard, tiring work and there are storms that make us stay together in our tent. Six men, together in a tent far smaller than this stage. You can imagine that I know this man, Henrik Gylling" – he turned to wave a hand at his colleague – "as well as any child knows his brother. And we argue as much, too."

The members of the audience chuckled at this. Gylling, for his part, did not deign to smile. He reached out to a low table positioned at the side of the stage, and retrieved a large placard which he held over his head. Upon it was drawn a sketch showing six men lying side by side in formless gloom, two of them resting forward on their elbows in conversation, one reading a book and another – Nansen himself – jotting notes in a minuscule journal.

"The Lapps read their New Testament at any chance they have," Nansen said, indicating the team member with an open book. "We others take air samples and write our diaries and make readings of meteorology." Then he pointed to what I had taken to be blankets wrapped around each of the team members. "We have but two sleeping bags, each made of reindeer skin, each to hold three men. The heat of a body is a resource not to waste, when the temperature is forty degrees below zero! Each bag has a hood that buckles over the heads of the sleeping men. A strange way to sleep, but most comfortable, and most effective against the cold."

He glanced at Gylling, who bowed his head in agreement.

"And the cold is something to fight at all moments of the day," Nansen continued. "My friend Gylling will now show to you our clothes that we wear."

Gylling rose from his seat obediently. Now that he was standing, I saw that his trousers and boots were as formless and bulky as his fisherman's jersey.

Drawing closer to his colleague, Nansen said, "We have no furs. We wear wool everywhere. Wool shirts and drawers next to our skin, then this thick and rough jersey. Then on the outside a short coat" – he waited as Gylling took from beneath his chair a garment, then drew this garment around himself and tied it tightly – "and knickerbockers and gaiters, and on the feet two pairs of stockings – one pair wool, one pair goat-hair – and then these 'lauparsko' boots from Norway. They are not beautiful but they are warm, and the soles they never come away!"

Now Nansen reached beneath the seat to retrieve a mass of canvas. Though I first assumed it to be a tent, when he shook it out I realised it was another garment. With difficulty, he helped Gylling push his already bulky arms into its sleeves.

"Wool is good for heat but does not do well in snow," Nansen explained. "This suit is thin but keeps fine-driven snow from touching the wool." He reached out, but Gylling brushed his hand aside to pull up the hood of the coat himself. Nansen hesitated, then continued, "And with the hood up we are as well away from the cold as possible. But it is still very cold, is it not, Gylling?"

I supposed that Gylling nodded in response, but his attire made him so shapeless and his body so difficult to discern that the gesture was all but invisible.

Nansen performed a pantomime of a shiver, his arms wrapped around his torso, his teeth gritted. The audience chuckled dutifully.

"Then of course there is the snow under the feet," Nansen said. "It is sometimes very deep and our boots sink into it. A great annoyance and a great difficulty. So, we adopt the most perfect tools for the task."

Gylling plodded to the rear of the dais again, and returned holding two long strips of wood each a few inches wide.

"These are the pride of Norway," Nansen said, "and it is my pride in turn to demonstrate their usefulness in Arctic exploration. These are 'ski'" – (I should add that there was widespread confusion in the room at this point, due to the fact that Nansen pronounced the word as 'she', though I have since determined the correct spelling) – "which are given to all Norwegian children to master by the age of four. In my country, to ski is as important as using the feet to walk."

He placed the 'ski' on the dais and then helped Gylling to place one foot after another into leather loops with bands to secure the heel. My neighbours in the audience involuntarily rose from their seats to see over the person in front and catch a glimpse of these strange contraptions.

"Gylling, show these men how you walk now," Nansen instructed.

With an expression that spoke of humiliation and the desire to be anywhere but here, Gylling trooped up and down the stage, at first lifting his feet high and keeping his legs apart to avoid the wooden strips coming into contact with one another and tripping him up, but after that he adopted a sliding motion, pushing each ski in turn forward without breaking contact with the floor. Then, in response to Nansen's urging, he dropped down heavily from the stage and paced along the narrow aisle beside our chairs, his dour frown never diminishing.

"With these 'ski', we keep above the snow instead of falling under it," Nansen said proudly. "It is my feeling that all Arctic expeditions will make use of 'ski' in future. Perhaps one day we Norwegians will make '*skilöber*' of you all!"

Gylling appeared decidedly foolish, less due to his immensely bulky clothing and more due to his manner of alternating scraping his way along the floor and tramping up and down with exaggerated, almost clown-like steps. However, I recalled the few times I'd taken to snowshoes to avoid sinking into snow, and determined that these 'ski' must fulfil their purpose.

Nansen watched Gylling indulgently for a while longer, then gestured for him to return to the stage, which he did with his cheeks glowing red. Gylling went immediately to the rear of the dais and stripped off his huge canvas outer coat before sitting to unfasten the loops that held his skis tight.

Instead of helping his friend, Nansen launched into the next part of his presentation. He detailed the decision to change course, the team setting their sights not on Christianshaab but Godthaab, hundreds of miles south on the far coast. His cheeks reddened to a colour almost matching Gylling's when he conceded that this new route had reduced the crossing journey by a little under one hundred miles – though he was quick to claim that the hope of reaching habitation before the last ship of the season sailed was the sole reason for the diversion. He had a duty to return his men to their families rather than condemn them to spend an entire winter in Greenland.

Now that Gylling had shed his coat and 'skis', he resumed his role of supporting Nansen's narrative with images, including a map showing the original and revised routes. Beyond the part of the story at which Nansen and his men had ascended the ice mountains and had commenced tramping on the vast expanse of inland ice with their sledges tied to them by ropes, Nansen's account faltered. Perhaps it was only that the following days merged one into another, but he seemed less certain of events and preoccupied with minutiae related to packing and unpacking the tent, and the team's supplies of food. We were told about the craving for fat due to the cold and the energy spent to stay warm, and the importance of a tinned preparation known as 'pemmican', a mixture of dried meat and fat, the latter comprising a third of the overall quantity.

The latter part of the trek across the inland ice appeared to be characterised by mishap and confusion. Nansen spoke of severe frostbite on every man's face, and also the need for slatted eye protectors to avoid the glare of the sunlight reflecting from the snow, but despite these latter useful tools there was more than one instance of snow-blindness, which had to be treated with cocaine. Nansen's men were frequently disoriented, and even now, in the present, Nansen seemed uncertain whether his described phenomenon of 'mock-suns' were an effect of the refraction of light through fine falling snow, or simple giddiness. Several times members of the team fell into crevasses which appeared without warning, the snow dropping away to reveal nothing beneath. One episode, which Nansen related with something approaching glee, had him rigging up sails for the heavy sledges, to allow the strong winds to push them along like ships upon the sea – an effort that paid dividends until one sledge was almost sent hurtling into a deep fissure, and another overturned and deposited its riders into the snow, then sped on far into the distance before being recovered. At this final admission Nansen turned to look at Gylling, who stood beside him holding up a placard with a sketch of the sail-fitted sledge. Gylling met his leader's eyes only for a second, then resumed staring straight ahead, and Nansen blinked rapidly as though he had been soundly rebuked.

This apologetic attitude only became more pronounced as Nansen announced, "Finally we know we are close to the end of the inland ice. But fjords are between us and Godthaab. Our sledges they cannot be dragged into this place, and we are fearful of leaving behind our supplies." Again, he glanced at Gylling, as if for some sign of agreement, but Gylling did not respond. Nansen cleared his throat and continued, "So we decide that Gylling and I will go on, and the others will stay behind with the sledges. They have the tent and enough to eat, and we take only what we need. We are the ones who take the true risk."

He continued, "In Ameralikfjord is the first true land we have seen for more than forty-five days. The descent is steep and rocky and after that there are bogs which slow us down. We are relieved when we come to a glacier, where we take our supplies from our backs and drag them along behind us on bamboo poles – a new sledge to replace the ones we leave behind. But the ice is not as thick as we hope, and many times it breaks and we fall in. When we reach its other side we are very tired and hungry. We—" He broke off, breathing heavily.

For the first time, I saw a hint of compassion in Gylling's dark eyes. He stood, then lifted one of his large hands and placed it on Nansen's shoulder. Nansen nodded heavily, as though he were experiencing all of the exhaustion he was describing anew.

"But we go on," Nansen said. "We reach the bottom of the fjord and then we build a boat from our bamboo poles, and tarpaulins, and willow for the ribs. We work together and we work hard. Then by this little boat we row out to sea, and soon around the headland to reach Godthaab. We are welcomed like heroes, and of course we send immediately for the four members of our expedition who are waiting east of the fjord. We have completed our crossing of Greenland."

Hearty applause erupted around me. I turned to look at Holmes, who was inert, leaning forward in his seat, a look of intense concentration on his lean face.

CHAPTER NINE

As we ate, I watched our companions intently. The conversation had been superficial, relating to Nansen's observations about London and comparisons with Christiania, though I perceived that that city had no more claim on his emotions than did our own capital. Nevertheless, Nansen appeared determined to play the part of a city gentleman on tour. Frequently, he turned to look at our surroundings, nodding amiably at fellow diners at their tables, then leaned back in his chair, his hand resting on his belly to signify his enjoyment of the food. Earlier, when we had been presented with the menu, he had made a great show of deliberation over the contents of the table d'hôte, humming thoughtfully over the decision for each course and enquiring as to my own preferences, and Holmes's.

For his part, Gylling had been content to duplicate Nansen's choices with mute nods to the waiter, and when the hare soup arrived he waited for Nansen to taste it and pronounce it delicious before he took a single mouthful. Otherwise he was taciturn and silent, pulling at the collar of his shirt and evidently uncomfortable with every aspect of our meeting.

Oddly – or appropriately, perhaps – it was boiled turbot which seemed to revive Gylling's spirits. He muttered something to Nansen, who responded with a snort of laughter and then began to push his own fish around his plate, stabbing and missing with his knife as though it were alive and evading capture.

"This fare must be a far sight different to your sustenance during your expedition," I ventured, addressing Gylling, whose smirk instantly evaporated.

Nansen composed himself and replied, "As I say in my talk to-day, we eat pemmican, pemmican, pemmican. Meat and fat. That was what we eat on our expedition, and though it is dull it takes up all of our thoughts all day."

"The fat is needed for warmth, I suppose?" I said, glancing at Holmes, who seemed disinclined to pursue the matter, watching the three of us placidly.

"Yes, and for strength," Nansen replied. "Fat gives slow release of energy, and let me tell you that pulling a sledge all day is tiring."

"But not only the pemmican," Gylling said. Both I and Nansen turned to him, Nansen appearing as surprised as I at this unexpected contribution to the conversation. Gylling continued, "We had a weekly ration of butter, an event that provoked rejoicing amongst us all. Though our attitudes to it varied a great deal."

A broad smile grew on Nansen's face. Addressing Holmes and I, he said, "I tell them 'Eat only a part, and save the rest', and some did – such as Gylling here. Others—"

"Martin Dahl," Gylling said solicitously.

Nansen nodded. "Dahl, he eats the butter whole, at once. A greedy man. Then every time we stop and cut off a corner of our ration, he watches us—"

"Like this," Gylling said, bending over his plate, staring at me intensely with lowered brow, his eyes flicking to the food before me and then biting his lower lip in anguish. He chuckled. "It was like being watched by a hungry wolf."

"Your family are foresters, Mr. Gylling, is that correct?" Holmes asked abruptly.

Gylling blinked and retreated. He nodded curtly. "So I know all about hungry wolves."

"Your English is very good indeed," Holmes said.

I realised it was true that Gylling spoke English most fluidly, his Norwegian accent only occasionally detectable. Quite why Holmes had chosen this moment to note the fact, though, was beyond me. I could only conclude that he wished to make Gylling uncomfortable in the hope of provoking some sort of revelation.

Holmes seemed determined to prolong the moment of awkwardness. He said, "Nansen, your wife also speaks English very well."

I wondered if Holmes was merely attempting to make a connection between Mrs. Nansen and Gylling. While suspicion about the threats had naturally fallen first upon Gylling, who had been present both in Lysaker and here in London, I realised that there was, of course, another: Nansen's wife.

If Holmes's observation had been meant to provoke Nansen, it achieved nothing of the sort. He only beamed. "My wife is a very good singer, and studied with the great Désirée Artôt in Berlin. My name is known well in Christiania to-day, but when we first were engaged, Eva was much more famous than me."

Holmes offered a pleasant smile. "How was it that you and she first met?"

"At Frognerseteren." Then Nansen registered my lack of recognition of the name and added, "It is a Norwegian skiing resort. I see legs sticking up out of the snow, and I pull them out, and there before me is Eva Sars. She is a fine skier – the best woman skier in Norway."

"Your courtship was brief, was it not?"

Still, this did not appear to offend Nansen. "Yes!" he replied. Then he nudged Gylling in the ribs. "Gylling here says 'It is too fast', and so do Hagen and Hassi when I write to tell them my news. But when I make decisions I never turn my back on them."

"Her family were not perturbed at the speed of your courtship?"

"They are good people. Her father, Michael Sars, he is a marine biologist, a man of science like me. Her mother's side gives her her artistic feeling – Eva's uncle is the poet Johan Sebastian Welhaven, who died some years ago. These people understand me. Anybody who makes the decision to walk across ice for fifty days has both science and poetry in his blood."

He looked at Gylling, who now stared at his empty plate. As if hoping to restore the earlier good humour, Nansen said, "We are pioneers in many ways on our expedition," he said jovially. "We create new dishes using what is available to us. Such as lemon snow."

With some degree of trepidation, I said, "Is that meant as a euphemism? I hardly think—" But Nansen's expression was blank. "Never mind," I said hurriedly.

"It is made by pouring lemonade mixture upon snow and oatmeal biscuits. It is most delicious." Nansen pointed at his own plate with his knife. "Earlier my friend reminds me of a time we fail to catch fresh fish, when we are still on the ice floes before reaching the east coast and the start of our trek. We consider ourselves expert fishermen, but our skills escape us when we are tired. We catch no fish, and catch no seal."

I experienced a sudden change, as if the lights had dimmed, or the room had grown cold. I looked around to ascertain that all was as it had been. Then I turned back to our companions and concluded that it was their manner that had suggested such an abrupt change. Gylling was inert, both his hands placed on the tabletop in a distinctly unnatural pose. Nansen, too, had frozen. Neither man looked at the other, and yet I had the distinct impression that they were more acutely aware of each other's presence than they had been moments before.

I had no idea how to proceed, so I looked to Holmes, whose eyes did not stray from the Norwegians.

"I suppose that supplies of food were a particular issue in the latter part of your expedition," Holmes said after a long silence, still maintaining a casual tone.

Nansen said quickly, "What we are speaking of is an attempt to capture a seal while upon the floes. A big one with a full-grown bladder on his nose, he flaps around on the ice, away from my seal-hook and Gylling's boathook, and we fail again and again, then bring out a rifle. The rifle does its work, but all the same the seal finds a way to slip away into the water. Soon dead, but gone to us." He sighed. "It is good luck that at this point we still have horseflesh. A good meal."

Apparently, Nansen mistook my expression for one of interest. With great animation, he continued, "It is good with salt and marrowfat peas. First, I chop up the horseflesh on the blade of an oar—"

I held up a hand to stop him. "I can well imagine, thank you."

"I was rather referring," Holmes said, "to the point of the expedition at which you left the greater part of the team in the tent, and struck out alone for Godthaab. Knowing that they would be obliged to wait on the ice for a number of days more, you would no doubt have left a correspondingly large share of your food behind."

Nansen cleared his throat. "Yes, of course."

"So I will ask you directly: was food an issue of concern during your final trek to Godthaab?"

Nansen hesitated. While he did not look at his friend, I sensed that he was attempting to gauge Gylling's own response.

"I see," Holmes said sternly. "Then I will supply my own answer. Something occurred during that final stretch – something which remains a point of contention between you. I noted as much during your speech at the Royal Geographical Society and I have noted it again during this conversation. Perhaps I might spend more time and energy prying the information out... but I will remind you, Nansen, that you came to me as my prospective client, and that I would be forgiven for not exhausting my deductive capabilities on your own person as opposed to the case you have brought to me. Now, before our next course arrives, might we move to the central reason that we are conducting this meeting?"

Now Gylling was watching Nansen overtly. Nansen said, "I have no secrets from Henrik Gylling. We may all speak freely."

Holmes merely raised an eyebrow in an invitation for Nansen to do precisely that.

Wearily, Nansen said, "Gylling knows about the threats that I receive, and yet his idea of it is different to mine."

"Let us begin with your own conclusion, then."

"Well…" Nansen hesitated. "Not a conclusion, then, but a sense of the answer. The meat is placed by somebody who wishes me ill. A rival, as you suggested yesterday, though I do not know who. And I tell you I do not care. These strange occurrences alarm my wife, but I am stronger than—"

Holmes cut him off. "Very well. And you, Mr. Gylling?"

Gylling's mouth opened, but he did not speak.

"Be assured," I said, "that whatever you say is in confidence. We will not judge nor leap to unreasonable conclusions. But you possess information that we will require if we are to help you, and help your former expedition leader. Who do you believe is making these threats?"

Gylling's face had become pale. I could easily imagine it was the same pallor he might have exhibited when caught in a Greenland snowstorm.

"Nansen jokes about the idea, but I believe…" he began, then faltered. When it became clear that nobody would speak in his place, he managed to conclude, "That they are gifts."

At the corner of my field of vision, I saw Holmes place his hands together beneath his chin, a gesture which always betrayed his fascination.

It struck me just how different Gylling's manner was from Nansen's, when he had used the same word in his first account of the case at Baker Street. It was abundantly clear that Gylling did not use the term as any sort of joke.

"Gifts of raw meat?" I said incredulously.

Gylling nodded.

"And do you use the word in its literal sense?"

"Yes."

"Then from whom are these gifts sent?"

"I… do not know."

"Well, then, how on earth might you reach the conclusion—"

Though Holmes spoke softly, his interjection stopped me from continuing. "Then you yourself have experienced such a gift before?"

"Yes."

"When you and Nansen were alone at the end of your expedition."

"Yes."

My eyes flicked to Nansen. "What happened, exactly?"

Nansen sighed. "Mr. Holmes is correct. We took little food with us at that time. We had guilt about leaving members of our team behind. Even if all proves to be well, we will arrive in Godthaab before them, and will enjoy the applause of the people there. We will know whether a ship is available to take us to our homes. We will not be required to wait – just *wait*, and nothing else – in the cold wind, full of worry. But we are fools. Before that point we keep our supplies on each of the sledges, and some part in one of our own packs. Now, it is all together. And when we go down into Ameralikfjord – exhausted, carrying everything – we sleep with no tent and then in the morning our supplies are gone."

"I fail to see how this corresponds to the more recent events that you have described," I said. "The loss of your supplies is a theft, not a gift."

Holmes made a quiet sound indicating his exasperation. Addressing Nansen, he asked, "How did you lose your supplies?"

Finally, the two explorers turned to look at one another momentarily.

"We do not know," Gylling said.

Nansen put a hand on his friend's shoulder. "Gylling is kind. I believe I lose the supplies myself. Before we reach the fjord we cross ice that is thin, fragile. I fall into a crevasse and Gylling drags me out. My bag splits and perhaps I drop the package of food. I am careless."

Gylling's expression was impassive. I found myself wondering whether he had another explanation for the loss, but equally I was certain that he would not contradict Nansen directly.

"Very well," Holmes said. "That explains the difficulties in which you found yourselves. You were very tired, and you lacked a boat to make the final stretch of your journey, so there was much work to be done."

Gylling said, "We were very hungry. We took it in turns to hunt. Unlike the days on the inland ice, in the fjord we saw life once again – but the gulls kept away from us and our tiredness made us poor shots. Crowberries grew only sparsely, and were not enough to restore us. Building the boat was a challenge, but a bigger challenge would be steering it out to sea and then around the peninsula to Godthaab. When we had finished the boat we slept again, but we feared the coming morning. We feared being so close to our goal and yet being too weak to achieve it."

"Yet achieve it you did," Holmes murmured.

Nansen put a fist on the table, perhaps with more force than intended; the plates and cutlery shook just as a startled waiter arrived to take them away. Nansen's cheeks flushed and he mouthed an apology. When the waiter had retreated with the dishes balanced on a tray, Nansen said in a low voice, "What happens is only good fortune."

"But what *did* happen?" I demanded.

It was Gylling who answered. "In the morning, on a broad, flat rock mere yards from where we slept, we discovered a gift."

"No," Nansen said forcefully. "That is not the right word. I like the joke, but it should not be taken as serious."

Gylling ignored him. "It was a bladder-nose seal, just like the ones we hunted from the sealer ship before we commenced our expedition, and just like the seal we failed to capture on the ice floes. It lay there, split open down the middle. An invitation for us to feed ourselves."

"And we do feed ourselves," Nansen said. "Though even then we are weak and clumsy. The copper hoop of our cooking-pot melts, and the pot overturns. We are forced to eat part of the seal raw to raise our strength before cooking the rest."

"What is important," Gylling said quietly, "is that without it we would not have reached Godthaab by boat. And if not by boat, perhaps not at all."

"One question remains, then," Holmes said. "Who was it who presented it to you?"

Nansen looked at Gylling, who closed his eyes with a frown.

To Holmes, Nansen said, "We are very tired. We see things all the time. For example, on the inland ice, fine snow known as 'frost-snow' makes tricks. When the sun shines through, it makes bright lines and mock-suns. It is worse than snow-blindness. It shows you things that are not there."

"At this point you were not on the inland ice. You were in a fjord."

"But tired all the same. So what Gylling sees may also be a trick."

"What does he see?" I asked. "I mean, what did you see, Mr. Gylling?"

Gylling's eyes raised. "I saw a shape, above the fjord, on the ice-horizon above us."

"What nature of shape?" I asked. "One of your fellow team members? A wild creature?"

Gylling shrugged. "Perhaps. But I think neither."

"Then—"

"A spirit."

Silence fell among our company, all of us preoccupied with our own thoughts. The murmur of conversation from the surrounding tables now seemed alien, and difficult to make out distinctly, like a constant hush of wind.

"Mr. Gylling—" I began in a faltering tone.

"I know that it must be strange to hear," Gylling said sharply. "I assure you it is stranger still to say it aloud. The thing I saw was large and stooped, and its outline was most ragged, suggesting a thick mane of hair – or that it was one with the snow. I mean to say that perhaps its shape could not be defined as can your body or mine, but that it was a form *made* by the shifting snow. It was entirely still, and yet it was moving, moving, moving. Yes, I believe that a Greenland spirit presented us with that meal which allowed us to continue on our way. I will not be convinced otherwise." Then he shuddered visibly.

Holmes said quietly, "You appear to find no solace in your conclusion."

Gylling shook his head morosely. "Some gifts signify goodness and kindness. Others signify nothing of the sort."

"And this one?"

"The latter, Mr. Holmes. We were being instructed to leave. Whatever that devil was, it wanted us away from Ameralikfjord, away from Greenland, away from that part of the world entirely. If we had only read the signs from the start, from the very moment the floes contrived to take us away from even commencing our expedition." He looked up. "Close to the east coast we were set upon by mosquitoes. We could barely get a scrap of food into our mouths without it being wrapped in a mantle of the buzzing things. We beat the air like lunatics and whirled tarpaulins around our heads. We tried everything we could to free ourselves of the plague, but finally we were forced to succumb and plod onwards in misery, and we lost a great deal of blood between us. I see now that we should have turned back and allowed our boats or the floes to take us away from that place, which summoned everything it could to prevent our passage."

Nansen's head bowed. "Gylling, Gylling. We have spoken of this. There is no cause for your sorrow. We complete the crossing, do we not? We are well, are we not?"

"Yes," Gylling said blankly.

"Then—"

Gylling cut him off. "Then why are you receiving these mutilated animals, Nansen? Why do they persist?"

We all turned to look at the expedition leader, awaiting his reply.

"I do not know," Nansen said.

In a quavering voice, Gylling continued, "They are gifts *and* they are threats. That morning in Ameralikfjord, you cheered as you ate the bladder-nose seal, but my heart was heavy. I understood the message we had been sent. It meant: *Take this and go. Next time the body you find may be one of your own men.* And these gifts you have received since our return, they mean the same thing. *Take this and never return. Next time—*"

"But it is absurd!" Nansen cried, and I saw several diners turn sharply in response to his outburst. In a quieter tone he added, "There is no 'next time'. Next time the gift is another dead animal – that is all. If these are threats, they are hollow threats, and I will not concern myself with them."

"And yet your wife is most concerned," I said, though I had barely meant to say the words aloud.

Nansen's expression clouded. "Yes. I must think of Eva. When we return to Christiania the day before Christmas, I will set my mind to making a team for my expedition to the pole. I cannot have her always worry about who I choose to trust. That is why I come to you for help. I may be strong, but for her this mystery must be put away forever."

We all ruminated on this. Then Holmes said, "During the other parts of your expedition, was there any evidence of a figure at all like the apparition that Gylling saw above the fjord?"

"No," Nansen said. Then the two explorers exchanged glances, and he added reluctantly, "Not during the expedition."

"Afterwards, then?"

Nansen made a gesture to his colleague, inviting him to take up the tale.

"Soon after our return, my family joined Nansen and his wife for a night at Lysaker," Gylling said. "My wife and daughter were eager to meet the great leader about whom I had spoken so much… Also, during our expedition Nansen and I had become used to lengthy discussions, and yet we had no chance to do so once we arrived at Christiania, and wished to resume our conversations." He smiled. "I understood his reasons for living in Lysaker. It is not far from the city but it is remote, calm, like the inland ice of Greenland. Not quite so cold, perhaps." Almost apologetically, he added, "Though that is hardly a consideration. These days all indoor spaces feel far too warm to me."

Again, he looked to Nansen before continuing. "You did not speak of it at the time, but you had received one of the gifts of meat already, is that right?" When Nansen nodded, he murmured, "You should have told me before we agreed to come. I brought my child to your home." Then he composed himself and addressed Holmes and I once more. "As you will have guessed, the next morning a dead animal was found on the doorstep by Eva. A mountain hare, already skinned and ready for cooking."

Involuntarily, I cast a glance in the direction of our departed waiter, thinking of the hare soup, my nose wrinkling.

"But what is important," Gylling continued, "is my daughter, Marta. She saw the spirit."

Holmes and I leaned forward in our seats immediately.

"She was excited," Gylling said. "Fridtjof Nansen is a hero to all Norwegians, and especially our schoolchildren, and now Marta found herself staying in his log house with its high-pitched roof, hearing of his adventures from his own mouth. How could she possibly sleep? So she read books, and wrote in her diary, and looked out of the window. That is why she saw it, in the early hours of the morning, before dawn."

"How did she describe what she saw?" Holmes asked. "Use her exact words, as close as you can manage, if you please."

Gylling hesitated. "A beast. Black, darker than the night."

"Did she add any more to this description?"

"I pressed her, but she is only seven years old. She spoke of fur and she performed its manner of walking." Gylling looked around him, then slipped from his chair and circled our table, his shoulders raised high, his head bent low. When he retook his seat he turned again to look at our fellow diners, none of whom appeared to have paid him any attention, and said, "She saw no more than that, though when I bring the image to mind I confess that the stooped figure is surrounded by whirling snow, its silhouette shifting all the time as it was on the horizon of Ameralikfjord. But it was very dark that night in Lysaker. And I must allow that I am not sure what part of her tale might have been real or what might have been the product of sleep, or half-sleep."

For several seconds I stared at Gylling. Then I turned to Nansen and asked, "Why did you not tell us of this yesterday?"

He spread his hands. "It is a child's tale. And it is nonsense, and I do not want my wife to worry more than she does."

"Was this the only sighting, or suspected sighting, of the bringer of these gifts?" Holmes asked.

Both men nodded.

"It is a most interesting addition to the puzzle," Holmes said. "I am glad of my decision to pursue it. Indeed, pursuit will be our next step."

At this moment, the waiter returned with our next course. My nose wrinkled once more as I regarded the plate of roast gosling that he put before me; I could not help but imagine the bird spread on a doorstep by an unknown creature, and the idea of consuming it filled me with revulsion.

"What do you mean by that?" I asked Holmes.

Holmes addressed Nansen rather than replying to me directly. "I mean that we will stand guard at your current lodgings, and we will watch for this beast, or spirit, or whatever it may be. And we must hope that it brings you another gift."

CHAPTER TEN

My arrival at Baker Street the next day, December 18th, was later than I might have wished, and I was in rather a hurry and somewhat disoriented by my activities that morning. So, it was with no small amount of fumbling that I made my way into the upper room at 221b Baker Street, and when I saw the disarray of the contents within and the activities of its occupant, I stood motionless and stupefied in the doorway.

Sherlock Holmes stood on the dining-table in the centre of the room, reaching up with both hands to the ceiling. He wore his dressing gown and his pipe was clamped between his lips, his teeth biting down in concentration. Around him was utter chaos. Cupboard doors were open and spilling their contents onto the floor. Dozens of books had been removed from the shelves and were scattered all around – I noted with dismay that this included some of my own volumes that I had left here when I had vacated the premises upon my marriage. The chairs that Holmes and I habitually used when entertaining clients had been moved from their places, revealing deep marks in the rug. Bottles and vials littered Holmes's chemistry bench, some of them leaking dark substances onto its surface.

"Do you mind explaining what you are doing?" I asked helplessly.

Holmes only now registered my presence. "It's here after all," he muttered.

I stared up at him, watching his fingers brush against the plaster. "What is? The ceiling?"

"A hole, Watson, produced by a round from a Webley .422, some months ago – by myself, I should add, in the pursuit of evidence related to variations in trajectory at close quarters. The case involved an assailant of diminutive stature, so I was obliged to crouch before a dummy victim of my own creation in order to replicate the shot. For a moment I became convinced that it was missing."

"Forgive me," I said uncertainly, feeling rather as if I was in a dream, or Wonderland. "So was it the dummy that appeared to be missing?"

Holmes climbed down. Then he took from his desk a lamp and replaced it in its usual place upon the table. He pointed up at the ceiling. "I am speaking of the *hole*. And it was only my having moved the lamp, and thereby altering the shadows that I am accustomed to seeing, that produced the effect of the hole having been filled in."

I looked up, and now I saw the divot in the ceiling to which Holmes referred.

"Ah. Good," I said. "Now might you explain the other – ah, *changes* – you've made to the room in my absence?"

Holmes ignored my question. "Before you enter," he said, "I would be grateful if you would describe the contents of your pockets."

Involuntarily, I patted them, then froze under the severity of Holmes's glare. I knew better than to protest, so I said immediately, "My pocketbook. A notebook and pencil. My pipe and tobacco pouch. A small box of matches. Half-full," I added, rather proud of my accuracy.

"Then you left your revolver at home?"

"Yes. Ought I to have brought it?"

"That is not the issue. Very well. Pocketbook, notebook, pencil, pipe, tobacco pouch, matchbox – and a scrap of newspaper within which is a small pair of scissors. Now, please place all these items onto the table here so that we might ascertain that they are all present."

I had already begun to obey when the discrepancy occurred to me. "Holmes – you're right! How did you know about the scissors, which I failed to mention myself?"

Holmes looked up, but this time I determined that he was not inspecting the ceiling but responding in world-weary fashion to my slowness. "Yesterday your moustache was noticeably longer – almost shaggy, I would venture to say. To-day you are a great deal more presentable, but you have addressed the issue imperfectly: the hairs to your left are still distinctly longer than those on the right. This is consistent not only with your having trimmed your moustache in a hurry, but also having carried out the act at your hallway mirror, where daylight from the transom above the front door would illuminate one half of your face far better than the other."

I found myself reaching and touching my fingers to my moustache, though I could detect no difference in the hair lengths.

"Furthermore, the distinct aroma of mincemeat and sherry upon your breath suggests that you have made merry this morning. I conclude that you visited more than one house on social calls. Something seasonal, I imagine," he added in an uninterested tone.

Indeed, my wife, Mary, had arranged for us to visit several of our neighbours to present them with cards and Christmas wishes, and each call had seemed to take longer than the last. By the time our neighbourly duties had been fulfilled, my stomach was full to bursting with mince pies and my focus affected by the three sherries I had consumed.

"Your wife insisted that you neaten up your moustache before you embarked on this series of calls," Holmes continued. "No doubt she had suggested this some time before you left the house, yet you only did so at the last possible moment – and then, in your hurry, you put the scissors into your pocket, where they remain." He pointed at my left jacket pocket. "That fact is no great mystery, because the metal tip is visible as it has been boring a small hole there."

I looked down to see that he was entirely correct.

Holmes continued, "The fingers of your right hand are stained with newsprint, which I suppose occurred when you realised your mistake at stowing the scissors away unprotected, and you took from the grate of one house or another the nearest piece of paper with which you might wrap them, after which time you promptly forgot about the matter again."

I chuckled. "You are entirely correct, Holmes. I have barely considered it since the blade jabbed into my thigh while we were being entertained by the Freers."

I withdrew from my pocket the offending article. The point of the scissors had indeed worn through the impromptu pouch of newspaper. I placed it on the table, and then alongside it the other items I had listed.

"All present and correct," I said. "Do I take it that you are in pursuit of more 'thefts without theft'? And that this same investigation is the reason for having upended every item of furniture in your rooms – and which inspired your search for a part of the ceiling that ought to be missing, but which seemed to have been reinstated?"

"Indeed," Holmes replied drily. Then in a more contrite tone, he added, "Though I have been quite wrong to imagine that she might repeat herself."

I did not know what to say about Irene Adler that would not cause offence. Instead, I said, "Has Eva Nansen approved your scheme to watch their lodgings for the Greenland spirit?"

"Yes," Holmes replied, but seemed disinclined to supply any more detail.

"I will have my revolver upon me to-night, then," I said. I added jovially, "And perhaps my grooming scissors, too, if I fail to restore them to their proper place."

"Good," Holmes said simply.

I hesitated. "Holmes – do you think that this preoccupation with the Adler Variations is…"

"What?" he snapped.

"Well, ah, is it *healthy*?"

Holmes stared at me blankly as if I had begun to speak an unknown language.

"Never mind," I said hurriedly. "Perhaps I might help, then. I suppose you have made some preliminary undertakings to determine the next clue in her challenge?"

"I have thought of little else these last days," Holmes confessed.

I did not dare to suggest that this was inappropriate, given that he had since been employed by a legitimate client, and that mystery was itself far from straightforward. I reminded myself that the application of only a little of Sherlock Holmes's mental faculties was worth as much as most people's full attention.

"I imagine you have checked the newspaper for clues each morning?" I asked.

Holmes subjected me to an unwavering stare.

"Of course you have," I said. "Did anything attract your notice?"

"Everything attracts my notice. But yes, upon close inspection a number of possibilities were raised – but they have come to nothing. In truth, to-day I am as replete with food as you are, having been fed incessantly by an elderly dowager." In response to my raised eyebrows, he went on, "My first hope was that the advertisements in the agony column might include a message of some sort—"

"Because that is the method you would deploy if you were setting the challenge," I suggested.

Holmes frowned. "In point of fact, I did employ it in one part of the puzzle I set last year. Perhaps you are right to say that I ought not to apply my own predispositions to the solving of another's challenge."

I had intended to say no such thing, but I nodded in agreement.

"And a fool's errand it proved to be," Holmes said. "Yesterday I was attracted by an advertisement that referred to a heart having been stolen – which certainly fits the description of a 'theft without theft' on the assumption that the woman still possesses a working heart despite her claim – and so I sent a telegram immediately to arrange a rendezvous. Consequently, this morning I found myself in the unhappy position of being expected to eat a vast quantity of crab-paste sandwiches while I attempted to determine whether my correspondent had any relation to Irene Adler." He put his hand on his stomach and grimaced as if reliving the experience. "Of course, she did not, and it was with no small amount of difficulty that I managed to extricate myself from the situation and the wrath of that lonely woman and her servants, due to their disappointment about my leaving so soon."

I stifled a smile, imagining Holmes in such an unlikely predicament. I had no doubt that Irene Adler, too, would relish his mistake and its repercussions. Might she have some means of observing his progress in the challenge she had set?

"Were there other promising leads in the newspaper?" I asked.

"The only other that promised – briefly – to bear fruit was the case of the Attorney General's missing briefcase."

"I read about that yesterday. Do you mean to say that you suspected Irene Adler of contriving that far more serious theft?"

Holmes waved a hand. "I did, but no longer. Until our appointment at the Royal Geographical Society, I spent much of yesterday in the environs of Westminster, interviewing civil servants and junior department staff, and I can safely conclude that the matter is the most straightforward type imaginable."

"Then it was truly stolen?"

"Of course – and I know who was the culprit."

"Who?"

"Mr. Walter Martin, junior assistant to the Attorney General himself."

"Oh," I responded, somehow disappointed that the name meant nothing to me. "And why did he steal it?"

Holmes shrugged his shoulders. "I venture I could find out, if it interests you."

I goggled at him. "If it *interests* me? This is a matter of the security of our nation, Holmes! What was in the briefcase?"

"I did not enquire."

"But… what was the response of the Attorney General, when you restored it to him?"

Holmes pursed his lips. "I suppose I ought to drop him a note to inform him of its whereabouts. I confess that it did not occur to me."

Without seeming to give the matter another thought, and without registering my amazed expression, he went to his chair where a newspaper was opened out. He held it up. "This last hour my focus has been upon the *Times* crossword."

I saw now that the margins of the newspaper were filled with untidy scrawled handwriting.

"I have never known you to take so much trouble over the crossword," I noted.

I was rewarded with another hard stare. "I am not attempting to complete the crossword, Watson. I am currently occupied in its deconstruction."

I shuffled my chair back into its correct place before the fire, then sat down. "What does that mean?"

"It means that if she has managed to infiltrate the crossword – if that is her method of conveying the next clue in the challenge – then she is unlikely to do so overtly, attracting the notice of everybody in the country."

"I hardly think that many people are likely to be scouring it for further puzzles than are already provided," I retorted.

"Nevertheless, I have found some elements which give me hope," Holmes said. "Look here: two across. 'Taking things the wrong way', seven letters."

I blanched. "It appears that you have no better idea than I. You have not filled in any of the answers."

"I do not see that I need to write them in, if I am content that I am correct."

"Then what is the answer to two across?"

"Larceny."

"Oh." Then I brightened. "Oh, I see! 'Taking things the wrong way' – very droll. I must say, that does rather neatly seem to apply to the theme of the Adler Variations. Then perhaps it is the reference 'Two across' that is significant. Have you searched the contents of the second page of the paper?"

"Once again, she would not be so overt," Holmes replied. Then he added, "And yes, I have."

"Now that I think about it, I suppose it does not really fulfil the 'without theft' part," I said at length. "It would hardly satisfy to simply see the word 'theft' written anywhere and consider that an instruction related to her next challenge."

"Quite so. There is another crossword clue that I hoped might suit. See here – five down."

I read it closely, several times. The clue for five down was 'Lacking hidden clue for "microscopic"', and the word had nine letters.

"The word 'lacking' is certainly promising," I said, "as is the reference to a microscope. You will have to supply the answer again, though."

"Minuscule."

I considered this at length. "Minuscule, meaning tiny, or microscopic – very well. And minus signifies a lack. Minus… clue? Ah, yes – the word 'clue' is hidden as an anagram." I blew out my cheeks. "It is tiring, this sort of brain work, is it not?" When Holmes did not answer, I went on, "And do you have a sense how this clue might relate to two across?"

Holmes shook his head slowly. "I have tried all combinations of two and five in this newspaper and those of the previous days. I have unearthed nothing. Perhaps…" Then, seized with new energy, he said, "Perhaps 'larceny' is itself anagrammatic. Let me see… *nearly C* – that might be a reference to another part of her musical score, might it not? Or it might just as easily be a rearrangement of *can rely*, though that would amount to mere reassurance rather than a new clue." He blinked rapidly. "Or… *can lyre*? It is another musical instrument so is arguably thematic, but the 'can' part is less satisfying. *Clan rye*… there is a River Clanrye in Ireland. Equally, it may be *lane cry*, an allusion to a call for distress in one of the narrow alleys of this city—"

"Stop!" I cried.

Holmes obeyed, staring at me in astonishment.

"Do you not realise, Holmes, that you are gabbling? You are seeing mysteries where there are none!"

He blinked several times very quickly, as if my statement required the same intensive processing as his earlier logical deductions.

"You are quite right," he said finally.

"Irene Adler is driving you to distraction, Holmes."

Holmes snorted softly and I saw on his lips the faintest of smiles.

I took the newspaper from him gently. "There can be no sense in poring over every word printed here. In the state of mind you find yourself, any piece of information might be twisted to appear to fit the criteria you have identified." By way of demonstration, I flicked through the pages of the newspaper, stopping at random, then placing a finger on a headline. "Look – I am sure with some effort we might work together to make this one appear significant."

Holmes's head tilted to read the words I had selected. His eyes narrowed.

"Yes," he said, the word barely more than a breath. "I believe you may be correct, Watson."

"Then can we now put this matter away, to concentrate on the threats against Fridtjof Nansen?"

"What?" Holmes said in alarm.

"Your *client*, Holmes."

"We will go to him to-night as promised," Holmes said distractedly, "but I see no cause to abandon this far greater challenge at the very moment we have glimpsed the sky through the clouds."

"But only moments ago you agreed—"

"I did, but then you yourself discovered another lead to investigate. A theft without theft."

It was only then that I looked down at the small half-column article I had unconsciously chosen, the headline of which read:

BEWILDERED LOCALS REPORT RIVER
EMPTIED OVERNIGHT

CHAPTER ELEVEN

The windows of our carriage were rimmed with heaped snow, making the view something rather like an elaborately framed image on a Christmas greetings card. Every aspect of the whitened landscape was almost as inert, too. The distant, snow-covered hills were as smooth as pebbles and the glimpses of villages indicated no life but for rising smoke from chimneys. In addition, our slow speed reinforced this sense of gazing at a fixed tableau. The snowfall appeared to cause a great deal of consternation among the train staff, and our speed frequently slowed to a walking pace. More than once I saw engineers stride alongside the engine, watching for banked snow ahead that might derail us.

Holmes had spoken little during the journey, so I looked to Toby the dog for companionship. The peculiar-looking creature, his half-lurcher and half-spaniel pedigree resulting in off-centre features and a baleful stare, had planted himself on the seat opposite me – alongside Holmes, who stared out of the window, dwelling in his thoughts – and frequently regarded me with a puzzled expression. I pulled faces to amuse him, but my actions roused no hint of a response. When our tickets were collected, the inspector frowned at the dog but seemed placated by Toby's absolute inertia, and I had to concede that I had never known a more placid, dejected animal. If only Toby did not emit such a powerful odour, anybody might view him a pleasant companion – and it was difficult to conceive of him being of any more use than a lapdog, so great was his disinterest in his fellow travellers.

Finally, our journey came to an end, having taken fully an hour longer than anticipated. We alighted at Cheshunt station and immediately proceeded east, trudging in the thick snow, and within minutes we arrived at a canal.

While the banks of the canal were as thick with snow as anywhere else, the centre of the river was clear and low boats moved along it at a rapid speed.

"There certainly seems nothing untoward here," I said.

Holmes made a sound of impatience. "Nonsense."

"Oh? But the report stated that the river had been emptied. Yet here it is, full to the brim."

"Quite so. But this is not the River Lea, Watson. We are looking at the Lea Navigation, a man-made canal that travels parallel to the River Lea proper, from Hertford Castle in the north all the way to the Thames at Bow Creek. We will walk north to find the section of the river that interests us. Even here, however, we may identify evidence for this 'theft without theft.'"

I stared at the river and its floating occupants. "All I see are boats travelling to London."

"Indeed. And what of those travelling in the opposite direction?"

Only now did I register that there were indeed other boats, which were stationed against the banks. Some of them towed flat barges with goods covered in tarpaulins. While the vessels travelling south were unimpeded, those that had paused at the banks were all pointed north. Even more surprising was the fact that the southbound boats were travelling more rapidly than seemed usual, despite the fact that no smoke came from their chimneys.

"The river is flowing too quickly," I said. "It is preventing any vessel from travelling north."

Holmes hummed and tugged on Toby's lead, but the dog refused to be goaded to move, sitting on his haunches and watching us with disinterest. Instead of attempting to encourage the animal, Holmes looked at me. Wearily, I took a biscuit from the bag that the dog's owner, Mr. Sherman, had given to us. Toby immediately took interest in the rather pungent foodstuff, and in total contrast to his earlier idleness he leapt up and gobbled the biscuit in one. After this point he became decidedly more animated, darting in all directions and investigating every cranny and frozen molehill along the canal path. Holmes did his best to direct him and I followed after, trying to put out of my mind the image of myself as merely another pet being taken for a walk. My mood had been somewhat sour ever since we had called on Sherman's house with its gruesome examples of taxidermy in the window, when Holmes had requested the use of Toby from the elderly proprietor. The look of delight on Holmes's face when the dog had lumbered out into the corridor was one which I saw rarely in any other context.

The canal path was not only perilous due to banked snow, but also because the overflowing river water continually lapped onto the path, turning the snow to slush in some places, and in other parts transforming it into a film of black ice. We must have looked a picture; while Holmes seemed to stride ahead with no need to check his pace, I walked with the exaggerated high footsteps of a circus clown and Toby's claws skittered continually and he produced plaintive yelps in protest as he drifted away in unexpected directions.

Presently, after we had travelled perhaps a mile and a half northward, we encountered a lock. Now I saw the cause of the issue downriver. A southbound boat was currently within the lock, and though its owner conducted himself in the usual way, turning the wheel while his mate remained on board the vessel, it was clear that the lock mechanism was operating improperly.

As the boat descended, it remained perilously high within the confined space, and it swung continually from side to side as its stern was pushed by rushing water from behind. Having nowhere else to go, this overflow pressed at the lower gate, spilling over it in a miniature waterfall. We watched as the two men navigated the troublesome obstacle, and finally the lower gates were opened and the boat rushed out upon a swell of water – so quickly that the bankside man was forced to work hurriedly to reclose the gate and then sprint along the canalside to where his colleague had finally managed to slow their craft to a halt.

Holmes pointed south along the canal to the other boats in a similar situation. "See, they are all able to move towards the lock in short bursts, but when it is operated they are compelled to take refuge at the banks. It will be a slow journey north, but an exceedingly fast one in the other direction to the Thames. I must say that I am relieved. Having discovered the newspaper article belatedly, I had feared the issue might already have been addressed before we arrived. Shall we go to the source of the problem?"

I nodded agreement and we crossed the canal at the lock. It was only now that I noticed a tributary that fed into the canal a little south of this point – or I should say it would *ordinarily* feed into the canal, whereas to-day it was heaped with snow that suggested no movement of water beneath.

"Is that where the River Lea ought to rejoin the navigation canal?" I asked.

Holmes nodded. Very soon we were within sight of the River Lea, which in contrast to the canal weaved a circuitous path around copses and peninsulas. For the most part, its route was only identifiable due to the thick snow within it being more sunken than on the banks. In other places the snow was sparser, and I was able to see through to the bare soil and rock of the riverbed.

Presently, we were joined by three men coming from the direction of Wormley. They wore caps and worn suits, and ambled with the dogged purpose of simple tradesmen, clapping their bare hands together to ward off the chill.

"It appears that we have arrived only barely in time," Holmes said to me.

"Here to sort the trouble with the river?" he asked the lead man affably, and I noted that he had adopted a sing-song tone which always seemed to put working men at ease. Indeed, Holmes's gait had changed, too, and he allowed Toby to get ahead of him, exaggerating the dog's straining at the lead as if the animal were even less within his control, a feisty beast requiring a lengthy walk. Toby seemed eager to participate in the charade and barked several times – the loudest sounds he had made since we collected him from his owner. At times he ran in circles aimlessly. I marvelled at the thought that Holmes regarded the dog as a useful tool in his investigations.

The effect worked admirably. The workman looked Holmes over, appeared to see nothing to rouse suspicion, and replied, "Heard about it, did you?"

Holmes gestured over his shoulder with a thumb. "Saw with my own eyes, back there. The Lea's dry as a bone all the way to the lock. Funny business."

The man snorted. "Ain't no mystery. I was sent out here this morning to see what was what, and any fool could see it. *Fixing* it's another matter, mind you. That's why these fellows are needed, plus the tools."

"I thought locals were bewildered?" I said in confusion, unconsciously repeating the newspaper headline.

The lead workman scowled at me. "Thought you said you'd heard nothing?"

"They… looked bewildered," I said haltingly, and pointed vaguely to the south, "and so did the men clinging onto their barges."

The man snickered, clearly relishing this idea. "Seems it was the farmers over to the east of here that told the papers," he said. "At Holyfieldhall, Hayes, Marsh Hill. Course, they could only see the empty tributary exit, and elsewhere the Lea's filled with snow. The only easy way to get here to Kings Weir itself is from the west. If they had, they'd've had the answer soon enough."

"Ah," I said, at which point the man seemed to lose interest in me. Holmes puffed his cheeks as if this information meant little to him.

The workmen seemed to pay no mind to our following them along the central promontory between the canal and river to approach the weir itself. Sure enough, the reason for the empty river was evident immediately. Kings Weir was angled sharply from the original river, and at thirty degrees or so from the canal, as if the Lea Navigation were the true course of the river rather than the Lea itself. No water passed this point to proceed along the River Lea. This was due to a row of five weir paddles that made an impassable obstacle to the water so that, having failed to split into two parts, it was forced to travel exclusively along the man-made canal in much greater quantity than was ever intended. Raising the paddles would have solved the issue instantly, but this was complicated by a great quantity of thick rope that wove in and out of the sticks atop each paddle, like willow woven to form a fence panel, which appeared to be bound tightly at various points and then reinforced with sticks and clods of earth. The overall effect was more like a beaver's dam than any human invention.

"Holmes, do you really imagine that this might be the work of Irene Adler?" I whispered.

Holmes shot me a warning look. Luckily, my question had not been overheard by any of the three workmen.

"It's a mess all right, Jim," one of the men said to the leader.

I could not agree – in fact, there was a strange beauty to the craft required to create the barrier – but nevertheless I sympathised. It would be no small matter to clear away the foreign elements of earth, sticks and rope in order to operate the paddles. The leader – Jim – leapt fearlessly from the snow-covered bank to the makeshift wall that blocked the river, and kicked at the ropes to demonstrate just how tightly they were bound.

"Absolute madness," muttered one of the pair of workmen still standing on the bank.

"Who'd go out of their way to do such a thing?" the other asked, though it seemed a rhetorical question. He bent to a canvas bag and began to take tools from it: two saws of different sizes, pliers with rusted jaws, a crowbar with an evil sharp tip.

"You'd think whoever it was might've left some trace behind," Holmes added. Then he paused for several seconds and said, "I wonder if the dog would find anything."

The two workmen looked at one another.

"He's got a keen nose," Holmes said. "Reckon your boss will hold off for five minutes, let us check the place over?"

The man with the tools rose and shrugged at his colleague. "Worth a try, Ed. We *were* told to look into it. Can't have folks meddling with the river whenever it suits them, can we?"

The other man turned to the weir and shouted, "Jim! Fellow here's got a dog good at sniffing things out. Let's give him a try, and I've got fresh rolls we can eat before we get started."

This seemed to convince Jim. He returned to the central promontory and the three men set to work consuming the large bread rolls produced from Ed's bag.

Holmes lost no time. He moved away from the group and bent to Toby. Though his body obscured my view to some degree, I saw him produce something from his pocket; I could not see what it was, but I took it to be some fragment of fabric. Once again I found myself wondering at his previous dealings with Irene Adler, presuming that this was something that held her scent.

Toby, however, seemed entirely uninterested in the item. All of his former energy seemed to have dissipated in an instant. Once again, he sat heavily on his haunches, gazing up at Holmes. When Holmes urged him to rise, the dog reluctantly waddled a few paces towards the end of the promontory, then peered down at the basin in the lee of the weir barricade, where at a glance the banked snow masked the fact that the River Lea was empty. Then the hound lowered itself to its belly and promptly rolled onto its side as if preparing to sleep.

Holmes bent to address the dog, and once again Toby stared balefully up at him. Slowly, Holmes rose and turned to face the huddle of workmen, and I saw utter dejection written on his face.

"Sorry," he said simply. "There is nothing to be found."

Jim looked across at Toby, who was still lying listlessly on the snow. "Don't know why you expected any more of that brute," he said, though not unkindly. "Looks like he's given up the ghost."

Holmes nodded sorrowfully.

"Right, then," Jim said, jamming the remainder of his bread roll into his already bulging cheek. "Let's get to work, lads."

Holmes and I stood side by side on the promontory, stamping our feet to keep warm as we watched the men begin to dismantle the barrier, beginning with the clods of earth, which they tossed down into the empty riverbed, followed by the loosened sticks. By the time they came to the wound ropes, the river water had begun to lick at their ankles and several times it appeared that one or more of them might slip and hurtle from the wall.

"Adler must be nimble, if she did this," I noted, "or at least she must employ nimble fellows."

Holmes only exhaled thoughtfully, his breath making a cloud before his face.

Despite his silence I was keen to initiate a conversation, if only to distract myself from the biting cold, and the fact that the wetness of the snow had begun to seep through the leather of my shoes.

"It certainly fits the criteria of a 'theft without theft', though," I said. "The river may well be described as 'stolen', at least as far as the farmers to the east are concerned – and yet the water remains available to all in the navigation canal. Quite ingenious, though ultimately pointless."

Holmes gave a hollow laugh, which I supposed represented a commentary on my thoughtless statement. To Holmes, no ingenious puzzle could be accused of being pointless, because he relied on such puzzles as others might rely upon tobacco or alcohol – or perhaps it was even more fundamental than that. To him, such complex challenges represented sustenance as essential as food or water.

"I'm sorry that Toby has disappointed you," I said.

"It is regretful," Holmes replied, "that my faith in him has been misplaced."

"Then you are convinced that there is a clue to be had in this area?"

"I am."

"And where do you hope it may be found?"

Holmes did not reply, but the direction of his gaze was my answer. The three workmen had been busy sawing away at the ropes at the centre of the barricade, and now Jim let out a cry of triumph and wrested the heavy rope up and away. Other parts of the knotted length came with it, now free to be lifted above the poles of the weir paddles, and together the three men carried it like an enormous python, skipping across the barrier over which some amount of water now spilled, to deposit it on the central bank. I saw Holmes glance down at Toby, perhaps hoping that he would respond to the rope – an object that ought to suggest to any dog an opportunity to gnaw, at the very least – but the animal paid it no heed.

Presently, Jim returned to the weir. Beginning at its far side, he used all his strength to pull up the first paddle. Water gushed from the main river along this new course, and Jim was forced to hurry several steps back, teetering like a tightrope walker, to avoid being caught in its force.

I watched the rush of water carve a channel through the heaped snow, curving up the side of the far soil bank before righting itself and following the correct path of the Lea. The mass of snow in the riverbed continued to be eroded, providing glimpses of rock – and then revealing something which at first I *took* to be a large rock, until I recognised what it was and cried out in alarm.

Holmes was already sprinting towards the weir, shouting, "Put it back! Put the paddle back, I say!"

Jim stood holding the paddle like a messageless placard, his mouth open in utter confusion. Rather than continue to state his case, Holmes darted onto the weir, wrenched the paddle from the man's hands and pushed roughly past him. Then, with three long strides he reached the position the paddle had occupied until moments ago, and with a show of surprising strength he slotted it back into place and pressed his entire weight upon it to force it down. The rush of water narrowed by degrees and finally, with Holmes's body shaking with exertion, the waterfall became a trickle and then stopped.

Holmes raised his head to look at the riverbed below. Jim's outrage was forgotten, and his colleagues were equally silent. I, too, stared down at the area beneath the barricade which had been cleared of snow by the river water.

I shivered involuntarily, despite being no longer conscious of the cold. Lying prone in the bed of the river and facing the sky with pale, sightless eyes, was the body of a man.

CHAPTER TWELVE

"Here comes a policeman now," I said, pointing.

Holmes did not even glance in the direction of the bridge, where Jim had appeared with a village policeman in tow. Instead, he continued to stare down from the promontory at the body lying in the riverbed, despite it being partially obscured by Ed and the third workman, who had without discussion adopted the roles of guardians of the corpse. They had muttered several times about 'covering our backs', which I took to mean that they feared that if the body was disturbed, then blame for the death might somehow find its way back to them.

When the policeman arrived he listened, nodding, as Jim provided an explanation of events – no doubt not for the first time, but now with the benefit of a visible location. The policeman peered into the riverbed, baulked, and rather than venture down into it he asked each workman in turn whether they had any notion who might have tampered with the weir paddles in such a way. Finally, he turned his attention to Holmes and I. Holmes was barely able to muster replies to his questions, so I spoke for us both, informing the officer that we had simply been walking Holmes's dog at the time of the discovery.

Finally, the policeman deigned to make his way slowly down the bank into the riverbed. Though it was now empty of both water and snow, moisture had left the bank tacky with mud, in contrast to the hardened earth elsewhere. The policeman skirted around the body, grimacing with each step. He half crouched near to the head, then appeared to think better of it.

He looked up to where we all stood on the bank. "We'll have to carry it up there. Will one or two of you fellows give me a hand?"

Holmes leapt up immediately, as did the third, nameless, workman, who yanked Ed's hand to draw him along. Jim and I watched as they struggled down the incline. Holmes bent over the body, as if he were gauging how best to raise it, though I knew that he must be making a hundred observations during this brief opportunity. On the police officer's command, the four men hoisted the body by the shoulders and knees, and set to climbing the slope. Several times one of them faltered, and the corpse threatened to slip out of their grasp and back into the hollow, but eventually they made their way up to the central promontory and deposited the body flat onto the snow. Jim and I edged forward. The skin of the man on the ground was pale, almost grey, the discolouration evidence of the early stages of decomposition. He appeared to be in his middle years, with a mat of mouse-brown hair, plain features and only a hint of stubble on his chin. He was dressed in a rough cotton shirt and trousers which were worn at the knees, and he was slight, though perhaps that was partly a consequence of the sagging flesh. His protruding tongue signalled drowning – a most unhappy way to die – but it was his meagre amount of sodden clothing on this bitingly cold morning that made me shudder.

Holmes's eyes continued to dart over the body. A little further away, the policeman discussed arrangements with the three workmen. I had been left holding Toby's lead, and as the dog flopped lethargically onto the bank overlooking the riverbed, the lead tugged at my hand, making my gaze shift in that direction, to the position that the corpse had occupied. Puzzled, I turned and signalled to Holmes, who moved to join me.

"What do you suppose that is?" I asked.

Holmes did not answer. Together, we hurried down the slippery bank.

The object I had seen was a small tin box, its surface rust-free and glinting in the low sunlight. Fixed to a metal handle on its lid was a thin chain which coiled snake-like in the mud.

As one, we looked up the bank to reassure ourselves that nobody was watching. Then Holmes lifted the tin. The greater part of the length of chain came with it, and now I saw that its other end was wrapped around a dense rock approximately the size of a rugby ball.

Holmes and I shared a glance, and then Holmes eased the lid of the tin open.

At first I saw nothing inside. Then, with infinite care, Holmes retrieved between his thumb and index finger a small square of paper. Upon one side was inscribed clearly a letter D.

I have never, before or since, seen such an expression of dismay on my friend's face. One might go so far as to describe his features as crumpling, having lost all his vitality in an instant.

The reason was clear. Since the discovery of the body he had evidently been in denial – and yet here was evidence that this ugly business was truly the work of his much-admired Irene Adler.

CHAPTER THIRTEEN

The return train journey was even less pleasurable than the outward one – but at least it was swift, the track having now been cleared adequately. Holmes stared directly ahead, not even paying the passing landscape any notice. Unwilling to sit in a position that might make me the object of his scrutiny, I sat beside him with the dog on my lap.

Once or twice I attempted to rouse my friend from his reverie.

"It is often said that one can never truly understand a woman," I ventured, "and a woman such as Irene Adler perhaps less so than any other. She is a complex creature, Holmes."

When Holmes turned and stared at me absently, I retreated into the safety of silence.

After some time I asked in a quiet voice, "Will you inform the authorities about the Adler Variations?"

The answer was a terse, "Certainly not."

"But questions will be asked. And if you have any desire to unravel the mystery of the body in the snow—"

"The broader matter is hardly the concern of the police force."

I hesitated. "But Holmes, you can no longer consider this a

challenge between friends – or whatever it is that you and Irene Adler are to one another. A murder has been committed."

"That does not follow. A body has been discovered. That is all."

"You are grasping at straws, Holmes. And even that village policeman will sense that something is amiss – I mean, even more amiss than simply finding a corpse. The tin box, the chain fixed to the rock... you saw his puzzlement when he saw what we had discovered. The fact that you took Adler's clue from it is immaterial. What remains clear is that there is a complex motivation behind the death of that man."

Holmes's head bowed – it seemed not quite an indicator of agreement; it struck me as more akin to defeat.

"It is an untidy matter," he said ruefully. "If only we might have had access to the body before attracting undue attention, then..."

I could not conceive how events might have proceeded any differently. A corpse is a corpse.

My friend's attention became fixed on Toby, who had fallen asleep on my lap. Holmes did not speak for the rest of the journey, or the brief walk from the station to Baker Street.

In the hallway, Holmes stopped on the lowest of the stairs that led to his rooms, and turned to look at me.

"I must have time to think," he said sharply, "and I cannot bear to have that dog in my sight. I would be grateful, Watson, if you would take him back to Sherman immediately."

I had never before been an admirer of Toby, whose lopsided features offended me, and whose talents had always seemed to me overstated. At this moment, however, Holmes's tone rankled, partly due to his misplaced anger at a benign animal, and partly due to his expectation that I might act as his errand-boy. I found myself wondering about the way in which Holmes saw the world, and whether he felt that colleagues who had exhausted their usefulness might sensibly be disposed of.

My thoughts were interrupted by the opening of the door beyond the staircase. Mrs. Hudson emerged, nodding at each of us in turn. Her doleful attempt at a smile was more than I could bear.

"I have an idea," I said. "Holmes, do you suppose that Mr. Sherman might allow us to hold on to Toby for a time – another week, for example?"

"I have no doubt that he would be delighted, as it would represent one less mouth to feed, allowing him to concentrate on the stuffed and mounted members of his animal collection. But what purpose might that serve? Toby is of no use to me."

"It is rather that we might be of use to him," I replied.

Holmes grunted. "Watson, this is far from the sort of riddle I enjoy."

I gestured at Mrs. Hudson as she moved to the front door to check the letterbox. She returned empty-handed, appearing more morose than ever. Then her eyes alighted on the dog at my heels and for the first time she smiled.

Holmes appeared to have caught on to my scheme. He bowed his head.

"Mrs. Hudson," I began, bending to scoop up the dog into my arms, "we wondered if you might perform a great favour."

She blinked, looking first at the dog and then at me. I felt sure that she had not been listening to our conversation up to this point.

"What is that, Dr. Watson?" she replied.

"This is Toby," I said, raising the dog to her eye level. "Through a fluke of circumstance he finds himself without anybody to care for his needs. Ordinarily that would present no concern – he is a most retiring, pleasant dog who demands little, and could no doubt fend for himself – but during this season… Well, it strikes me that nobody ought to find themselves alone at Christmas."

The landlady's eyes glinted, and I hoped I had not gone too far. I could not bear the thought of her weeping.

"Now, if his owner agrees, Holmes and I rather hoped that you might look after the dog yourself – just until after Christmas."

"Of course!" Mrs. Hudson said immediately. She held out her arms, and I slid the uncomplaining Toby into her embrace. His body must have been heavier than she had imagined: he slid down so that she barely held onto his flanks, though his face remained level with hers.

I handed her the bag of biscuits that I had been carrying in my coat pocket and with some difficulty she succeeded in taking one out and offering it to the dog. Instantly, Toby came alive, and snatched the treat into his jaws. Then, abruptly, a fat, flapping tongue emerged from between his lips and licked at Mrs. Hudson's nose. She giggled with glee.

"He's a smelly old thing, isn't he?" she said.

It was true: now that the dog had been raised up, it was clear that the sharp tang I had detected at various times during the day was certainly produced by him.

"It is to be expected," I said. "And though he may be getting along in years, he has much still to contribute, and he is a fine friend."

Both Holmes and his landlady stared at me in puzzlement, but I found I had no easy means of explaining my sudden empathy for this faithful beast. I cleared my throat and said, "Well, then. I will leave you both be, and I will drop by Sherman's premises on my way home to confirm the arrangement."

Nobody appeared to be listening. Mrs. Hudson giggled again as she pressed Toby's wet nose to hers, and then she scurried away in the direction of her kitchen. Holmes had already recommenced stumping dejectedly up the stairs to his rooms, where he would no doubt distract himself by other means.

CHAPTER FOURTEEN

The cab journey north to Nansen's lodgings was brief, but when we arrived our surroundings could scarcely have been a greater contrast to our usual environs in central London. The farm at Child's Hill was within striking distance of Hampstead Heath, and the cottage was surrounded by a dense orchard which itself lay within snow-blanketed, empty grounds. When we stood before its door, we might as well have been fifty miles away from all civilisation.

It was Eva Nansen who led us into the cottage and when I repeated my observations of our surroundings, she laughed and said, "My husband insisted that we would not stay within the city. He does not sleep when there are very many people nearby. If he had his way, I wonder if he would do without me, too. Perhaps he would allow Gylling to stay. After all, Gylling has shared a bed with my husband as often as I."

It was eight o'clock in the evening and all occupants of the cottage had already eaten. We passed the remainder of the evening pleasantly, gathered around the fireplace of the cosy drawing-room, indulging Nansen and Gylling in their tales of exploration. Now that they were in relatively familiar territory, both men appeared at ease, and there was no reference to the reason for us joining them at Child's Hill. Mrs. Nansen watched her husband throughout his storytelling, displaying a more tender attitude towards him than she had during discussions of the threats levelled against them. Now she only chided him softly when his enacted pantomimes of crawling from crevasses or climbing ice walls threatened to become so animated that the furniture was rocked or he came too close to the open fire. Gylling's part in the delivery of the Greenland tales was more modest, and he preferred to sit with his legs splayed apart, a glass of whisky resting on his belly as he confirmed his leader's statements with slow, serious nods of the head.

I found myself responding to the stories with exaggerated displays of appreciation, due to the fact that Holmes reacted barely at all. We had spoken about the corpse in the riverbed during the cab journey, but he had offered no further insights and it seemed obvious that his thoughts were preoccupied with that mystery and, consequently, the involvement of Irene Adler. The sole piece of information I had been able to glean was that there would be an autopsy in Waltham Cross the following day.

Perhaps it was Holmes's taciturn behaviour that hastened the end of our evening's entertainment. A little after ten o'clock Nansen yawned and Gylling made a joke about their custom during the Greenland expedition of sleeping as soon as darkness fell. Eva Nansen said goodnight and retreated into one of the two bedrooms – the building was single-storey, with both bedrooms located at the rear. Presently Gylling, too, made his excuses and retired.

"I cannot thank you for staying here to-night," Nansen said to me.

At first I took this to be an insult, but I reminded myself of Nansen's imperfect grasp of English, and I nodded and shook his hand. Nansen glanced at the silent Holmes at the fireside, then retreated into the depths of the house.

"Well," I said, clapping my hands together. "Will we take it in shifts to watch out for any sign of the Greenland beast?"

Holmes simply nodded and continued gazing into the fire.

"Perhaps I ought to take first watch," I said.

Holmes waved a hand dismissively. "As you wish."

So my guard duty began. At first I behaved like a sentry, every half an hour performing a tour that took in the views from the windows of the drawing-room, then the hallway, and the small window positioned between the two doors of the bedrooms. Gradually, however, I became less active, and when there came a sound from outside – which proved to be nothing more than the hooting of an owl – it was Holmes who leapt from his seat first. Seeing that my friend was more alert than I, even when his mind was elsewhere, and that he betrayed no desire to rest, I allowed myself to sink into the armchair by the fire, muttering that I would take a brief moment before renewing my vigil, and slipped gradually into sleep.

I awoke to the sound of voices and the smell of frying bacon. I shivered and for a moment I imagined that I was in the polar north, sharing a tiny tent with five other men who were currently occupied in cooking breakfast at a stove. I soon realised that the cold was due to the open windows – beyond which was still the blackness of night – and the fact that I had had no blanket over me as I slept. The voices and delicious smells were coming from the kitchen.

To my surprise, it was Holmes who I discovered dishing up bacon from the pan onto five plates, upon which were thick, buttered slices of bread. Nansen and his wife were seated at the table, and Gylling was pouring tea from the pot.

"Finally, Watson!" Holmes called out, and all eyes turned to me.

I stifled a yawn. "I am sorry for sleeping so late." Then I looked around the room in search of a clock. "What time is it? It is still dark outside."

"Half past six," Nansen replied. "A good sleep."

It would not be light for another hour and a half, but I reminded myself that Nansen's preference would have been to retire to bed at dusk and rise at dawn. Evidently he had also trained himself to be satisfied with a minimal amount of sleep. I glanced at Eva, who appeared noticeably weary, one elbow propped on the wooden farmhouse table and her hand covering her mouth.

To Holmes I said, "And what of your own sleep?"

"What of it?"

"I had meant to relieve you at two o'clock. Have you rested?"

"Yes. But rest and sleep are two very different things."

Startled, I said, "Then you did not sleep at all last night?"

Holmes smiled and finished his task, then returned the pan to the stove and took a seat at the table.

I followed suit – then I gasped audibly, as it was only now that I remembered the reason for our being here. I glanced at the bacon on the plate warily. "I suppose that no gift of meat was found this morning?"

"None," Nansen replied cheerfully. "This meat is a gift of Gylling, yesterday."

"I assure you that it has been nowhere near a doorstep," Gylling added.

In response to my silent appeal, Holmes shrugged his shoulders slightly. "I suppose our Greenland spirit was in no mood for deliveries last night."

I noted that Eva Nansen did not react to Holmes's unusual description of the bearer of the gifts. She only covered her mouth and yawned.

I said, "Perhaps it was put off by a fuller house than usual."

Then I concentrated on my bacon sandwich. Plain and unseasoned though it was, I had to admit that it was most delicious.

"What are your plans to-day?" I asked Nansen.

Nansen waved his half-eaten sandwich vaguely. "We meet the Prince of Wales."

I stifled a splutter. "Really?"

"Is that a surprise?"

"I suppose not," I replied, trying to compose myself. "But it is a great honour."

Nansen shrugged. I looked in turn at Gylling and Eva, who seemed entirely unaffected by the prospect of meeting a member of the royal family.

Mrs. Nansen yawned again and then said, "We ought to apologise for your wasted evening." I saw that she had not yet touched her own food.

"There is no need," Holmes replied. "The absence of information is often as valuable as any acquisition. I desire to know about the pattern of these deliveries, particularly in this new location, and now we have another reference point."

"Then do you intend to return this evening?" Mrs. Nansen asked. Her tone was difficult to determine, and I sensed an actress's control over her emotions, or at the very least her voice. I recalled that she was accustomed to performing on the stage as a singer.

"I regret that we cannot," Holmes replied. "We have another engagement."

Mrs. Nansen's neutral façade slipped immediately. "But you promised to uncover whoever is making these threats!"

Holmes did not reply, and my attention was occupied more with Henrik Gylling. In response to Holmes's announcement I had heard him exhale, then had seen him attempt to mask his reaction by lifting his cup of tea to his lips.

Afterwards, when we had said our farewells and were walking along the lane towards the railway station, I asked, "What is it that prevents our return to the cottage, Holmes? Surely it is paramount that we maintain our vigil even after this initial disappointment."

"You are quite correct, Watson," Holmes replied.

"But you told Nansen that—" I halted. "Ah. It was a lie, then?"

"Indeed. We will perform another watch over the house to-night, but from without rather than within."

I sighed. "I'm glad that I chose to sleep last night, then, as there will be little opportunity to do so in the chill of night-time, and in the bushes. Is it Gylling that you suspect, or Eva Nansen?"

"I am receptive to all possibilities. We must learn more before pronouncing who is the culprit."

"Be that as it may, Holmes, something has occurred to me. I have not been certain whether it warrants sharing."

"I imagine you will do so all the same."

"Well, yes. I have been considering the case of Henrik Gylling. If Gylling must be considered a suspect in the matter of the threats now being made, then it does not seem unreasonable to wonder if his duplicity might extend to the fanciful tale of the 'Greenland spirit' and its initial gift of raw meat. Even further back, ought we not to interrogate whether he was responsible for the loss of the rations during the final portion of the expedition, when he and Nansen trekked alone? That was the cause of their trouble in the first place, which resulted in these stories of spirits and beasts."

"Yes," Holmes replied simply. "Those are all good questions."

"And yet they do not appear to concern you greatly."

"For the moment, they do not."

Until now I had resisted suggesting a connection between Gylling and Irene Adler's challenges, but it now seemed the only way to ensure Holmes's interest. So I went on, "If Gylling did dispose of those rations, then the status of that loss must be in question. It occurs to me that casting food supplies into an ice chasm, for example, is a crime that involves stealing from a person, and yet no other person is the beneficiary. That is, one might argue that it qualifies as a 'theft without theft.'"

I noticed a change in Holmes's bearing – his strides became stiffer, and he pressed a curled index finger to his lips.

I resumed walking beside him, casting occasional glances at my companion. Now that all of the good humour I had seen at breakfast-time had vanished, it was clear that it had been a pantomime for the benefit of the occupants of the cottage. In truth, there was only one subject that occupied his mind.

"I imagine we are not going to return directly to Baker Street," I remarked.

"No, we will not."

"Then we will travel to Waltham Cross, for the autopsy?"

"Yes," Holmes replied, and he would speak no more until we alighted from the train in that town.

CHAPTER FIFTEEN

The clinic at Waltham Cross was smaller than my own practice, and the idea of such a demanding procedure as an autopsy being performed on the premises inspired horror in me. When we called at the front desk a young man hurried out from a room at the rear of the building, wiping his hands, and he immediately refused us access despite my medical credentials. It was only Holmes's insistence that he worked on behalf of Scotland Yard that made the young man yield finally, and with great reluctance he showed us into the rear parlour. Here, we discovered the same body we had seen the previous day, naked and laid out on an operating table, the chest splayed open and an elderly, white-haired coroner peering into the cavity. Instantly, Holmes railed against the man having begun his work earlier than scheduled – an antagonistic stance that ensured that we were even less welcome than we had been already.

"I insist that you halt your work for five minutes to allow us an uninterrupted examination," Holmes said.

The young man we had spoken to earlier bent his head to whisper to the coroner, who blinked in surprise and shook his hands in a pantomime of refusal. The young man muttered something more, and finally the white-haired man stepped away from the corpse upon the table.

"Now, Watson," Holmes snapped, "let us see what secrets this body may divulge. No doubt they will be fewer than if the autopsy had commenced at the agreed hour, but we will make do."

I noticed the elderly coroner blanch at this indirect accusation. His eyes flicked to the body upon the table, as if he was seeing afresh the effects of his morning's work spent cleaving it open.

Holmes and I both leaned over the cadaver. First I examined the face, which I had only glimpsed momentarily the previous day, though I was able to confirm my initial assessment that drowning had been the cause of death. Both the hands and feet were bloated, though the skin had not sloughed away and the putrefaction and discolouration suggested an arrested decomposition, which had no doubt been due to the icy cold within the heaped bank of snow.

Next, I turned my attention to the exposed interior of the body. The chest cavity was overhung by broken ribs which had been sheared away inexpertly, leaving ragged stubs which were themselves discoloured with stains of fluid. I saw immediately that the lungs, liver and kidneys were all notably swollen.

"There seems no doubt about the matter," I said in a quiet voice so that only Holmes could hear. "Drowning is the only conclusion. Though it is no thanks to this coroner that we are able to determine so. Perhaps he was not strong enough to break the ribs more cleanly."

Instantly, Holmes whirled around to face the coroner. "At what time did you begin your work to-day?"

"An hour ago," the coroner replied.

Holmes nodded, then his eyes flicked to the young man. I felt certain that he was performing his usual miracle of minor observations, all of which would supply a character summary greater than the individual under scrutiny might provide if questioned directly.

After concluding this brief assessment, and apparently satisfied as to the young man's irrelevance to his immediate concerns, Holmes demanded, "Where are the personal effects?"

"He had none," the coroner said before his assistant could reply.

"His clothes, man!" Holmes snapped. "Where are they?"

The assistant looked at the coroner for approval, then went to a closet and retrieved a shapeless pile of fabric. Holmes snatched the garments from him and held them up: a pair of coarse work trousers and a rough cotton shirt which had now dried and turned stiff.

"Were there undergarments?" Holmes asked.

"No," the young man replied.

Holmes considered the clothes at length, then tossed them aside. He made a circuit of the room, pausing at the table upon which the coroner's tools had been laid out neatly, shining under the light from the lamps.

"I would be grateful if you might tell me your name, sir," he said to the elderly coroner.

"Bastable."

"Bastable…" Holmes repeated. "Bastable, of Waltham Cross. Is that correct?"

"Of Whitechapel," the coroner replied.

"Then your presence here was specifically requested?"

"Indeed. I came yesterday evening and have stayed overnight at the local inn."

"Naturally," Holmes replied, though his tone conveyed his suspicion.

"Now, gentlemen," Bastable said, rising to his full height, which was only a little over five feet, "I would be grateful if you might allow me to resume my work. Or ought I to send my assistant to fetch a representative of the local authorities?"

With a final look at both men and then the body on the table, Holmes exited the room and I followed after him.

"That was hardly a pleasant experience," I said once we were outside the building.

"Do you tend to relish autopsies, Watson?" Holmes asked.

I was about to protest, but then I realised that this was a rare example of Holmes making a joke.

"The assessment of drowning is a simple matter," I said, if only to reach more familiar ground for conversation, "but there is one aspect I don't understand. Why would the corpse have been wearing only shirt and trousers, and no undergarments?"

"That is the least of the mysteries with which we have been presented," Holmes replied good-naturedly.

His tone rankled after our confrontation within the clinic, and I found I was unable to shake off my irritation. "You appear surprisingly cheerful," I said, "given our recent, rather tense experience – not to mention the fact that we must yet suspect Irene Adler of murder."

I saw instantly that this had been the wrong comment to have made. Holmes fell silent and would not respond to my further questions.

CHAPTER SIXTEEN

I spent the greater part of the day with my wife, whose opinion was that the Yuletide season was primarily a time for family. I called in to Baker Street at seven o'clock in the evening as agreed, wearing an additional thick jersey under my jacket and overcoat, plus woollen leggings beneath my trousers, in preparation for a cold night spent lying in wait outside Nansen's cottage. When Mrs. Hudson answered the door and invited me inside, I became immediately warmer than was comfortable, and I was forced to shed my overcoat, doing so carefully to avoid disturbing the revolver contained in its pocket.

"Mr. Holmes has not been home all day," the landlady said brightly. She turned to fiddle with a pine bough that was resting upon a sideboard next to the door, which was festooned with red ribbons. I looked around and saw that other such boughs had been placed all around the hallway. Mrs. Hudson went on, "I thought that he must be with you. Will you come in for a moment and have a cup of tea? It's dreadfully cold out there."

I dabbed at my forehead and removed my jacket, feeling far from cold. Yet, remembering my earlier promise to Holmes to spend time with his landlady, I followed her past the bottom of the staircase towards her kitchen, growing warmer with every step I came closer to it. The smell of pine was almost overpowering.

"Did he not return home even briefly this morning?" I asked.

"I have not had a single sniff of him."

By coincidence, as I entered the kitchen it was a single sniff that overpowered my senses – though it was now not only the scent of pine that made me reel and lean heavily against the door frame before I was able to compose myself. I detected cinnamon and aniseed, which perhaps came from the pan simmering on the stove, though they were mixed with something far less palatable. Very soon I saw the author of the noxious smell: Toby the dog sat in a new basket by the hearth, his head lolling on his paws.

Mrs. Hudson followed me inside and then stood, arms folded and head tilted, watching the dog as if he were a favourite child performing a newly learned skill.

"I see that Toby has made himself quite at home," I remarked, "and that your mood is much improved."

The landlady beamed. "He's a darling. We've been having a wonderful time together."

I could scarcely imagine what nature of activities they might have performed together, given that I had rarely known Mrs. Hudson to leave her home. I reminded myself that all recent evidence suggested that Toby was no longer enthusiastic about being taken for walks.

The landlady set to making a pot of tea, humming as she worked. Before long, Toby's smell ceased to be so appalling – or at least my senses grew used to it, and it mingled with the scent of pine and whatever confection was responsible for the aniseed and cinnamon – and I bent beside his basket to pat him on the head, which he endured stoically. I began to wonder whether I might not prefer the unfortunate creature now that he possessed a little less character. Perhaps he had been worked too hard by Sherman – or by Holmes, in his pursuit of clues. This thought led me to the same odd feeling I had had the previous day, of both Toby and I being led around by Holmes, acting as our master.

Mrs. Hudson turned to see me in consultation with Toby. "Mr. Holmes really has no feeling for unthinking creatures," she said wistfully.

"I am not an unthinking creature!" I retorted. Then I realised my mistake, and my cheeks flushed.

Mrs. Hudson was kind enough to refrain from passing comment. She simply placed a cup before me and poured the tea in silence.

"It must be a bother when Mr. Holmes performs his vanishing act," she said finally.

"It is infuriating," I agreed. "Then again, what aspect of Holmes's character is *not* infuriating at times?"

She patted my arm. "You know that you're welcome to come here whenever you like, whether Mr. Holmes is here or not."

A discomfiting image came to mind, of Toby and myself trapped in this kitchen, our only purpose companionship.

Experiencing a strong need to establish that I lived an independent life, I said, "I am often required at my practice." But the words sounded hollow to my own ears – how many days had it been since I crossed the threshold of that building? Though I remained convinced there must be some other activity to demonstrate that my contribution to the world was not only in relation to Sherlock Holmes, I could think of none. I added weakly, "Perhaps I will bring Mary to wish you a merry Christmas, in the coming days." I looked again at the immense amount of ribboned pine boughs which distracted the eye at every turn, and thanked my good fortune that my wife's enthusiasm for the festive season did not manifest itself so invasively. In comparison to this almost medieval – and most pungent – seasonal display, Mary's tastes were decidedly modern.

"How lovely!" Mrs. Hudson said, clapping her hands.

I rose from my seat. "Thank you for the tea. I must go if I am to make my train." I hesitated. "I can only hope that Holmes will be at the station, or that he will meet me at our destination."

"It's awfully late to be travelling," the landlady said, "and cold as the Arctic."

I grimaced, struggling to pull my coat over my thick jersey. "It'll be colder yet to-night. We are due to spend a good deal of it outside."

"You poor dear!" she cried. "And you will be alone?"

"As I say, my hope is that Holmes—"

Mrs. Hudson clucked her tongue. "You must not rely on him. Here, why not take Toby?"

I looked doubtfully at the inert animal. "I hardly think that—"

"It will do you both good. I've overfed him and he'd benefit from some fresh air. He's ever so lively sometimes, but a moment later he seems to lack any energy at all."

I thought of the task at hand. While Toby had singularly failed to track any scent at Kings Weir, he might fare better if he was called on to chase some beast in the wild. Though I was fully aware the chances were that he would be of no use, the idea of huddling in the bushes at night with a dog for company was notably less unappealing than doing so alone.

"Thank you, Mrs. Hudson," I said. "I would be glad to take him with me."

CHAPTER SEVENTEEN

There had been no sign of Holmes at the stations at either end of my journey. As I tramped in darkness to Child's Hill, Toby trotting at my side, I began to lose hope entirely. By the time I reached the orchard which surrounded Nansen's cottage it was almost ten o'clock and the trees made a black, almost impenetrable barrier before the building. Nevertheless, if I angled myself just so, I could see that a lamp was lit in the window of the drawing-room, and behind it was the ruddy glow of a fire in the grate. I circled the cottage at a safe distance and determined that no other lamps were lit elsewhere in the house.

I returned to a vantage point that overlooked the front doorstep, then hissed, "Holmes!" in the hope that he was already present and hiding far more effectively than I. Yet there came no answer.

Fighting a growing sense of resentment, I cast around in the darkness, searching for a site that might protect me from the worst of the cold while allowing me an uninterrupted view of the front of the cottage. The ground was littered with uneven heaps of snow which had penetrated the canopy of the fruit trees, and I realised now that I had taken no care to hide the tracks I made. I reassured myself that it hardly mattered – there ought to be no reason for anybody to emerge from the cottage unless it was in pursuit of the very perpetrator of the crime I was here to witness, at which point it hardly mattered whether I had hidden myself. All that mattered was to determine who was delivering the gifts of raw meat.

A nearby bush beneath a large apple tree seemed equal to my needs. I huddled within it and tried to urge Toby to lie at my feet – though his energy had mysteriously returned and he seemed far more intent on investigating every sharp noise that came from within the foliage. I sighed, held tight to the dog's lead and tried to ignore his sharp odour – a mixture of pine and something more distasteful that eluded me – to concentrate on watching the building.

Around forty-five minutes later, the light was extinguished. I waited, squinting in the darkness, and was rewarded with another glimpse of light at a side window. Conjuring the layout of the building in my mind's eye, I determined that this was Gylling's bedroom. The room which the Nansens shared was out of sight, and I cursed Holmes for his failure to appear – if there had been two of us watching the house, one of us might have waited on its opposite side, affording a clear view of both bedrooms.

After half an hour more, this final source of light disappeared. I settled myself, preparing for a long wait. The moonlight was sparse due to the overhanging boughs of the orchard trees, producing only patches of greyness amid the black. This near-uniform darkness produced a strange effect in me: before long I lost any perception of depth, seeing only vague patterns of grey and black, like the spots on the flank of a dappled horse. I lit my pipe and muttered to Toby in an attempt to maintain alertness – but then I saw that the dog had fallen asleep.

I continued to speak, now addressing only myself and repeating anything that came to mind: stories I had read recently in the newspapers, aides-memoires related to medical knowledge that I had long ago committed to memory, even childhood rhymes. Shivering alone in silence was unbearable for any length of time.

Presently, I stopped. A sound had interrupted my thoughts. I checked my watch: it was a quarter past one.

I held my breath, identifying each sound I could hear in turn: a faint breeze moving the leaves above me, the clicking of some unseen insect, the occasional stirring of something small. I told myself that nothing of the size to make such a sound could be the Greenland beast.

Toby's head lolled on my left shoe. I shook him free gently and rose to my haunches, my legs complaining at the motion. I realised that my fingers were numb despite my gloves, so I pressed my hands together, then flexed the fingers and interlaced them, trying to restore life.

Still, I could not hear the same sound that had roused me. Now, I could scarcely recall what I had heard, I had fallen so deeply into my own senseless ruminations.

Then it came again: a voice.

I rose sharply, then stifled a cry as my head struck a branch. I kept still, watching and waiting, but saw no sign of anybody. Then, perhaps due to the cold breeze changing direction slightly, I caught another snippet of speech – I could understand none of what was said, but this time I judged by its pitch that it was certainly a man. Moreover, the voice was muffled. I no longer believed that whoever was speaking was stalking around in the orchard, but rather that he was within the cottage.

I gazed at the doorstep for a time, regretting the need to abandon my vigil in order to investigate the new sound. Nevertheless, it seemed inevitable. I bent to wake Toby, fed him a biscuit, and together we crept to the right, keeping a good distance from the building and making our way to its rear.

As I moved, the voice grew louder. It came in fits and starts; the pauses now seemed to have little to do with the direction of the wind. Now it occurred to me that there might be not one voice, but two, with pitches varying between low muttering and higher, more urgent appeals. Both certainly came from within the cottage.

I reached the corner of the building, where the coverage of the trees was sparser and the snow correspondingly deeper. I looked around, reminding myself that the mystery of the voices was all well and good, but that I must not forget about the possibility of the Greenland beast – or whoever was posing as it – being close at hand. Still, though, I saw no evidence of any other person. Beyond the orchard, the snow was flat and uninterrupted by footprints.

Toby began to run in circles around my feet and I hissed at him to be quiet.

At my new position, moonlight shone over my shoulder and towards the house. There were no lamps lit in either of the bedrooms, but I was able to see into each room – no curtains were drawn at either window, and each sash was wide open. I supposed this was a habit both explorers had adopted since their return from Greenland, where they had become accustomed to far lower temperatures at night. In the rightmost room, which belonged to Fridtjof and Eva Nansen, I saw nothing to suggest that the couple were not asleep in their bed, but in the left bedroom I perceived an upright figure. From the spike of his beard I knew immediately that it was Henrik Gylling.

Gylling's hands were raised as if in supplication. He was looking in the opposite direction to the window, perhaps towards the door of his room. I could not see his lips, but his body shook whenever the other voice spoke, making higher-pitched entreaties. I could now hear the words quite well, though I could not understand them – belatedly, I realised that both he and his interlocutor were speaking in Danish, or rather its Norwegian dialect. However, the name of 'Nansen' was clear even amid this gabble.

I moved to one side, but I could see nothing of the other person, who I assumed was Fridtjof Nansen. The right side of the window, and therefore the entrance to the bedroom, was blocked by some solid object.

My gaze travelled from this unknown object down to the windowsill, and then I froze in shock. Something appeared to be leaning in at the window at this side, apparently in the act of either climbing in or climbing out. It was beyond the beam of moonlight and wreathed in shadows, but I could make out some aspects: it was not large overall, yet its head was bulbous and disproportionate in relation to the size of the body.

I gasped, and instantly I fancied that the apparition turned sharply. Though I saw no eyes or muzzle, I was certain that the movement of its head – or its pelt, or its mane – indicated that it was now facing me. I thought of Henrik Gylling's description of the figure on the ice-horizon. Was this creature's silhouette shifting as if it were composed of whirling snow? In my panic I could not begin to make an assessment.

At my heels, Toby growled and pulled at his lead.

The moment seemed to stretch interminably. Then I told myself that the creature was not large, and that I had a revolver and a hound. I fumbled in my pocket, managed to locate my gun, and pulled it out, but my fingers were so cold (and fear also played a part in my clumsiness) that I could not handle it properly. It fell from my grasp and I bent to scoop it up – but by the time I had risen, the beast was gone.

For a moment, all was silent save for the thudding of my heart. I stared at the open window, entertaining the awful thought that the creature had scampered inside – but within the room Gylling still sat on the edge of his bed, and he had become silent and calm. The idea crept into my mind that the beast had existed only in my imagination, a phantom produced by exhaustion and morbid tales.

Then a sound came from the foliage at the right side of the building. The thing was making away.

"Toby!" I cried, releasing the lead. "Go after it!"

To my surprise, Toby leapt forward. I followed at his heels, brandishing the revolver wildly as we hurtled into the thickets to the north of the cottage. The strobing effect of the moonlight dazzled me, but I kept the dog in view, shouting encouragements and caring nothing if I woke every sleeping person in the county.

It was only when we had performed two circuits of the same small bush that I lost hope. Toby, too, seemed to give in: he turned to look at me, one ear raised as if in apology. Then he slumped onto the snow, panting heavily.

I grunted in frustration and raced back to the cottage. Now lamps were lit in both bedrooms, and I heard cries of alarm. In moments I was at the front of the building, and as I approached it at speed, its door began to open from within. I reached the doorstep first, and so it was I rather than Eva Nansen who discovered the large, skinned hare draped there, its arms and legs awry as if thrown down in a great hurry.

CHAPTER EIGHTEEN

The next day, December 20th, was a Saturday, and I had once again promised to accompany my wife on a Christmas errand. Ordinarily I might have been reluctant to visit the market selling trinkets, where visitors congregated to stand idly drinking mulled wine and discussing gift ideas. My usual conception of shopping involved striding at a high speed into whatever premises I was unfortunate enough to need to visit, then swiftly taking items from the shelves and hoping for the best.

To-day, however, I found this slow, calm business most comforting. In between purchases of sweet treats for the children that lived in our street and crackers for the Christmas dinner-table, we stood in pleasant contemplation of a group of carollers performing enthusiastic renditions of 'Once in Royal David's City' and 'Joy to the World'. However, I soon found my thoughts wandering – particularly when the carollers moved on to 'The Twelve Days of Christmas', the repetitions of which soon became associated with the Adler Variations in my addled mind. I had slept little the night before, naturally, and I was forced to blink in an exaggerated fashion in order to clear my eyes. Several times when

Mary left my side to enquire after one item or another, I leaned on a counter-top or the pole at the side of a stall, and might easily have fallen asleep if not for her jogging my arm upon her return.

Later, we received our cups of mulled wine and sat before a fire beside a chestnut-seller's cart. I listened to my wife's tales about the festive plans of some people we knew, and I nodded to bid her continue. Before long, though, the nodding of my head had an entirely different significance. As if from a great distance away, I saw myself reeling forward, my cup overturning and its contents spilling onto the pavement, and Mary gripped my arm to stop me from toppling into the fire.

"Goodness, John – what is the matter with you?" she said when she had restored me to an upright position.

"I am only a little sleepy," I replied, then yawned as proof.

Her mouth set into a frown. "This is Sherlock Holmes's doing, no doubt. Has he kept you awake all night as he expounded some theory or another?"

I watched her, gauging whether or not to tell her the truth. To this point in time, Mary had always supported my work alongside Holmes, in part because of the trust she had once placed in him during a case relating to herself. However, she had made it clear that she did not wish to be informed of the precise nature of our work, as it only made her worry for my well-being.

"In truth, Holmes played no part in the events of last night," I replied.

"Then you were not at your old rooms in Baker Street?"

"No. Until the very early hours of the morning I spent the night crouched in a bush, and very much awake." I shivered as I recalled another crouched figure: the Greenland beast hovering before the window of the cottage.

My wife stared at me. Her expression was unreadable at first – and then her lips turned up at the corners and she began to laugh.

"It is no laughing matter," I hissed. People around us were turning to look.

"I'm sorry," Mary said, grasping my arm as if to anchor herself. With great concentration, she managed to stifle her mirth. "And you say Holmes was not there? You were entirely alone?"

"I had a tracking dog with me," I said, then added, "but he fell asleep quite promptly."

This prompted another burst of laughter. Then, composing herself and fixing me with an exaggeratedly serious expression, Mary asked, "So you have not slept a wink?"

"A wink is a good approximation of the amount of time I did sleep. It was in an armchair in Fridtjof Nansen's cottage, after the hullabaloo had died down, and after I had made my apologies for watching the house in secrecy – apologies which were accepted readily enough by Nansen but were received coldly by his wife. However, the house was far from quiet and I dreamed fitfully of being chased by a wild beast."

Mary reached out to put an arm around me. "Oh, John." Then she hesitated. "Did you say Nansen – the explorer who was to meet with the Prince of Wales yesterday?"

I nodded. "And he did so, during the daytime. I regret that I forgot to ask anything about the visit when I woke Nansen from sleep."

"You woke him from sleep," Mary repeated in surprise.

"That is to say, I watched over the building as he and his wife and colleague slept. Early in the morning I saw an intruder, and I raised the alarm." Abashed, I added, "Nansen has told me not to return this evening – he says that he would prefer for everybody in his household to have a full night's sleep, regardless of what they may find deposited on their doorstep come the morning."

"Deposited on the doorstep... Does this relate to your watching the house at night?"

It was the simplest of questions, but to answer it would take a great deal of time. I weighed up the merits of withholding details from her against the benefits of speaking freely. It did not take me long to decide. My wife is the most capable sort, and as far from judgemental as any woman might be.

I told Mary everything about the singular threats against Fridtjof Nansen, the peculiar behaviour of Henrik Gylling during the night and the awful stunted creature which had been at his window. After the discovery of the hare I had made another circuit of the building, but could see no trace of footprints other than my own – though the cover of the orchard trees meant that there might have been ample opportunity for the perpetrator to skip from patch to patch without alighting upon any snow-covered area.

Mary considered what I had told her, then asked, "After the hare was found, did you enter the cottage immediately?"

"I did, and I was most grateful for its shelter."

"And did you check the rooms?"

"Naturally. There was nobody but the three usual occupants, and no sign of any disturbance save the throwing away of bedcovers as the sleepers rose."

"Even in this man Henrik Gylling's room? Was there no indication who he had been addressing?"

"None. I even checked for dirt or dampness from snow on the rugs. The only accusation one might level at Gylling is an untidiness that one might find surprising in an explorer who is used to packing his possessions neatly into a single bag. The door of his wardrobe was wide open and its dishevelled contents were scattered upon the foot of his bed."

Mary nodded. It was the same curt nod of approval that I might have expected from Holmes if I had performed a task correctly but deserved no particular recognition for it.

"And during all of this, where was Sherlock Holmes?" she asked at length.

"I do not know. And I still have no idea of his whereabouts to-day."

"But this business with the Nansens is *his* case, is it not?" Mary asked indignantly. "And yet he dispatched you to deal with it alone."

"I am sure he has good reason," I said weakly.

"John. I know you very well, and I know when you are lying."

"One cannot lie about such a statement. It is an opinion."

"And yet it is not *your* opinion."

I took a deep breath, then said, "You are quite correct. I fear that Holmes has become distracted. Or rather, that was my initial fear, at the beginning, when the puzzle was merely a frippery, a friendly challenge. Now I fear something else entirely. Holmes has got himself embroiled in something dreadful, and yet I find that I cannot rely on his judgement in the matter. I do not know where it will end."

"Then you had better explain it to me, and perhaps I will be able to unravel some part of it."

I clasped my wife's hand gratefully. I found that I was no longer tired – at least in physical terms. I was merely weary of trying to understand Sherlock Holmes. If Mary might shine any faint light on his recent actions or predict those in the near future, it would be all the better for me.

Mary rose and gestured for me to do likewise. She gestured at the people sitting around the fire and said quietly, "Let us walk around a little as you speak."

Arm in arm we passed through the market, and I began at the beginning of the tale, with the delivery of the opera tickets purportedly from the jeweller, Matthew Jacchus. Then I halted, realising that I must go even further back in time, to explain the circumstances of Irene Adler's first encounter with Sherlock Holmes, in which she secured possession of a photograph of herself with the Crown Prince of Bohemia, who had since become king and desired the return of the offending article in order to protect his honour rather than be discovered to have consorted with a known adventuress. I detailed Holmes's eventual conclusion that that incriminating photograph would be used only to ensure Adler's security, and not to blackmail the royal family, and his great admiration for the means of her acquiring the picture using techniques of secrecy and diversion equal only to himself. Mary responded with frequent exclamations at this story, and did not hurry my explanation, asking questions only where necessary. Finally, I returned to the present and related the development of the Adler Variations which so gripped Holmes.

When I had concluded the story, Mary asked, "How many of these 'thefts without theft' have there been?"

I paused to think. "Let me see... The first was the statue of Veritas in the British Museum, which was removed but not taken from the room. Then the painting in that same building, which *appeared* stolen but which had never truly hung in that dummy frame. Holmes's violin strings were certainly a theft, and Adler returned them even before their absence was discovered, by placing them in my own pocket. Finally, Holmes maintains that the River Lea is another example of 'theft without theft', as it was emptied but its water continued to flow along the navigation channel. So that makes four in total."

"Quite ingenious," Mary remarked. "I can well understand why Holmes is so fascinated by this woman."

I turned to look at her, surprised that she did not condemn the actions of either Holmes or his correspondent – or, as I was beginning to think of Irene Adler, his tormentor.

"But now the body in the river changes everything," I said.

"Of course."

"And yet you do not seem the least horrified," I noted.

My wife raised an eyebrow. "I am not so straightforward as that, as you ought to know. I have seen something of the world."

"Quite so," I said. For the first time in almost half an hour, I looked around to notice our surroundings, and saw that we were now in Marylebone. "But what are we doing here?"

Mary gestured along the road, to the junction where it met Baker Street.

With a smile, she said, "We are going to call on Sherlock Holmes."

CHAPTER NINETEEN

All was confusion at the entrance to 221b Baker Street. The very moment that the building came into our view, we saw a man emerge from a cab parked outside to approach the door. He wore a fine black coat which was as pristine as his carriage. He was still waiting on the doorstep when we arrived and stood behind him, and he turned to look at us in surprise before turning to face the door resolutely, evidently having decided that he was now in a queue and his place at its head must be defended.

Before I could explain, the door opened and Mrs. Hudson appeared, the unfortunate Toby pressed to her bosom and a large holly wreath held in her free hand. She gazed up at the stranger, then over his shoulder at Mary and me. Before she could speak, a boy in an oversized cap emerged from behind her in the hallway, nodding first at the landlady and then peering up in curiosity at the trio standing on the doorstep. Embarrassed, he bowed his head and pushed past us to leave.

"I'll hang it up at once!" Mrs. Hudson called after the boy as he hurried along the street, and then she held up the elaborate wreath against the surface of the door, covering the more meagre one already attached to the knocker, and gave a sigh of satisfaction.

Finally, she snapped out of her reverie and remembered her visitors. "Well – not only Dr. Watson, but Mrs. Watson, too!"

The man who stood before us cleared his throat and said, "I believe I arrived first. I wish to speak with Mr. Sherlock Holmes."

"Is he a friend of yours, Dr. Watson?" the landlady asked in puzzlement. She put down the wreath.

"No, he—" I began.

At the same time, the gentleman said, "My dear lady, I must insist that I be seen first. These people came later than I and must be told to wait."

"I'm not going to leave Dr. Watson and his wife on the street," Mrs. Hudson said shortly. "Why don't you all come in?" She stood back to allow us to enter.

Once we were in the hallway, a transformation seemed to come over the stranger. He took off his hat, revealing a mass of dark curls, and stood before Mrs. Hudson, his legs bent in order to lower himself to the height of the lolling dog in her arms.

"He's an extraordinary fellow," he said, reaching out his free hand to nuzzle behind Toby's ears. "Full of character. What is he?"

"Oh, I don't know," Mrs. Hudson replied. "Some sort of dog, that's all I can say. He's a lovely boy, though."

"Indeed he is," the man said. Then, to my amazement, he adopted the sing-song tone of somebody simple-minded, or somebody addressing an infant, saying, "Isn't he now? Isn't he?" – all the while rubbing the back of Toby's neck vigorously.

Toby bore this embarrassment with great dignity, and I found my regard for him rise correspondingly.

The man turned to face Mary and I. "Edward Langtry, at your service. Allow me to apologise for my short temper. My mind is occupied and it is all I can do to think straight."

I was ready to reprimand him, but Mary spoke first. "No apology is necessary. In fact, we are not here to stand in line. My husband is an associate of Sherlock Holmes."

Langtry's eyebrows rose. "Is that so?"

I bowed my head. Then I turned to Mrs. Hudson. "Has Holmes returned?"

"No, he's not been back since you brought Toby back this morning – that is to say, I've not seen him for two whole days now."

Addressing Langtry, I said, "Then I am afraid that this has been a wasted visit. Sherlock Holmes is conducting a matter that has required him to be elsewhere, and he will take on no new cases at this time."

Langtry's face fell. "That is a blow. I had hoped—" He halted, drawing in air. "I see that I was foolish to hope that this issue might be resolved before Christmas, but anybody might have wished it so."

"What are your circumstances?" Mary asked bluntly.

I turned to her with narrowed eyes.

Langtry's mouth opened, but he seemed to think better of providing an explanation. "It hardly matters, if Mr. Holmes is not available to be engaged." He placed his hat atop his wild hair and said, "I shall bid you all farewell and return in a fortnight."

However, he did not leave immediately. Instead, he seemed not to be able to help stroking Toby's coat again, this repeated action seeming unconscious and indicative of great despondency. I even fancied I saw the glistening of tears at the corners of his eyes.

Mrs. Hudson, too, observed this sorrowful behaviour. Then she fixed me with a stare. I realised that Mary, too, was watching me closely. I shook my head subtly, then froze as Langtry noticed the motion.

"I hardly think—" I began to say, but then stopped when Mary nudged my elbow forcefully.

I saw that I had no choice in the matter.

"Mr. Langtry?" I said. "Perhaps you might stay for a short time, and join us in the upstairs room. Holmes may be absent, but I might take down the principal details and your address, in order to supply them to Sherlock Holmes at the first opportunity."

By force of habit, I took my usual seat and gestured for Langtry to sit in the cane-backed chair which we customarily offered to clients. So familiar were these actions that I forgot the circumstances, and so I was unprepared for the sight of my wife taking Holmes's chair. I almost ushered her away, but then told myself that a chair was only a chair, and our seating arrangement had no particular importance. All the same, as Langtry began to speak, my eyes darted continually to my wife, who sat primly on the edge of the seat, demonstrating her concentration, in stark contrast to Holmes, who at the start of such discussions tended to lounge in a display of inattentiveness.

"Thank you for allowing me entry," Langtry said. In repose his wide, handsome face suggested haughtiness or even disdain. "While I understand that no solution to my troubles will be forthcoming soon, perhaps simply by stating it aloud I might push it from my thoughts, however temporarily."

"Please," I said, reaching into my jacket for my notepad and pencil, "speak freely, and I will record all of the salient details."

He nodded and looked at Mary. "It concerns the fairer sex."

"Are you comfortable with my wife's presence?" I asked. At the edge of my field of vision I saw Mary's posture stiffen.

"Certainly, so long as she is comfortable hearing of matters of infidelity," Langtry replied. "The woman in question is my own wife."

I winced. I knew Mary well enough that I felt certain she would rankle at being referred to in the third person when she was present in the room. I did not speak, to allow her to do so for herself.

"Please, go on," Mary said softly. "You have no reason to hold back any details, and all will be received in confidence."

Langtry bowed his head, then passed his tongue over his lips as though this might allow his words to pass more easily from them.

"My situation is a remarkably simple one," he said. "I believe that my wife, Emilie, is conducting an affair."

We both waited for him to continue. When he said nothing more, Mary prompted him, "What more do you know about it?"

He sighed. "You are not surprised, I see. Perhaps there is something about me that makes me appear suited to the part of jilted husband."

"Nonsense," Mary said. "Is there somebody in particular you suspect of having become your wife's lover?"

"None – all I know is the frequency of their meetings." Langtry uncrossed his legs, then crossed them again, this time left over right. It struck me as a particularly affected mannerism, intended to convey some internal mental process; perhaps deep consideration, or discomfort. "Every fortnight I am obliged to be out of town for two days, conducting business—"

"What nature of business?" Mary asked.

I frowned at her – this interrogative manner hardly seemed necessary; the man would provide such details in his own time, and hearing a tale unprompted often produced valuable insights.

Langtry seemed as perturbed as I. He hesitated, then replied, "Financial matters. Related to my family."

"The Langtry family," Mary said. "Of what county?"

"Northumberland."

"That is quite far away."

"Indeed."

"Perhaps a day's travel in each direction."

"The discussions are held in Cambridge."

"Why is that?"

"That is where my brother lives."

Mary smiled to indicate that she was satisfied, and I perceived that Langtry was most grateful for the respite. I sympathised with him; when my wife pursues a matter, she rarely lets up.

"My most recent visit, exactly a fortnight ago, was cancelled at the last possible moment, due to illness," Langtry went on. Then, in response to Mary's parted lips, he added, "My sister-in-law was unwell, and did not relish the thought of hosting a guest. What is important is that I returned to my house only a short time after the train I ought to have taken would have pulled away from the station. I found my house empty. I fretted all night, as you can well imagine – I paced the hearthrug until it was almost threadbare. In the morning I demanded information from our housekeeper, certain that she knew something that I did not. At first she maintained her silence, but under threat she revealed that she had seen Emilie leave the house the previous evening – and furthermore she confessed that this was not the first time my wife had done so. In fact, it is her custom to leave the house in this fashion each fortnight, always after seven o'clock on the Saturday – the day I always leave, and a time at which my train would be certain to have departed. The housekeeper would say no more. I spent all that day in wait, ready to apprehend my wife on her return, consumed by anger. However, after another night spent alone, my rage had dissipated and all that was left was grief at this duplicity. The next day, Monday, I relieved the housekeeper of her duties, warning her that any contact with my wife would result in severe recrimination, and left the house early. When I returned in the late afternoon, Emilie was in the sitting-room as usual, sewing and eager to hear news of my brother's family. I said nothing about her disappearance, and my subtle questioning elicited only shameless lies. She claimed that she had hosted a party for two of her friends at our own house – but at that very moment I had been present in the building myself, entirely alone."

He turned to the window, one finger pressed to his lips, his chin trembling noticeably. It seemed a strangely literal signifier of great emotion.

"Perhaps there is an explanation for your wife's actions that does not relate to infidelity," I said, then glanced at Mary, who did not respond.

"I am convinced she has been stolen from me!" Langtry cried, then slumped back into his seat with a groan. "And I cannot prevent her being taken again this very night, as it would be impossible for me to put off my visit to Cambridge again."

Mary retorted, "Your wife is hardly a mere possession, Mr. Langtry."

Langtry considered this. "Perhaps not – and yet I am as bereft as if I had been robbed of something more precious to me than all my other belongings put together."

"She is valuable, then?"

He blinked. "Yes."

Mary watched him closely until he baulked and looked away.

Langtry seemed to have reached the end of his tale. I closed my notebook and said, "I will convey all of this to Sherlock Holmes. However, I am bound to tell you that his habit is to search out problems of great complexity and with unusual features—"

"And is your opinion that my situation is attractive in neither respect?"

Carefully, I said, "I am simply forewarning you of Holmes's response, or at least what I imagine it may be. Now, the only remaining formality is for you to provide your address."

Langtry retrieved a pocketbook and took from it a slim card upon which was written an address, but which stated no occupation or hinted at any other detail of his livelihood. I slipped the card into my inner jacket pocket and then rose, gesturing towards the door.

Evidently, though, my wife had not yet satisfied herself with information. She did not stand as she said, "What sort of a woman is your wife?"

Langtry froze, bent in an awkward position halfway between sitting and standing. "She is a wonderful creature," he said.

"That is subjective. What are her interests, for example?"

Langtry hesitated. "I already mentioned her sewing, did I not?"

Mary did not reply, but simply waited for him to continue.

Our guest's face had paled visibly, but I knew better than to come to his rescue.

"And…" he began. "She has friends."

"Yes, you mentioned them as well."

They watched each other wordlessly. Langtry made a show of realising he had left his overcoat upon the chair arm, and then busied himself putting it on carefully. When he had completed this action, he said in an almost triumphant tone, "She adores animals. She goes often to the zoo, and she delights in walking the dogs that belong to her friends. She has been known to draw portraits of them and give them as gifts. We have two cats and she dotes on them."

Mary received this information impassively, then rose and moved to stand beside me.

"We will take your case," she said.

Shocked, I protested, "But we cannot speak for Holmes."

"I did not mean Holmes. *We* will take this case. You have supplied your address, Mr. Langtry, and you have already told us that shortly after seven o'clock is the time we must expect Emilie to leave the house on her mysterious errand. We will follow her."

I stared at my wife in dismay – but I understood that it would be a grave folly to object. Instead, my thoughts turned to plans for a long nap that afternoon, in case of another night without sleep, in the harsh cold of winter.

CHAPTER TWENTY

To my dismay, when my wife and I left our home together I found that the evening was even colder than recent ones – and moreover, a freezing mist had descended which seemed to cling to the exposed skin of my face. In the afternoon I had caught forty winks and yet my head was still heavy with tiredness, and the cloying mist produced the effect of severe myopia, adding to my disorientation. Even our own street was unrecognisable, and the street lamps that lined the suddenly unfamiliar stretch of road glowed only dimly, like hovering fireflies, providing no particular illumination and, indeed, they appeared less bright than the white fog itself.

"Are you certain that you wish to spend your evening in this way?" I asked. "In my capacity as a doctor I would warn against it. It is perfectly possible that we will both spend Christmas Day nursing severe head colds."

Mary gripped my arm and led me onwards. She possessed a preternatural ability to determine her whereabouts even in this white void. Though our house was only a short walk from the busy main thoroughfare, I supposed that it would have taken me far longer to reach it if I were alone, and that I would have been forced to reassess my location at regular intervals. Furthermore, the pavements were becoming ever more slippery, the mist transforming into a thin veneer of ice as it touched the ground, and several times I clung to my wife's arm to avoid falling. Finally we saw a cab emerging from the mist, and after a great deal of hand-waving I succeeded in flagging it down.

We arrived at the appointed place in Stoke Newington in good time, and I ordered the cab to stop at the end of the street. Upon my suggestion, we adopted as casual stroll as the snow covering the pavement allowed, directly past our client's house. Then, when we reached the end of the street, we skirted around a small area of parkland in the centre of the crescent and paused at its far side. Only now did I realise that from our new location the Langtry house was enveloped entirely in mist, so we were obliged to creep through the park, coming to a halt against the railings closest to our target. For the first time I was grateful for the dreadful weather, as at least it would prevent us from being seen by people in the neighbouring houses and attracting undue suspicion.

As we watched the door of the house, we huddled together for warmth. It struck me that there were worse places I might find myself, despite the cold.

"How do I measure up?" Mary asked, her voice muffled by her scarf and the turned-up collar of her coat.

"Against what?"

"Against *him*. Sherlock Holmes."

I laughed softly. "There is no comparison."

"Oh."

"No!" I protested. "I meant that you are incomparable. You are my wife."

At first Mary did not reply. Finally, she said, "Thank you for trying to say the right thing. I find that I am enjoying acting as his understudy for a time. Do you think I'm a fool for insisting that we pursue this case?"

"It is only as I said to Langtry himself: Holmes would not have considered doing so. And I suppose I was surprised that you were so adamant that we ought to help Langtry. All the evidence suggested that you did not like him."

Mary exhaled softly, and even without looking at her I knew she was smiling. "I'm glad that you are attuned enough to my thoughts to have seen that. No, I did not like Edward Langtry – and I do not wish to help him."

"Then why on earth are we out here inviting frostbite?"

"For Emilie, of course."

"But you have never met her."

"No. And yet I sympathise with her plight."

This sent me immediately into a dark mood.

"John, I do not mean that she and I are in similar positions."

"Oh. Good."

"I merely mean to say that I believe she is the person we ought to help – or at least we ought to investigate in order to determine if she *needs* help."

"But she is the only perpetrator of this crime, if indeed there has been one."

Immediately, Mary pushed me away. "John! How can you say that?"

Startled, I replied, "What?"

"You spoke of a crime – what do you mean by it?"

"I did not – that is, what I meant to say was—"

"All that we have been told is that this woman has been conducting her affairs in secrecy. Is that a crime?"

"Of course not. And yet—"

"And yet if it transpires that she has been meeting a man, or that she has taken a lover…"

"Well, yes."

"Then what? Is *that* a crime?"

"No. I use the word as a convenience. Edward Langtry is our client, and rather than 'crime' I ought to have said 'problem.'"

Mary made a sound of disgust. "Quite so. His wife is behaving in a way that does not suit him, and that creates a problem for him. Yet what Emilie Langtry may require has not featured in the discussion one bit. She may as well be a possession, just as her husband intimated."

"Perhaps to-night we will learn a little about Emilie Langtry, then, and the balance of our opinion will shift."

"It is very difficult to imagine it shifting in favour of the husband," Mary said petulantly. "His account of his circumstances in Holmes's rooms was a calculated performance. And do you remember how little he knew of his wife's character? A marriage like that is no marriage at all."

"He did provide details eventually," I said. "I think you rather scared him into silence at first."

"That is not how I see it at all. What was it he claimed? A love of animals, their two cats, trips to the zoo, portraits of dogs – and yet none of these notable characteristics occurred to him when I first asked my question. That man is either an unthinking monster or a fraud, John, and his vague financial dealings related to Northumberland but conducted in Cambridge only provide further ammunition. Any woman finding herself in thrall to such a man would desire to escape."

While I felt certain that there were gaps in my wife's logical process, I could not at this moment identify them – so it was with some gratitude that I saw that the door to the Langtry house had opened and a figure was emerging. For a moment her face was visible, and I saw that she was equally as handsome as her husband, with a thin face and a strong Roman nose. She wore a dark cloak with a wide hood, so that when she turned away to walk along the street, her figure became only a shapeless form.

Mary had also noticed her, and she bustled me in the direction of the gate of the little park before I could speak.

"Now, Mary," I whispered, "it is paramount that we disguise

the sound of our footsteps as much as possible, and that we do not come close to her for fear of scaring her away."

My wife glared at me. "We are not on the savannah hunting antelope, John. And what you are saying would be obvious to anybody."

"Oh." I had thought that my years at Holmes's side had afforded me some experience. I resolved at a later date to list the skills I had learned that few others might be able to deploy – for there must be some. "Very well. Let us proceed cautiously."

However, our pursuit of Emilie Langtry was far from as noiseless and furtive as I had hoped. She walked at a brisk pace, and her shoes produced little sound, or perhaps the noise was drowned in the moisture of the fog. At times Mary and I were forced to jog along the slippery pavement, then stop suddenly when we saw that our quarry had paused before crossing an empty road. I reminded myself that the difficulty we found in following her must surely apply in reverse; that is, she would be unlikely to hear the sounds that we ourselves were making.

I knew little of Stoke Newington, and even if I had, the conditions meant I would have had little understanding of the route Emilie Langtry chose. Her path seemed to change direction at every possible intersection. Presently we were led away from the road and onto a desolate field blanketed with snow.

"I wonder if this is Finsbury Park," I remarked. "Or it might be the wetlands that are somewhere nearby. If it is the latter, we must be careful not to slip into the reservoir. The snow makes every part of it look alike."

We hurried after Emilie Langtry, stumbling occasionally on the rough ground hidden beneath the hardened crust of snow that crunched with every footstep. We were now forced to keep a greater distance from our quarry due to the additional noises that we made.

"Are all your adventures like this?" Mary asked, attempting to pull up her collar even further as an icy breeze passed us.

"Some of them," I replied, "though I much prefer to conduct outdoor pursuits during the warmer seasons."

She laughed. "Perhaps you and Holmes ought to place an advertisement in the newspaper – a request for the criminal class of London to be considerate about the timing of their schemes."

"I hope you are not referring to Emilie Langtry as a criminal, given your earlier defence of her?"

A squeeze of my arm indicated that my joke had been registered, but that I ought not to pursue it any further. Then there came another tug, far more urgent.

"John—" Mary said. "Where has she gone?"

I squinted, peering ahead. "She cannot be far away."

We increased our pace – but presently we came to a dense hedgerow with snow piled against it, through which I could see no possible means of access. We turned and retraced our deep footprints as far as we were able, but soon came to a stop again. I could see no sign of Emilie Langtry's tracks.

"I have no earthly idea where we are," I said.

"There is no need to panic," Mary said. "On the other side of that hedge is a road. We need only to skirt around it and we will find ourselves in some area that is populated, and from there we can navigate. No doubt whoever Emilie Langtry is visiting lives somewhere in that area."

"Yes – but how can we possibly—"

Mary held up a hand to stop me from speaking. Then, without warning, she made a sound of exclamation and darted away to my right.

"Mary!" I hissed.

I stumbled after her through the thick snow, keeping close to the hedgerow in the assumption that Mary sought to work her way around it. From here I could make out the faint sounds of horses' hooves on the road on its far side. But I could not see my wife anywhere.

"Mary!" I cried, no longer caring whether or not I alerted others.

I sprinted with difficulty along the hedgerow, travelling at a rate which I felt certain was faster than my wife might move, considering my longer strides. When I still saw no sign of her, I broke away from the edge of this open space, into the snowbound downs – then I faltered as I remembered my own earlier warning about the reservoir. I came to a halt, listening for clues of anything nearby – there was no sound – and peering in vain into the fog which was uniform in its whiteness and thickness in all directions.

"Mary!" I called again, but my voice sounded small to my own ears.

Now any direction was as good, or as hopeless, as any other. I set off at a run, deciding that making progress in one direction was better than vacillating and moving nowhere. As I stumbled across the uneven terrain, wetness seeping through my shoe leather, I attempted to reassure myself that Mary had proved herself better than I at navigating in these conditions. At this moment she might well have resumed the trailing of Emilie Langtry, and might be cursing my failure to follow.

Then I saw a shape. My first thought was of the Greenland spirit that Henrik Gylling had described: its silhouette appeared to shift constantly and for a moment I fancied that the whiteness that surrounded me on all sides was not fog but whirling snow. It is trite to say that my heart skipped a beat, especially as a medical man, and yet in this instance I maintain it was the case. Gathering my wits, I peered into the pale gloom and reassured myself that the shape I saw was not furred, and that its posture was not stooped. A billow of fog passed and I recognised the same long cloak that Emilie Langtry wore – or at least the figure was certainly not my wife, as I would know her manner of movement in an instant, in any conditions.

I hesitated momentarily. It was all very well that I had found my way back to Emilie Langtry, but what of Mary? She was stranded in the fog. I conjured my wife's voice in my mind, hearing her as clearly as if she were standing at my side: she told me to continue. I had to trust that Mary would find her way to safety. As I lumbered on, I told myself again and again that we were not on some desolate moor, but mere parkland in Stoke Newington. The fog that was causing us such problems was no true threat at all. However, it was so complete that even if Mary had also been tracking Emilie Langtry only a few feet away from my own position, I might know nothing of it.

I attempted to put such thoughts out of my mind to concentrate on keeping the woman in sight. Soon, I stumbled once again, but only because the ground beneath the crunching snow had become less uneven rather than more so: I was now following my quarry along a gravel path. Though I was now forced to tread more carefully, it was now far easier to maintain a constant speed, as I was no longer forced to watch my footing.

Presently, balustrades arose from the whiteness and I saw that I was now crossing a bridge. Faint murmurs from either side, and a suggestion of the snow shifting ever so slightly, indicated that I was passing between two parts of the reservoir – so we were indeed at the wetlands as I had suspected. I tried to picture the maps Mary and I had consulted before our departure, but I could not recall what was beyond the two pools of water in either direction.

The path forked, and Emilie Langtry chose the narrower route. The snow must have been cleared here at some point, and her pace quickened accordingly. The path took us down a shallow incline and then into back streets which were unlit and which I judged must be far from any main thoroughfare. Shortly I saw the woman pass through a gateway in a high fence; the gate creaked as it swung closed behind her. I could see through the fence slats to some degree, so I waited until she had passed a little distance away before I ventured through the gate, and I eased it back into position very carefully after passing through to avoid making any sound. When I turned around to face the yard I had entered, I could see no sign of her.

I fought rising anxiety about the possibility of her effecting an escape. I told myself that the placement of the yard slightly below the reservoir embankment suggested that the only exit would be the same gate by which we had both entered. I ventured forth, peering at the vague, blocky shapes on all sides of the yard, each of which was dusted with only a light covering of snow.

I came close to the object to the far left of the yard, then gasped as I came across a distorted, leering face, even though it was immediately clear that it was merely a painting. Only when I saw the curlicued writing above it did I understand – it read: *Hall of Mirrors*, and below that was the slogan *See Yourself As Never Before*. Thankfully, the door near to the sign was fixed shut, and when I stepped back again I saw that it was not a true building but rather a collapsed wooden façade, folded away for safekeeping. Evidently this yard was home to a wintering and temporarily unemployed travelling fair.

Further along was a large truck with writing on its side which boasted of containing one of the world's greatest menageries of animals – fortunately I could see or hear no evidence that they were currently housed inside it – and in the corner of the yard was a large, curved shape covered with an enormous oilcloth. I pushed the cloth away, producing a miniature flurry of snowfall, and peered into an empty space. Its purpose baffled me at first, until the sparse moonlight glanced against a protruding form of a caricatured cockerel, and I realised that it was nothing more sinister than a merry-go-round with a circular roof.

I made my way carefully around the periphery of the yard, aware that if I had not found another exit then there was a great likelihood that Emilie Langtry, and whoever she was meeting, were close at hand.

At the rear of the yard were parked a series of carriages, some of them ornate living wagons belonging to the fair-folk and others fairground businesses. I stopped before each one in turn, listening for any sign that Emilie Langtry might be within them. When I heard nothing, I continued along the periphery of the yard, past untidy heaps of wood, and soon I had returned to the gate.

I began to wonder whether it was possible that she had gone out again. If she had recognised that she was being followed, it would have been shrewd to have entered an enclosed yard, but then waited directly behind the gate and slipped out the moment I came inside. I had wasted a great deal of time peering at carnival signs.

Though this idea became more solidified in my mind, I did not leave. I could not be certain that Emilie Langtry had left, and if she *was* still present in the yard, then she already knew that I was following her, and continuing my policy of secrecy would be absurd. I would reveal her and we would have a frank conversation, and then we would see where things stood.

With this new resolve, I repeated my circuit of the yard, this time testing each door and looking beneath every oilcloth – all the while checking around me for signs of my quarry bolting for the gate. I reached the carriages and opened the door of the first, which once had been occupied by a 'living skeleton', then the second which had a painting of a harlequin on its side, and then the home of 'Tilda, the Fattest Woman in the World'. All were empty.

The final carriage belonged to 'Palmist Professor Atbar'. Visitors to her premises were invited to *Speak With Prof. Atbar And She Will Convince You Of Her Ability*, with the further assurance that *She Is An Expert Not a Novice*.

I pushed open the door, then recoiled as I saw a glow from within the depths of the carriage.

The faint light came not from the lamps affixed to the walls, which were unlit, but from a pale blue orb upon a table halfway along. Still standing in the doorway, I waited for my eyes to adjust, and it was only after some several seconds that I saw the outline of a figure sitting on the far side of the fortune-teller's glass orb.

"Please, sit," a woman's voice said calmly.

I did not obey. "Mrs. Langtry," I said sternly. "There is no need for this rigmarole. Shall we abandon our pantomime chase and speak frankly?"

"You may abandon anything you wish, Dr. Watson. And I rarely speak in any manner but frankness."

I gripped the door frame. "You know my name. Did your husband speak of me?"

"He did not."

It occurred to me that my modest fame preceded me – that is, anybody working in service of the great Sherlock Holmes must be his friend and biographer, Dr. Watson.

As if reading my thoughts, she laughed and said, "We have met before, in passing. Please, sit."

I told myself that there was no cause for concern over my safety, despite the Grand Guignol surroundings. Leaving the door wide open, and with an exaggerated display of reluctance, I moved into the carriage and sat on a cushioned stool before the table.

"So, then," I said, "you have been well aware that you have been followed." I thought again of Mary, perhaps still wandering the grassland in search of Emilie Langtry or, if she had abandoned that chase, in search of me. I determined that I would return to her as quickly as possible.

"Of course. If one is leading somebody, then one is invariably followed."

On instinct, I turned sharply in my seat, half expecting an accomplice to lurch out of the shadows to strike me with a cosh. Though there was nothing there, I let my hand rest upon the revolver in my pocket.

"Let us get to it," I said. "Your husband suspects you of conducting a love affair with another man."

She gasped. "Does he?"

I strained my eyes to see her face, to determine whether she really was upset by my comment or whether her response was no more than a charade, but I could see nothing but her silhouette, which was oddly large and round – then I recalled that she was wearing a hooded cloak.

"My word," she said. "That is too much. I see no grounds for such an accusation. I am in correspondence with another man, but no more than that."

"But you have been meeting him, too. That is why you left your house under cover of darkness this evening, when your husband was away on business and you believed he would not learn about it."

"There is nobody here but you." Now the mocking lilt of her voice was unmistakeable.

"On other occasions, then."

"Never. And I assure you that my husband is asleep in our bed."

"Madame, I say with authority that Edward Langtry is in Cambridge."

She laughed. "I said nothing of Edward Langtry."

I was about to rise from my seat and insist that I was leaving – but the changing of the quality of light from the blue orb stopped me. I shielded my eyes, and despite the unusual circumstances I wondered how the device worked – a lamp hidden away beneath the table, perhaps?

Then I looked up. The more powerful light from the glass orb lit the woman's face from below – and with a start I realised that I recognised her. She had a square, almost masculine jaw and thin lips, but this severity was offset by smooth, pale skin and wide eyes. She wore a doleful, sardonic expression that I had most recently seen on the stage at the Theatre Royal – and the hooded cloak that framed her face completed the recollection of her looking up at me in my box seat.

"Irene Adler!" I exclaimed.

"It is a great pleasure to speak to you face to face at last," she said.

"But—" I found that I did not know what to protest about first. Finally, I said, "Then you were Emilie Langtry all along?"

Adler's thin lips curled. "No – you followed her most effectively, for a time. Your wife is a veritable bloodhound. I have no doubt that she will not have lost her quarry as you did."

"Then there were two women by the reservoir?"

"Three, including the estimable Mary Watson."

I clutched at my revolver again. "I warn you, if any harm has—"

"I assure you that none has."

I paused, trying to gather my wits. "Why do you wish to speak to me?"

"To protest my innocence, and to seek your help, like any other woman who comes to your door."

"Innocence?" I scoffed. "You have been leading Sherlock Holmes on a merry dance."

"And yet not all of its steps were my invention."

"I see. Then this is about the body in the River Lea."

Irene Adler bowed her head. "I did not put it there." Then, more hesitantly, she added, "Does Holmes believe that it was I?"

To my surprise, she leaned forward over the table, directly over the blue globe. The features of her face became grotesquely distorted by upturned shadows and partly obscured by the overhanging hood of her cloak. This leering visage captured my full attention, so that when she gripped the lapels of my coat firmly I cried out in surprise. I pulled away from her and she withdrew her slim hands, folding her arms in what seemed a defensive posture.

When I had composed myself I said, somewhat reluctantly, "The entirety of his response to the discovery suggests that he does not suspect you of that crime. But the others remain real and unsupportable. You do not deny that you mutilated beyond repair a statue in the British Museum, for example?"

"A worthless statue, yes."

"And you stole from both Holmes and I?"

"On more than one occasion," she replied.

"What?" My hand went to my revolver again, and then instinctively to my pocketbook. Both were in their proper place.

"How many thefts are there to be, before you release Holmes from your thrall?"

Her shoulders rose and fell. "While some of these details have been planned for some time, I enjoy a degree of opportunism – otherwise all my entertainment would have been exhausted weeks ago."

"*Entertainment?* Do you not see that you are driving Holmes utterly insane? He can think of little but your challenge, your nonsensical Adler Variations. He is hardly a complete human being at the best of times, but now his frustration and preoccupation are becoming unbearable. He gabbles about absurd concepts such as 'theft without theft'. And to top it all off, I have not seen him for days, since that blasted body was found."

Her eyes shone, reflecting the eerie blue of the globe. "He is easily frustrated, and though he is entirely correct about the theme of my challenges, you are right to say that I have teased him to the point of cruelty. Furthermore, I am untrustworthy. If there was a single word to encapsulate my character, it would be *mendacious*. But I must know that you believe me, Dr. Watson. I did not kill, or arrange for the death of, the man that you found. I did not put his body there."

"Then who was it? Who are your enemies?"

She exhaled softly. "There are any number of people who might have been responsible. There are only two people who trust me. One is asleep in my bed; the whereabouts of the other, as you have told me, are unknown. But only the latter knows me fully."

"Fully?" I scoffed. "Holmes knows you not at all. Your mystery is precisely your appeal."

"My appeal?" she repeated thoughtfully.

"Yes. I do not understand it, but he is contrary and hardly understandable himself. You are quite the pair."

I saw the ghost of a smile appear on her face.

"I hope you will give him my regards," she said.

"Even better would be for you to pass them on yourself—" I stopped as the light from the orb grew ever brighter, and I was compelled to shield my eyes against the glare. Then there came a violent popping sound – the shattering of an electric bulb, perhaps, as the glass orb itself remained intact – and then suddenly the carriage was enveloped by darkness.

I reached out across the table blindly. "Adler! Stop these theatrical tricks!"

My hands encountered nothing. I rose sharply, passing around the table to reach into the empty seat opposite. Then I turned and burst through the open door of the carriage, stumbling down the ladder-like wooden steps. The yard seemed intolerably bright in the moonlight, and at its far side I could see clearly the gate swinging loosely on its hinges.

CHAPTER TWENTY-ONE

It was well past eleven o'clock when I returned home. Despite Irene Adler's assurances, I had spent more than an hour on the snowy downs above the yard of the wintering fairground, calling my wife's name and casting around in the fog. On two separate occasions I slipped on ice patches and almost tumbled into the reservoir, and the second time I distinctly heard Mary's voice – albeit imagined – telling me that I was a fool and, in addition, I was far more likely than she to trip and perish in a location no more rural than Hackney.

Nevertheless, it was with immense relief that I entered the sitting-room of my house to find my wife rising from her chair to greet me. Our embrace lasted very long and she was obliged to push me away gently and hold me at arm's length. My entire body was shivering, despite the fact that I was now warmer than I had been for many hours.

"Goodness, you look a state!" Mary said.

Still gasping with relief, I nodded heavily. "Whereas you are as composed as ever," I managed to say.

"Here – come by the fire," she said, guiding me to sit like a child before the hearth. Then she sat opposite me and took my hands in hers, rubbing them.

"I am so very glad to find you here," I said.

"Where else might I be? I am the one who has been sitting here fretting about you."

"I have been—" I began.

Mary broke in excitedly, "I did it, though! I solved the mystery, or at least a part of it."

"The mystery," I repeated blankly, thinking only of Irene Adler in the fairground palmist's carriage.

"Emilie Langtry, of course!"

"Ah, yes."

"I hope you are not so absent-minded when you are assisting Holmes. Following Emilie Langtry was our reason for prowling around at night, was it not?"

"Of course. Forgive me. Then where did Mrs. Langtry go?"

"It was as I suggested. She made her way to a lane at the edge of that barren common…" She trailed off, looking down. "John, steam is coming from your shoes."

I saw that she was right: the heat of the fire was producing wisps of vapour from my sodden shoes and socks.

"I fell into some water," I said. "Twice."

Mary's eyes widened, but she only watched in silence as I took off the offending articles, feeling ever more like a child being made ready for bed.

"Never mind that," I said. "Please, continue."

"I had heard a sound from the other side of the hedgerow, and from the light tread I felt certain that it was Emilie. I dashed around – and you were too slow to follow me, you poor dear – and sure enough I saw her, striding along the street, away from the downs. I had a difficult decision, then: ought I to wait for you to catch up, or call out to you and risk being heard? I had to trust that you would fend for yourself. I followed Emilie a short distance, and then lost her again.

However, there was only one route she might have taken having left the path. I went into the grounds of a little church, certain that she was nearby. It was eerie, John, I must say! The gloom under the trees added to the ghostliness of that awful fog… I shan't forget the experience in a hurry. But I found her! And then all of my travails seemed justified."

I had been watching my wife's face, enjoying her animation and enthusiasm which had turned her cheeks pink. I scarcely noticed that she had stopped speaking.

"Well, then," she said, "aren't you going to ask what she was doing?"

"Sorry," I said distractedly. "What was she doing – and who did she meet?"

"She met nobody alive on this earth." Then Mary chuckled. "Sorry, John. I couldn't resist adding a Gothic flourish. It was a grave, you see. She was visiting a grave."

"In darkness, in a freezing fog?"

"She must have her reasons – and you will no doubt hazard a guess when I tell you what she placed on the grave."

I waited, and then when she did not continue, I prompted, "What was it?"

"Two things. Pink lilies, and a doll."

"Then it was—"

"I waited a short time until she left the graveyard, and then I went closer. Yes, it was a child's grave. The poor thing died four years ago, at the age of only two. It hardly bears thinking about."

I covered my mouth. "Then we must conclude that this has been her errand each fortnight. She is innocent of the accusation levelled at her."

"As I maintained from the start."

"Yes, but you—" I stopped short of making any criticism. "Then we will be able to inform Langtry and all will be well."

"Hardly, John. Now that we know the truth, it is as well that we keep it to ourselves."

"Why ever would we do that? Grief for the loss of a child is entirely understandable. I grant that Mrs. Langtry's routine has been peculiar, but her husband would not level any complaint at her, in the circumstances."

Mary reached forward to take my arm. "We are very comfortable together, you and I, are we not?"

Much confused, I replied, "Of course."

"That is the product of two years of closeness. Now, you are hardly the most possessive of husbands, but you must imagine others of redder blood. With that image in mind, how long do you suppose that Emilie and Edward Langtry have been married?"

"I could not possibly know that. We have not seen them together. In fact, neither you nor I have met Mrs. Langtry."

"Consider his attitude towards her. He spoke of her as a possession, and he did not know her interests or character."

"Then you believe they are newlyweds?"

"Or something close to it. There are aspects of his manner that I cannot understand. Anyway, if I tell you one more piece of information about that grave, you will see the situation as I see it. The name was a girl's – Georgia – and the surname was Hooper."

"Good lord. Then she was the product of a previous marriage?"

"Perhaps, or perhaps not a marriage. We do not know Emilie's maiden name."

I rubbed at my face, which was thawing, but my fingers were still like ice. "What are we to do, then?" I asked.

"I do not suppose that anything can be done for Emilie Langtry, in this respect. But I hope that you will not tell her husband the truth."

I frowned. "He has engaged our services. *You* made him our client, Mary. I have a duty to furnish him with answers."

"And what do you suppose will happen when you do?"

"That is hardly my concern."

Mary did not respond to this. She stared into the fire.

"Look here," I began. "Holmes and I cannot very well go around determining what truths are or are not for consumption by others. This is not a moral matter, Mary."

She turned to face me again. "No?"

"No," I said firmly. But already thoughts of the treatment to which Edward Langtry might subject his wife had begun to fill my mind. I groaned. "Do you suppose that she wishes to remain in her current marriage, and her current circumstances, despite this torture she evidently suffers?"

"That torture will remain, wherever she is. It is not for us to determine her wishes now – only to allow her the ability to decide for herself. But I will say this: I would not be surprised one bit if she escaped Edward Langtry before long."

"Why do you say that?"

"Because no woman desires to be a possession. The way he spoke of her was inhuman. When he said 'she is being stolen from me', I saw no evidence of compassion – only the theft of something of value. I wonder if it is Mrs. Langtry who is responsible for generating their income, rather than her husband with his vague financial dealings with a person he maintains is his brother."

I gasped. "Mary – what did you say?"

"Were you not listening to me?"

"Yes… but you mentioned her being stolen."

"That was the very word that Edward Langtry himself used."

I gazed into the fire, feeling distinctly hot and dizzy, after too little sleep for two nights in a row and the early symptoms of a head cold.

"John? What are you thinking about?"

I seemed to hear my own voice from very far away as I replied, "Langtry says she has been stolen from him – but each time he returns from his travels she is there in his house. It is a theft without theft."

CHAPTER TWENTY-TWO

My sleep was the deepest sort imaginable, and after I woke I lay motionless, simply relishing the comfort of my bed. Mary had already arisen, and when I came downstairs she provided me with a hearty breakfast and smiled at me continually as I ate. I supposed that her kind feelings towards me were prompted by a comparison with the unfortunate Langtrys. When she asked what my intentions were, I assured her that she and I were of a like mind, but that I must attempt to consult Holmes before reporting to our client – given that Edward Langtry had nominally engaged the services of Sherlock Holmes rather than the Watsons. I tapped my inner jacket pocket where I had put Langtry's calling card, and assured her that if Holmes was still absent, I would visit the Langtry house promptly and weave a tale that Emilie Langtry had indeed left the house, but had simply taken the air for a time and returned without incident. With luck, Langtry would conclude only that his wife found their house stifling, and perhaps changes to their lives might be introduced for the better. Mary seemed satisfied at this suggested course of action, and I left our home in a buoyant mood, with the hope of resolving several knotty problems in a single action.

However, my good intentions were dashed the moment I entered 221b Baker Street.

"He's still not shown his face," Mrs. Hudson said.

As now seemed habitual, she clutched Toby to her chest, and the animal seemed to have given up all pretence of being disgruntled about his lot in life, nuzzling against her lazily. My nose wrinkled at his pungent odour, once again mixed with other sweet flavours from within the building, and I struggled to focus on what the landlady was saying.

"And have there been any callers?" I asked.

"Nobody to speak of."

"What do you mean by that?"

"Nobody proper, if you take my meaning."

I forced myself to remain calm. "Then who came?"

"Only the telegram-boy. I've just this minute put the telegram on the table upstairs."

If he were in a bind, it was possible that Holmes might send word to his own home rather than to my house, knowing that I would not fail to come here. I told Mrs. Hudson that I would go upstairs momentarily in order to read it, and she nodded as if such invasions were entirely usual; I only hoped that she did not allow other visitors similar access to Holmes's private communications. Then, on pushing open the door to Holmes's rooms, I marvelled again at Holmes's failure to lock it, and I could only despair at the behaviour of all current occupants of 221b Baker Street – the malodorous Toby included.

The room was in a far neater state than was common, which was evidence not only of Holmes's long absence but also his landlady's lack of useful occupation. Every corner appeared recently swept, and the surfaces were now clear of the piles of detritus that constituted Holmes's chaotic 'system' when he was pursuing some new interest or other. I smiled at the thought that on his return, Holmes would be hard pressed to determine whether there had been another 'theft without theft' given the unrecognisable surroundings. Then again, might Mrs. Hudson's tidying itself encapsulate Adler's theme – a theft of the usual arrangement of possessions, yet everything present but not in its customary place?

I shook my head in wonder at my train of thought. Adler's nonsensical challenge was beginning to affect my good sense.

The telegram was placed in the centre of the table, framed by candlesticks and a collection of coins sorted into piles according to denomination, which I supposed had been found around the place by Mrs. Hudson and tidied together unnecessarily. I snatched up the note and read:

```
PLEASE VISIT. UNUSUAL BEHAVIOUR AND I
AM WORRIED. NANSEN.
```

Less than an hour later, I stood at the front door of Nansen's cottage. I could not help but look down at the doorstep, but it appeared clean and untainted by blood or meat juices – though the sight of it still provoked an involuntary shudder in me.

Nansen himself answered the door, and shook my hand warmly. "Thank you for coming," he said.

I noticed that his gaze flicked to a point over my shoulder. I turned, almost expecting to find Holmes standing behind me, but there was only the empty orchard.

"Holmes sends his apologies that he cannot join us," I said, and Nansen did a fair job of hiding his disappointment.

He emerged from the house, and I saw that he was wearing his overcoat. He gestured beyond the cottage and said, "The snow is crisp to-day. It takes me back to Greenland. Let us walk for a time."

I began to protest; I could see a lit fire through the window of the sitting-room, and after my trek from the railway station it appeared most inviting. However, something about Nansen's hasty departure from the building persuaded me, and I nodded and followed him through the orchard.

We tramped in silence for several minutes, breaking cover of the trees so that we were exposed to a chill wind from the east and our feet were plunged into deep snow. I shuddered and hugged myself with my arms, but Nansen seemed entirely unaffected by the cold.

We came to a halt on a slight rise, half a mile from the cottage. From here we could see the snow-draped trees of Hampstead Heath and Kenwood, with few buildings and only the subtle interruption of narrow roads as evidence of a nearby human population. Nansen heaved a great sigh as he contemplated the sight.

"In your telegram you mentioned unusual behaviour," I said. I turned back to face the cottage, but saw no movement in either of the bedrooms at its rear. "Did the creature appear again last night?"

Nansen shook his head. "No, but perhaps that is because I watch the house."

For a moment his use of the present tense puzzled me. "You watched the house overnight – do you mean from the inside or the outside?"

"Outside. I wait all night and nothing comes."

It had several times struck me as unreasonable that I had been the one to wait in the cold the night before last, whereas Nansen might have positively enjoyed it, his bodily temperature hardly comparing to those he had experienced during his time on expedition. Now that I knew he had indeed performed the duty himself, I experienced only a pang of regret at my lack of professionalism about this case – and the even more profoundly unprofessional manner of Sherlock Holmes, who had abandoned it entirely.

"When we are in Greenland, we do not worry about emotions," Nansen said, still staring out at the vista before us. "Life is simple. We walk, we stop, we set up camp. We eat, we get warm. We make our scientific notes, we write our diaries. We sleep. We wake up and we do it all again. If we discuss our homes we speak only of the landscape, or our work in the past. If we speak of the future, we speak of where we might live that is like Greenland, which we have learned to love. We do not speak of our feelings towards others."

I was still unclear what, precisely, we were discussing. "Do you suspect that Henrik Gylling has personal issues that might have a bearing on recent events?"

Nansen turned to face me. "No. He has a wife and child in Christiania and he is most happy. Why do you ask that?"

"Because of your telegram," I replied. "The 'unusual behaviour' to which you referred."

"But I am not speaking of Henrik Gylling," Nansen insisted. "There is nothing unusual about him."

"Then—" I turned back to look at the house. "Were you instead speaking of your wife?"

"Of course. Dr. Watson – you are married, are you not?"

"I am."

"Do you understand your wife?"

"I like to think so."

"Is she unusual?"

I thought of our actions of the previous night, and our conversation before the fire.

"She is," I said, "and I would have it no other way. But I suppose there is a difference between being unusual and displaying behaviour which is worrying. Perhaps you might tell me what your wife has done that concerns you. Or is it something more serious? I am a medical doctor, and I could examine her if you would like."

"There is nothing wrong with her," Nansen replied gloomily.

"Dr. Nansen, I am afraid that I fail to understand—"

"She is happy."

"Well… that is good, is it not?"

"She smiles more than since we leave Norway. Back then, she is happy to leave Lysaker, because she hopes that we will leave behind our trouble. When we arrive here, the trouble continues and she does not smile. Until yesterday and to-day."

"And this is what concerns you?"

Nansen nodded. "When my wife worries, I say things to help her. I am confident, I am strong, I protect her. I agree to hire Sherlock Holmes to stop the trouble. All of this I can manage even if I do not know who makes threats against us. But this is harder to understand. To-day, Eva tells me we should say to Sherlock Holmes: 'Do not come again.' And she says these threats are of no importance."

"I see." I chewed my lip for a time, then asked, "Nansen, two nights ago, did you speak to Gylling during the night-time, before I raised the alarm by chasing the intruder?"

"No. I sleep until you shout."

I nodded uneasily. I had not yet spoken of the small piece of information I had gleaned on that night. When Gylling had risen from his bed he had addressed somebody in his own language, and had spoken the name 'Nansen' more than once. If he was not speaking to Fridtjof Nansen, then might it have been the only other person in the house – Eva Nansen herself?

"Who is within the house presently?" I asked.

"Only my wife. Gylling is in town, buying gifts for his wife and daughter."

"I would like to speak to her, if I may."

Nansen thought about this. "Perhaps if you tell her that you come here for the last time. And do not mention the telegram I sent."

"Very well," I said, and having reached this agreement we began to trudge back to the cottage.

CHAPTER TWENTY-THREE

We found Eva Nansen in the sitting-room, curled in the largest of the armchairs and reading a book. Despite her husband's reluctance about her finding me here, she greeted me warmly and offered me tea, which I accepted gratefully. When she returned she gestured for me to sit, placed a tray on the table, but then retreated back to her book to indicate that she did not expect to conduct a conversation. Nansen was right: if the situation were different she would simply appear untroubled, and her casual inclusion of a guest to her home without question rather appealing – but in the circumstances her behaviour was baffling.

I glanced at Nansen, who shrugged his shoulders, and then I sipped my tea and tried to imagine what Holmes might say or do in my place.

"Mrs. Nansen," I said finally, "what are your plans for the day?"

She looked over the top of her book. "I do not know. I will take the day as it comes."

I checked my watch. "It is eleven o'clock already."

She grimaced. "Is that so? I had lost track of time. When I woke I intended to bake Fridtjof some kvæfjordkake, but I lost my good intentions. So perhaps to-day will be a day for reading and nothing more." She looked to her husband, who perched uncomfortably on his own seat. "We are on holiday, after all, are we not, Fridtjof?"

A thought struck me. "I suppose that your visit to meet the Prince of Wales was most interesting – though perhaps rather enervating."

She laughed. "It was neither of those things. I am sure the prince was well-intentioned, but he was something of a bore."

I looked at Nansen in horror. He grinned involuntarily and said, "Yes, he is not interesting. No royal person is, even in Norway."

I found myself unable to form words in the face of this impudence. All the same, as I looked from husband to wife, I saw in them a common attitude to the world, which reinforced quite how much they were suited to one another. Did Mary and I not share similarly shocking private opinions about all manner of things behind our own door?

Mrs. Nansen watched me with raised eyebrows, then said, "Perhaps I will bake after all," and she rose from her chair and left the room.

For several minutes I sipped my tea in silence, wondering how I might make another approach to speak to Eva, who was now humming happily to herself in the kitchen.

Abruptly, a sharp sound came from the rear of the house.

Nansen and I stood up immediately.

"That sound was not made by my wife," Nansen said, quite unnecessarily given that Eva's melodic humming continued unabated.

"You said that Gylling was away?"

Nansen nodded.

We approached the door and then passed along the hallway. I stopped at the doorway to the kitchen, where Mrs. Nansen was making preparations for baking, laying items on the table. When she was looking elsewhere I took the closest heavy item to hand – a wooden rolling pin – and held it above my shoulder as we continued to the rear of the house. The door to the bedroom

Nansen and his wife shared was open, revealing an empty room, but Gylling's door was closed. The faint thudding sounds we had heard undoubtedly came from behind it.

"Please, stay back," I said to Nansen, and he obliged, watching me carefully as I gripped the door handle.

I pushed the door ajar very slightly. The room was gloomy, the curtains having been drawn together at the window – though I saw that the sash must still be open, as the fabric drifted in the breeze and allowed occasional shafts of daylight to enter. In these flashes of light I perceived something moving at the bedside. The figure was stooped and peculiarly shapeless.

"Gylling... is that you?" I asked uncertainly.

There came no answer, but whatever was in the room moved. I had the sense that it was turning around, even though I could see no hint of a face.

The curtains drifted once again, and for a moment the figure was lit from one side by pale light.

I gasped and stepped back, the rolling pin in my hand now forgotten. I recognised this bent shape and its mane of unruly hair. It was precisely the same apparition I had seen from outside the cottage, climbing in at the window of this very room.

I was about to cry out for Nansen when the beast lunged – though not towards me, quite, but instead up and onto its haunches – and the words died in my throat.

My silence was not due to terror. Now that the figure stood upright, I saw that it was no beast, and neither was it incorporeal like a fairy-tale spirit. Moreover, it now possessed a face, and a face that I knew, at that.

"Holmes!" I cried in a hoarse voice.

The expression on my friend's face was close to jubilation. "It is good to see you, Watson," he said amiably.

"But what are you—" I began, but then a voice came from the hallway behind me, asking, "Who is it?"

I put a hand up to Holmes, then ducked out of the room. To Nansen I said, "It is only Sherlock Holmes – he has responded to your telegram after all. Given your wife's current disposition, it may be better that she does not suspect that he is in the house, or at least that he has entered it without her knowing. Go back to the sitting-room and behave as if nothing has happened, and I will speak to Holmes and explain the situation."

Nansen wavered, clearly suspicious, but then nodded and went away. I waited until he turned into the sitting-room, then listened to reassure myself that I could still hear Mrs. Nansen humming in the kitchen, and then I slipped back inside Gylling's bedroom.

The place had been transformed by as simple an action as Holmes opening the curtains. He stood facing me, smiling broadly as though discovering him crouched in the dark ought to have provoked no surprise or confusion. Over his suit he wore a shapeless coat with an enormous, baggy hood. Now, in the light, I determined that this was the garment which had deceived my eyes on the night of my vigil, appearing like the oversized mane of a wild beast.

"I hope you have not been gone all these days simply in order to play a trick on me?" I asked, not quite managing to stifle a querulous shaking in my voice.

"Certainly not. Though I do not deny that when I heard your voice, and knowing that you would insist on entering the room first, I determined that a trick would be appropriate."

"*Appropriate?* You had better explain yourself, Holmes." Then, without waiting for an answer, I went on, "Was it you that I chased in the orchard two nights ago, then?"

Holmes raised an eyebrow. "What was it that you saw?"

I waved a hand at him. "I saw... this. A squat figure with a wide mane. Now I understand that it was not a beast nor a Greenland spirit, but a rogue playing an absurd trick. I will ask you again – was it you?"

"It was not."

I grimaced. "But the coincidence is far too great!"

"There is no coincidence." Holmes held up a hand to prevent me from asking further questions. "Tell me what you witnessed, and I will explain myself fully."

I sat down heavily on the bed. "I waited in the snow for many hours, alone and as close to misery as I have ever been. Then a sound drew me to the rear of the cottage, out there—" I twisted to point out of the window, at the edge of the orchard. "I saw movement in this very room, where the curtains were wide open: it was Gylling, speaking to somebody, entreating them in his own language and repeating Nansen's name. It was only then that I saw a far more alarming vision. A figure that I took to be the Greenland beast was at the window." I broke off, then asked, "But, Holmes, if it was not you, then who was it that I saw wearing a coat like that one?"

"Please, finish your account," Holmes said.

"There is little more to add. I chased the intruder – once again, Toby was of no earthly use – but I soon lost it. When I returned to the front of the house there was a skinned hare on the step."

"And where were the three occupants of the cottage?"

"They all came to the door from within the building. Nansen was quick to understand why I was there, of course, and his wife was shocked but nevertheless she relented and invited me inside. At first Gylling made a show of being convinced that I had been the one to place the gift of meat on the doorstep, though he soon accepted that the argument was ridiculous, and then maintained that he was still half-asleep and not in his right mind. His response struck me as rather an overreaction, and even now I wonder whether it was an invented claim. He was, after all, already awake when I began to chase the intruder."

Holmes looked around the room. "Watson, be so good as to play the part of Gylling, when you saw him from outside."

For a moment I struggled with the change of perspective as well as the change of role. After some consideration I slipped off the bed and stood beside it, facing the open doorway. I raised my hands and clasped them together. Then I checked behind me, picturing my former position at the edge of the orchard, and said, "Yes, I think this is about right."

"And you could not see who he was addressing?"

"No."

"The bedroom door – was it open or closed?"

"I do not know. I could not see it."

Holmes nodded. "And the thing you took to be the Greenland beast – it was directly outside the window?"

"Indeed."

Then, to my great surprise, Holmes bounded across the foot of the bed and slipped through the open window in a single fluid movement. It was only now that I realised that this was precisely how he must have entered Gylling's room in the first place – it was a simple matter, given both explorers' tendency to leave their windows open at all times.

Now Holmes crouched before the windowsill, and once again his shapeless garment and large hood transformed him into the eerie figure I had seen that night. He looked up at me expectantly.

"The intruder was positioned more to the left," I said. "That is, to your right."

Obediently, Holmes shuffled to that side. "Here?"

"I think that is exactly right."

"Can you think of anything else related to the positions of each of these figures?" Holmes asked.

"No, I am sure that everything is as it was that night."

Holmes turned and looked into the orchard. "Where were you standing?"

I pointed. "Close to that old wooden cart which is half-buried in the snow."

"From there you would certainly be able to see the door of Gylling's bedroom, and anybody standing there."

I frowned. After a moment, I exclaimed, "There was something else – a large block that obscured the right side of the window. I have no idea what it might have been."

Without answer, Holmes reached through the window, contorting himself in order to reach the handle of a wardrobe beside the bed. When the door swung open, I saw that it made precisely the obstacle I had described.

"That's it!" I cried. "If the wardrobe door was open, I could not have seen past it to the door of the bedroom."

"Very good, Watson. The situation is becoming ever clearer."

"Is it? Then perhaps you will explain it to me."

"In good time. Now, we have much to discuss. It would be inopportune to speak to the Nansens at this point, so I will remain out here. Perhaps you would be so good as to bid them goodbye and join me."

CHAPTER TWENTY-FOUR

"I am gratified, at least, that you still have some thought for Fridtjof Nansen's plight," I said as we walked along the lane that led to the station. "Especially as he and his wife and colleague will return to Norway a mere three days from now. I had supposed that you had been entirely diverted by the Irene Adler business."

When Holmes did not reply, I sighed and said, "I see. So it was the Adler Variations that caused your disappearance, after all."

"I had to understand the business of the body," Holmes said.

"Then do you understand it now? Adler claims that she had no involvement whatsoever."

Holmes halted abruptly. "You have spoken to her?"

"Yes, at her invitation – if you can call a pursuit across wetlands and into unused fairground carriages an invitation."

Holmes's eyes sparkled. "You must tell me everything."

I thrust my hands into my pockets dejectedly. It was entirely in keeping with our usual arrangement that Holmes would demand to know everything that I knew, without supplying any information himself. All the same, I proceeded to explain all that had occurred the previous night, from the chance encounter with Edward Langtry to my conversation with Irene Adler in the palmist's carriage.

Holmes listened attentively to the tale, and when I had finished he asked, "What was her manner when you spoke to her?"

I waved a hand. "Rather like your own. Haughty and rather self-satisfied."

Holmes's upper lip curled. "And when she spoke of her variations, and about me?"

"A certain amount of pride – I mean in relation to her series of challenges. I suppose that does relate to you, as they have been designed for you alone. Other than that… I would go so far as to describe her attitude as surprisingly tender."

"That does not seem in keeping with her usual character. I wonder if it is a ploy."

I placed a hand on my friend's shoulder. "I do not think you realise, Holmes, how greatly your own character changes whenever she is concerned. Do not suppose that she is so much transformed in any other respect."

Holmes considered this, and nodded slowly.

"What was most important to her," I said, "is that you do not suspect her of foul play."

"In terms of altering the rules of her challenge, you mean."

"No, Holmes. In terms of committing a murder."

"Ah. Yes."

"She was most appalled at what has happened – and despite my suspicions I could not help but believe her. In fact, this appearance of the body seemed to prompt a great deal of soul-searching. She described herself as cruel and mendacious."

"Were those her exact words?"

"They were."

"How very strange," Holmes murmured, "given that the body had indeed no relation to her plans."

"Have you managed to prove as much, despite the fact that a man drowned in the very position where she hid one of her mysterious clues? It is stretching the concept of a coincidence."

"That is because there is no accidental coincidence at all. Even before I set out to prove her innocence in the matter of placing the body there, I had long dispensed of the idea that she killed that man *in situ* at Kings Weir."

"How so?"

"Because she would have had to drown him twice."

I sat down on a large stone at the side of the lane, not caring that it was covered with snow. The bottom of my coat and the seat of my trousers instantly became cold and damp.

"What do you mean by that?" I asked.

"Perhaps you have neglected your medical practice for rather too long," Holmes said. "You were present at the autopsy, and had the opportunity to perform the same observations that I did. The evidence was clear."

"Everything I saw supported death by drowning."

"Indeed – and no doubt that is what the coroner concluded the first time around."

I stared at him, unable to form an objection.

Holmes smiled genially. "The detail you neglected to notice was the fluid on the broken ends of the ribs."

"I did notice it," I said faintly. "The ribs were inexpertly sheared, and the ends were discoloured."

"Why would that be so?"

"I do not know. It did not strike me as strange at the time, but now that you mention it…" Then another image came to my mind. "I remember that you inspected the coroner's tools while we were there. Why was that?"

"I hoped to satisfy my expectations – and so I did. The tools were arranged neatly on the counter, and the shears were clean and had not been recently used."

"But that's preposterous!" I cried, leaping up from my rock.

"The man's chest had been opened wide!"

"Yes, and if you had looked more closely you would have seen the needle marks in the flesh, and traces of thread. What that shows, Watson, is that the body had been inspected in the usual way soon after death, and then it was sewn up again in order to be deposited into the River Lea."

I ran my fingers through my hair in dismay. My own failure to see that the chest cavity had been closed up was one thing, but the coroner could not have failed to notice the thread and the already snapped ribs. And yet this was not the question uppermost in my mind.

"But *why*, Holmes?"

"That is precisely what has taken me two days to determine."

I shook my head. "I still do not accept even the premise. A corpse left underwater for several days ought to have been in a far worse condition."

"There was no water, only snow, which preserved it."

"But you yourself said that it was deposited into the River Lea!"

Holmes tapped his chin. "When is a river not a river? Another riddle. As should have been abundantly clear to you, I meant that it was placed on the riverbed *after* the water was diverted."

I groaned. "Then we are back to where we began. Irene Adler was responsible after all."

"Irene Adler may be many things, but she has no access to the morgue at St Bart's, let alone any means of removing a body from it."

"St Bart's? Then have you been able to determine who the unfortunate man was?"

"No – and nor have the police. The only conclusion is that he was a suicide. The body was originally found washed up at Shadwell, perhaps indicating that the man threw himself from Tower Bridge. It hardly matters. What is pertinent is that the corpse was housed at St Bart's until, abruptly, it was not. There is no written record of its removal from the morgue, and indeed all records of the autopsy were also excised. It took no small amount of investigation to determine that the coroner who conducted the first autopsy was a man named James Bastable."

"The same coroner we met at Waltham Cross!" I cried.

"Yes, and an unscrupulous rogue, by all accounts. Nevertheless, he is only a pawn."

"Then who arranged for the removal of the body from the morgue?"

"A man who goes by the name of Getty."

"Should I know the name?"

"No, and nor would anybody else. I am confident that he uses other names for other purposes, presumably with full credentials to support each of his various identities."

In wonderment, I said, "He sounds like a formidable opponent."

Holmes shook his head. "He is no opponent at all. He is an irrelevance."

"And yet you have just told me—"

"This man Getty represents only the hands that enacted the business. The mind is elsewhere, secure and comfortable, avoiding any involvement that might suggest a direct link to anything that has occurred."

"And yet… you have uncovered such a link?"

"I have not – and I feel confident that I will never be able to prove such a link exists."

I sighed in exasperation. "But who do you *believe* is responsible? This person – this mind at the centre of such a dreadful project?"

"There are few men who find themselves in such a position, with access to the necessary institutions, and even fewer who might have any motivation to intervene in such a way. My suspicions formed immediately, and yet even after two full days of investigation at Westminster, under a range of guises, I found myself barely any closer to the truth. Yet all indications point to a single man."

"Yes, but *who*?" I demanded.

"Mycroft Holmes."

I laughed, then stopped short. "Are you being serious?"

"Deadly serious."

"But why would your brother arrange such a thing? The idea is monstrous."

"Is it? The man was already dead, was he not? And anonymous to boot."

"Yes, but to use a cadaver in this way… and for what purpose?"

Holmes plucked a twig from the hedge at the side of the lane and played with it. "To throw me off the scent, of course."

"The scent…" I repeated blankly. "You mean Adler's challenge? You mean to say that Mycroft knows of it?"

"There is little that occurs in this city that my brother does not know about. He, or rather his associates such as Getty, watch all events continually. I hope I do not flatter myself unduly to suggest that I might be under closer surveillance than most."

"The idea is intolerable!" I cried.

Holmes gave a wan smile. "I suppose every family behaves in a way that is different and alien to others."

I felt suddenly that I had gone mad, so implacable was Holmes's manner in the face of such lunacy. Holmes continued to watch me with a guarded manner, as though I were the one behaving strangely.

"Then I suppose Mycroft wished to cast suspicion upon Irene Adler," I said finally.

"Yes."

"Without making the matter public."

"That would hardly suit him. The corpse was a signal for me alone. But my brother is a fool to have imagined I would be taken in. I must drop him a note to suggest that he work harder next time. Furthermore, given the advanced age of James Bastable, and his inability to lie with conviction, Mycroft will certainly require the acquisition of another friendly coroner very soon."

I was barely listening, so deep was I in my own thoughts. I said, "Then it is the case that Mycroft Holmes, and presumably the

British government in general, are still concerned with the fate of Irene Adler – because of her association with the king of Bohemia."

"There is no longer a direct association between those former lovers, but I take your meaning. Yes, for a variety of reasons our government sees it as vital that diplomatic relations with the House of Ormstein, and Bohemia at large, remain cordial. Few would describe Irene Norton, as she is now sometimes known, as a citizen of England – and no other country would sensibly make a claim for her citizenship either – and yet she is here on our soil, and that fact evidently makes the British government exceedingly anxious."

My mind reeled at this new information, but I realised that, at heart, what I had been told was very simple.

"If all that you say is true," I said, "then Irene Adler's account of her actions can be trusted."

"Certainly. She was responsible for the diverting of the River Lea, and for placing in the empty riverbed a tin box containing her clue, the letter D. What is most impressive about her plan is that she must have been certain that heavy snow would fall, in order to cover up the tin temporarily. Only when the river water was reintroduced to its normal course would the tin have risen to the surface, anchored by the rock to which it was chained. It is something of a shame that we were denied seeing that mechanism in action due to the corpse that was later placed directly on top of it."

Holmes held up the branch to point along the lane. "Shall we continue to the station? Your cheeks are turning rather blue."

I roused myself, and we set off side by side. For a time we were silent, but then I remarked, "It still baffles me that you can allow Adler's puzzle to occupy your thoughts to such a degree."

"I can assure you that I have not forgotten our Norwegian friends."

"We must also contend with Edward Langtry," I reminded him.

Holmes did not respond. I wondered whether he was angry with me for having accepted such a straightforward case as

Langtry's. I hoped that I would not be driven to blame Mary for having done so.

"Even discounting those other matters," I went on thoughtfully, "I am surprised that you are not offended by Irene Adler's challenge as it stands."

"Offended?" Holmes repeated incredulously. "Why ought I to be offended?"

I thought again of my interview with Irene Adler in the fairground carriage, her references to teasing Holmes which had an almost gleeful aspect. Even her confession of mendacity had been tinged with something like pride. But it was something else that occupied the greater part of my thoughts.

"The clues," I said. "The scraps of paper with letters written upon them."

"What of them?"

"They represent an insult, do they not? An implicit criticism of you."

Holmes stopped dead in the centre of the lane.

"You had not thought of it?" I said.

"Of course," he replied quickly, resuming walking – yet every aspect of his bearing, from the length and stiffness of his strides to the faint twitch at the corner of his mouth, suggested that this was a lie.

I could not help but smile privately at the turn that Adler's teasing had taken. No matter how intimately I knew Sherlock Holmes, until this moment I might never have suspected that he might respond so badly to the suggestion that he was growing O, L, D.

CHAPTER TWENTY-FIVE

The next morning, at an early hour that would represent an unacceptable visiting time for most, I bustled into Holmes's rooms brandishing my copy of the *Times*. I found Holmes sitting placidly in his seat, which had been turned to face the window, as if he had merely been occupied watching the snow fall past the pane. The still-unstrung Stradivarius lay on his lap.

As I passed the laden breakfast-table I saw another copy of the newspaper, which had not yet been unfolded.

"Have you not read it yet?" I asked breathlessly.

"Are you referring to to-day's *Times*?" he replied, looking at the item I held before me.

"You need hardly be a great detective to deduce that," I grumbled. I put the newspaper onto the table, feeling a fool for having brought it unnecessarily. Even during the short journey from the cab to the door of 221b Baker Street it had become sodden.

Holmes rose, placed the violin on the sideboard carefully, and came to the table. He looked at the heap of crumpled paper I had brought, then picked up his own pristine copy.

"What page should I turn to?" he asked. "Or did you mean the newspaper in its entirety?"

"Page nine. Holmes, do pull yourself together. It's insufferable, this mooning around dreaming of Irene Adler—" Then, in response to Holmes's sharp glance at me, I corrected myself, "Or rather, her Adler Variations, which I know is what consumes you. But we have more serious matters to attend to."

Holmes said nothing as he leafed casually to the page I had indicated, then allowed his eyes to pass over its contents before reading the relevant article, though with no suggestion of particular interest.

"How strange," he said when he had finished reading.

I stared at him. "Yes – yes, it is strange, Holmes. *Arctic Explorer Fears Threats by Creature of Myth* – I have never known such an outlandish claim in a respectable publication!"

"It is certainly salacious."

"But if only the nonsense were constrained to the headline! The constant speculation about beasts of folklore is absurd – and there are a great number of inaccuracies even in the content that is purportedly factual. Look here – it states that the meat laid on the Nansens' doorstep is invariably liver. Why on earth would any journalist write that, when it is plainly untrue?"

"That is certainly a pertinent question," Holmes said. "I suppose that he had been told as much by whoever related the tale to him. Who do you suspect?"

"Who do I…" I blinked in surprise. "Why, Henrik Gylling, of course. He is the only person quoted in the article, after all, which indicates the writer has had direct access to him."

Holmes nodded, and his eyes passed over the text again, though still no more intently.

"I must say that he has presented himself as a most changed character from the man we have encountered," I continued. "Take this statement from him: 'Whatever these threats are intended to achieve, I say that they will not do so. I can only suppose that they intend to ward Fridtjof Nansen away from further exploration of the Arctic region. Yet he is the most committed and resolute man I have ever known, and he will achieve his aim and conduct his expedition to reach the North Pole – and I am proud to say that I will be at his side throughout, with unwavering loyalty. If anything, this outrageous series of threats has strengthened my resolve, and Nansen's.'" I looked up. "Would you agree that Gylling's true feelings are nothing of the sort? He has been far more wary of the threats against Nansen than Nansen himself, to the point of outright superstition about this Greenland spirit."

"Yes," Holmes agreed. "It does not sound much like his voice."

Then a thought came to me. "Holmes – did you explain your reasoning about the use of Gylling's coat to Nansen? I confess that I am yet to understand who you suppose wore the coat to impersonate the Greenland beast – surely it could not have been Gylling himself. I do not believe he would be capable of play-acting at the fear he has shown over the matter. Might Nansen have reassured him that the beast is false, resulting in the bravado Gylling displays in this newspaper article?"

"No, I did not. I replaced the coat in Gylling's wardrobe and went out by the window. No doubt Nansen was puzzled at my brief visit to Child's Hill, but he would have had no information to impart to Gylling."

I rubbed my forehead, now equally as dismayed at Holmes's lack of interest as I was at the offending newspaper article. I picked up my mutilated copy of the *Times* and attempted to smooth it out at page nine.

"Then again," I said slowly, "each puzzle related to this business seems to encompass not one but two people. Why do you suppose that the writer of this piece put so much focus on Eva Nansen? It is not only background detail – what newspapermen call 'colour' – but rather information that only she or somebody very close to her might possess."

"Such as what?" Holmes asked.

Stifling my annoyance at his disinterested tone, I said, "There is considerable attention afforded to Eva Nansen's career on the stage. That is all well and good, but I see no reason why there is any need to refer to her ambitions of one day performing in this country, or the fact that she is due to meet with the director of the Royal English Opera company to-morrow – it even states the time as eleven o'clock, for heaven's sake! These are private details which leave me wondering whether it might not have been Eva Nansen who has contacted this journalist, rather than Henrik Gylling... unless they are working together. Holmes, it has occurred to me more than once that Gylling might have been addressing Nansen's wife that night I saw him from outside his bedroom."

Holmes formed his fingers into a steeple, tapping at his lower lip. So closely did I associate the gesture with deep thought that I could not help but believe that he was engaging his mind upon the problem at hand, finally.

However, he then gestured at the full table and said, "Have you breakfasted, Watson?"

"Have I—" I repeated.

Holmes waited patiently for my response, and when none was forthcoming, he moved to take a seat at the table and said, "I find that I am rather peckish, myself."

"Holmes! You are *never* hungry. If you eat at all, it is fuel and nothing more."

Holmes shrugged his shoulders and reached for a slice of toast and the butter-dish. Then – an amazement upon amazements – he lifted the lid of a nearby platter and began to heap scrambled eggs onto his plate.

I dropped into the chair opposite his, positively stunned. For more than a minute, I could do nothing other than watch my friend eat heartily.

Finally, I said, "You are much changed, Holmes."

"Oh?"

"This challenge of Irene Adler's... I fear it is not good for your constitution."

"And is your supporting evidence that I am eating breakfast?" Holmes asked with his mouth full.

"Well... yes, among other things. When I came into the room, you were looking out of the window."

"Is that so very bad?"

"Not if you were ruminating on an aspect of a case. Were you?"

"I was watching the snow."

I raised my eyes to the ceiling in dismay. "Do not make me plead with you, Holmes. I only wish that you would try to concentrate."

Holmes finished chewing, then set down his knife and fork. "Very well. What do you think ought to command my attention?"

I pointed at the newspaper, but before I could speak, Holmes said, "Not that. The business with Nansen will be addressed in good time."

Oddly, this response gave me heart – at least Holmes appeared to have formulated an agenda related to the case, whatever it might include.

I cast around for something else to engage him, then concluded, "Edward Langtry."

"The jilted husband?"

"The very same. Or rather, he *hasn't* been jilted, as it turns out. I know that the matter is hardly your usual fare, Holmes, but there is certainly some mystery at its heart, and..." I trailed off hopelessly. Until now I had forgotten the suspicion that had crept into my thoughts regarding Langtry and his wife, and specifically the possibility that Langtry might have considered his wife's affair as a 'theft without theft'. The prospect of returning Holmes to rumination of Irene Adler's series of challenges was galling.

"You told me that your wife followed Emilie Langtry at the point you were waylaid by Irene Adler," Holmes said, "but you did not say what Mary discovered."

"Mrs. Langtry visited a child's grave in the grounds of St. Olave's Church, near Woodberry Down – a child we suspect may have been born and died before her marriage to Edward Langtry. While she is not guilty of conducting a love affair, it seems clear that this revelation may harm her, if her husband learns of it."

"You have not met Emilie Langtry in person?"

"All I have seen of her is her face as she exited her home, and then merely a cloaked figure in the fog."

"What of her husband, then? What sort of a man is he?"

I considered the question at length. "My wife has been more astute than I. On the face of it, his reasons for hoping to consult you, and his response to our questions, were all sound. Mary, though, has convinced me of irregularities in Langtry's behaviour. She has an eye for such things: she is able to determine a man's conscience merely in the way he behaves, even down to the movement of his eyes when he speaks."

"I have long suspected that your wife is innately suited to our line of work," Holmes said with a smile. "Perhaps we ought to consult her more often."

"No – I think she has had her fill for the time being," I replied quickly. I was conscious that my cheeks were warm, and no doubt had turned red, indicating my true feelings. In truth, I was anxious not to involve my wife in my 'other' life with Holmes, not only due to fears for her safety, but because of a certain degree of pride that I alone was indispensable to him.

Holmes bowed his head. "All the same, I would like to know what Mary perceived in Langtry's behaviour."

"In short, she believes he is a fraud."

Immediately, Holmes sat up straighter. "In what regard?"

"He seemed to know little of his wife beyond her basic role – and yet, when pressed, at length he supplied information about her preferences and habits with an unlikely amount of detail. It amounted to a portrait perhaps designed to rouse our sympathies. It was only when Mary pointed it out that I recognised that many of his own affections during our interview seemed somewhat exaggerated. Like this." I broke off, and adopted a posture that I recalled Langtry making at one point: one finger to my lips as if in thought, my head turned to one side as though looking far away, both eyebrows raised as though somebody had trodden on my toe. "Mary's remark was most accurate. She said that both his pronouncements and his gestures seemed rehearsed."

"Well done Mary Watson!" Holmes cried. "This is most useful information, and—"

He was interrupted by my groan.

"What is it?" he asked. "Does Mrs. Hudson's breakfast not agree with you?"

I pushed my plate away, its contents hardly touched. "No. That groan is merely the sound I make when I have realised something I rather wish I hadn't."

"Related to Edward Langtry, no doubt. I rather suspect I know what it is."

"No, that is quite impossible."

"Allow me one attempt. You now realise that you once encountered Edward Langtry before you interviewed him here in this room."

My eyes widened. "Yes! It was—"

"On the stage—"

"Yes!"

"—at the Theatre Royal—"

"Yes!"

"—alongside none other than Irene Adler."

I nodded morosely. Without another word, I rose from my chair and went to fetch my jacket.

CHAPTER TWENTY-SIX

When we were installed in the cab the driver called down and Holmes turned to me expectantly. I thrust my hand into my jacket pocket – then another pocket, then another. Soon I had turned them all inside out, and emptied the contents of my pocketbook, and yet I had not unearthed the calling card that Edward Langtry had given me.

Holmes appeared unperturbed by the loss – in fact, he appeared positively delighted.

"Why are you grinning?" I asked, my irritation only increasing when the cab driver called down again, asking where he was to take us.

Ignoring the driver, Holmes asked me, "When you met Irene Adler, did you come into physical contact with her?"

"We were either side of a small table, with a ridiculous crystal ball between us." Then an image formed in my mind, and I said wearily, "I am wrong yet again. She did lean forward at one point, and she took me by the lapels. I was distracted. The light from the globe was… Well, it hardly matters." I did not wish to add that the distortion of her features caused by the blue light from below had frightened me, even if only momentarily.

"Then she took the card from you," Holmes concluded with an air of satisfaction.

"But why? I have been to Langtry's house once already. If we go now to Stoke Newington, I will very soon locate the right place. In fact, I am able to recall the street name: Paget Road."

Promptly, Holmes turned in his seat to address the driver. Then he turned back to me. "You ask why she stole from you? Because of the challenge, naturally! It was another of her thefts without theft. Undoubtedly it was she who took the card, but as you had already absorbed the information upon it, the theft leaves you no worse off and in possession of the same knowledge."

I stared out of the window, watching the street as the cab bumped along. "It strikes me as an immature trick," I grumbled.

"An unnecessary flourish, perhaps," Holmes said, "though perhaps she could not trust that you would recall seeing Langtry's face on the stage, or that your wife would suspect him of presenting his case fraudulently. Eventually you would have realised that the card was missing, and that alone would have set us on our current course."

"Then you are convinced that Edward Langtry – along with his wife, no doubt – are simply agents of Irene Adler, in service to her ridiculous challenge?"

"I am certain we have picked up the scent once again."

I watched as my friend's head tipped back, and he inhaled thoughtfully as though his statement had been meant quite literally.

We soon arrived at Paget Road. Once again, I asked the driver to stop at the end of the street so that we might alight without attracting notice. I saw with some satisfaction that Holmes's impulse was to enter the same small park in the centre of the two halves of the crescent, from which point we watched the house for several minutes. When it was clear that there was no movement at any of the unlit windows, we emerged from the park and approached the house. Holmes leaned from the top of the steps to look in at the parlour window, then pronounced with no small amount of satisfaction, "It is as I suspected. The place is empty."

I took my turn looking in, and realised what he meant: not only was the parlour empty of any occupants, it also bore all the hallmarks of being unoccupied in a far more permanent sense. Though there was furniture visible – a table covered with a cloth, four chairs, a long bottle-green sideboard, a canvas screen – all of these items were grimy and in disarray, there was a ragged hole in the ceiling, and the table was coated in plaster dust.

"I feel quite the fool for not having thought to visit the place in daylight," I said.

"You were not to know, Watson," Holmes reassured me. He bent to examine the lock of the front door, reaching into his pocket for his tools.

"To all appearances, it seemed an entirely natural arrangement," I said. "Mary and I saw Emilie Langtry – or whatever the woman's true name might be – exiting the house, and then..."

Holmes seemed not to have noticed that I had trailed off. He was occupied in selecting the exact tool for the task at hand.

"Holmes?" I said.

"Be so good as to allow me peace for a moment," Holmes muttered.

"Yes, but Holmes—"

Holmes rose. "Watson, I must insist that you remain quiet. I shall not be able to concentrate on unlocking this door if you are twittering at my ear."

Rather than argue with him, I simply reached beyond him to the door handle, and turned it. The door swung open with a faint creak.

"What I was trying to tell you," I said, "is that Mrs. Langtry did not lock the door – no doubt because she did not possess the key."

Holmes stared at the open door. Then, without bothering to pass comment, he strode inside.

The air inside the house was thick with dust, and I found myself breathing shallowly in an attempt to avoid inhaling it in any great quantity. I paused at the doorway to the parlour which we had seen from outside, but did not enter as it was clear that the series of footprints visible in the dust of the hallway did not continue inside. The next room contained only an upright piano, a desk and some empty shelves. The room at the rear of the ground floor was a kitchen containing another table – this one wooden and bare – positioned before a fireplace, and at the back window a sink and scullery area. I supposed that it might once have been the exclusive realm of serving staff. One of the rough wooden chairs had been pulled away from the table and dusted down, and had evidently been used recently.

"Perhaps Emilie Langtry sat here while she waited for the appropriate time to leave the house," I said.

Holmes nodded absently. He betrayed little interest towards any evidence of Emilie Langtry's actions; instead, he went directly to the mantel above the fire, taking each of the handful of decorative objects down one by one. So far as I could see, none of them had been touched in a very long time. Furthermore, they were all distinctly unappealing objects, such as painted china representations of an elephant and a woman holding an umbrella, and two ugly grey plates inscribed with the year 1845, commemorating some unknown event. These plates captured Holmes's attention for longer than the other items, and he turned each of them over in his hands more than once.

After watching him for a time, I asked, "Is it the letters that you have in mind? O, L, D?"

"Indeed," Holmes said. "That clue is not much, but it is something. Perhaps you might look around upstairs, and report back if you find anything that heralds from before 1845."

Obediently, I left the kitchen, but returned promptly. "The footprints do not go upstairs," I said. "So surely there is no need to investigate there."

Holmes shook his head. "We cannot make assumptions. She is certainly wily enough to spread dust in her wake."

"By 'she', I presume you mean Irene Adler?"

"Who else?"

I shook my head in dismay and left again, tramping up the stairs. The rooms of the first floor were in a similar state to those downstairs, with wardrobes and sets of drawers abandoned and empty, and miscellaneous decorative objects left around the place: a music-box, a small chest filled with worthless bracelets and rings, an album containing a single photograph of a group of men standing before a memorial of some sort. It struck me that so disparate were these items that any one of them might have represented a clue in Adler's game, which left me singularly unwilling to investigate any of them closely. Though this challenge fascinated Holmes, to me it seemed only a diversion. That might have been well and good if there were nothing more pressing that might occupy our minds, but in the circumstances it seemed inexcusable, while Fridtjof Nansen yet feared for the safety of his wife and his own person – even if the deliverer of the threats against him was demonstrably human rather than a spirit from the Arctic.

Presently Holmes made his way up the staircase.

"Well?" he said. "Have you found anything of interest?"

"Possibly. That is, you might have an interest in any of these objects. I must confess that I have no opinion as to their worth or age."

Holmes did not respond to my glum pronouncement, and set to making his rounds of the three bedrooms. For my part, I removed a heap of blankets from an armchair and sank into it, as it was the least dust-covered surface I had yet found. I already had the beginnings of a cold after my tramping around on successive nights. Now I wondered if spending a great deal of time in this house might soon affect my lungs, and the idea of spending Christmas coughing and choking made my mood all the more dismal.

As anybody with any passing familiarity with his temperament might have supposed, Holmes displayed no such qualms. He worked fastidiously, examining each item in turn. Gradually the dust on the floor was pushed aside as he created channels by his movements from place to place.

Finally, he returned to stand before me. I gazed up at him blearily; I had almost fallen asleep. Holmes was holding an ormolu mantle clock featuring a horse and rider above the timepiece.

"Is that a gift for me?" I asked sardonically.

"It is the oldest item in the house," Holmes replied. "It dates from no later than 1840, so it is older than the plates."

"Well done you," I said in no less bitter a tone.

"I have examined it in minute detail, prising off the rear panel to see the workings. There is no sign of anything having been placed there."

"Then can we go?"

Holmes nodded wearily. He placed the clock onto a sideboard, raising a faint plume of dust at either side.

I could not bear to see my friend so downcast. "Perhaps we have made a wrong assumption," I volunteered as I rose from my chair. "We have been convinced of the meaning of the letter clues – there seems no room for misunderstanding that they spell out the word 'old'. But when you were searching within this clock, what did you hope to find?"

"Another scrap of paper."

"Quite so. But if the message were complete, then expecting to find another letter would make little sense."

Holmes stared at me. "You are right, Watson! How blind I have been."

I had only been speaking my thoughts aloud, but now I saw how wise my words had been. Pressing this advantage, I went on, "And so perhaps the letters do not spell 'old', but are constituent parts of some other message." I waved a hand while I thought. "Such as, for example, doll—" Then I gasped sharply.

"Yes, Watson. 'Doll' would certainly fit the pattern. Does your wordplay amaze you so very much?"

I shook my head. "*Doll*, Holmes!"

"Have you seen one here in this house? I have not come across one, and I have searched the place thoroughly."

"Not here. On the grave! Mary told me that Emilie Langtry placed a doll on the grave that she visited!"

To my surprise, Holmes made no exclamation. Instead, he tutted and turned away.

"Holmes, what is the matter? Surely you must accept that this is a development we must follow."

"It is slapdash, Watson. Irene Adler is meticulous, and her challenge ought to be correspondingly orderly – and therefore it must be predictable. Do you really suppose that she could countenance delivering clues in such a way that they might be taken out of sequence? We have only found the letters D, O and L of 'doll', so by your reasoning another L has been missed, which would have set us on the correct path. Conversely, what if Mary had examined that doll on the night when she saw it placed upon the grave? She might easily have unearthed a step in the puzzle long before its proper time. No, it is too untidy an approach."

"You say Adler's method must be predictable, and yet here we are, standing in a dust-infested house with nothing to show for several hours of effort." I took him by the arm and led him down the stairs. "Protest all you like, but we have a new line of enquiry, and I must insist that we pursue it."

CHAPTER TWENTY-SEVEN

St. Olave's Church was located on a narrow strip of land between two roads at the tip of Finsbury Park. Though I knew that Woodberry Down and its reservoir were very close behind the nearby row of houses, I could see nothing of that place, for which I was most grateful. The air was still bitingly cold and the memory of slipping partially into the water filled me with horror.

The churchyard was very small, and formed an unusual acute-triangular shape. In the narrowest part near to the park were several dozen headstones, but Holmes and I examined each of these in turn and none of them belonged to a child. Then we moved to the far side of the building, where the snow was less deep and where a scattering of newer stones were positioned near to the windows of the apse, beneath the boughs of a number of large pine trees.

It was I who found it. I cried out to Holmes, who hurried to my side.

"Georgia Hooper," I read. "She died in 1886, at the age of two years old. I am certain this is what Mary described."

Until this point Holmes had been notably unmoved at the prospect of reaching the church. Now, though, he displayed some enthusiasm as he reached down to a mass of pink lilies that had been placed at the foot of the headstone, still wrapped in brown paper. It was only when he moved them aside that a child's wooden doll was revealed. It had cherubic round cheeks and a dress patterned in red and green. Its hiding place beneath the flowers had prevented it from being touched by snow or frost.

"It is not at all old, though," I said. Then I realised my mistake and added, "Apologies. I am forgetting that we have dispensed with that line of thinking."

Holmes took up the doll and began to inspect it. Now it crossed my mind that I may have been entirely mistaken, and we were in fact no more than what we appeared to be: two men disturbing the gifts placed upon a child's grave. I looked around the desolate churchyard but saw nobody, though I could not help but wish us far away from this place. I dreaded the possibility that Holmes might suggest destroying the doll in order to see whether it was hollow.

As Holmes manipulated the doll, I saw the skirt of its dress unfold: evidently, it had been tucked up and secured at a shorter length. From this makeshift pocket fluttered a scrap of paper. I leapt forward and caught it before it touched the snow.

"Well done, Watson!" Holmes cried. "Had it been made wet, that might have been the end of our clue. Now, what letter is it?"

I turned the scrap over to reveal a handwritten letter S. Holmes responded with a grunt of annoyance.

"I presume the word is not 'olds', but 'sold'," I said.

"You were expecting an L, then?" Holmes asked irritably. "That would only have indicated the very location in which we found it, and would have led us nowhere else. Though I confess that 'nowhere' is precisely where we seem to have found ourselves, in any case."

I raised myself to my full height. "Holmes, may I remind you that you resisted coming here in the first place? You were certain that Adler would not have placed a clue here, and yet she did.

It suggests to me that we are following her formula accurately. There has been no missing letter L, and the word was never 'doll'. Rather, I identified an irregularity in the pantomime she put on, and it has paid off."

Holmes appeared chastened. "You're quite correct, Watson, and you deserve my apologies and thanks."

"You do not seem at all pleased about finding yourself on Adler's trail once more."

"I confess that I am disappointed. All that I said earlier about the untidiness of this arrangement remains true. I fear that she has lost her touch. This challenge has all the hallmarks of becoming indiscriminate."

I considered this for a time. "There is another explanation, Holmes. You must remember that this is a challenge designed for you – and you alone – to solve."

"What of it?"

"Perhaps there is no accident in this 'untidiness' which you have identified."

Incredulous, Holmes said, "But she knows very well that I am the last person in the world who would respond favourably to such a method!"

"Quite so." Growing in confidence, I went on, "When I met her in the palmist's carriage, she said a number of things which I am increasingly certain were not idle comments. In particular, she spoke of your frustration in attempting to solve this series of puzzles, and her tendency to tease you."

Holmes waited, then said, "Again, Watson, I am bound to ask: what of it?"

"Do you not see what I mean?"

"No, I do not."

I laughed hollowly. "Then that, too, is part of her design." Recognising that my friend's patience was wearing thin and that he might soon explode into anger, I added quickly, "I believe that Irene Adler is deliberately playing on your weaknesses."

My words were poorly judged, and the explosion occurred despite my best intentions.

"Weaknesses?" Holmes retorted. "Are you going to lecture me on my habits, now?"

I stood my ground, watching him with some interest, as his display of irritability supported the very point I was attempting to make.

"Irene Adler understands your intellectual capabilities very well," I said calmly. "She has set you these particular challenges for that very reason, and no doubt she knows that in a straight pitting of her wit against yours, you might well be the victor – which in this case would represent an unravelling of the hard work she has put into her puzzles. However, she intends to make their solution difficult for you. Though I have no doubt she wishes you to succeed in your task eventually, she would prefer to demonstrate her superiority all the same."

"Watson, I beg you to speak more plainly. What are you trying to say?"

"You are irascible, Holmes, and you are impatient."

"Then you intend to insult me and nothing more!"

"But you do not deny the charges?"

Holmes hesitated. "No. They are merely the consequences of a mind channelled into useful application."

"And they are the very aspects of your character that have been creating obstacles to your progress in these challenges. What is your attitude to this search for letters that Adler has planted as clues?"

With a grimace, Holmes replied, "I find it intolerably slow."

"There you have it, then. Adler knew this would be your response, and she has used it to her advantage."

"Neither to change, nor falter, nor repent," Holmes said in a faraway voice.

"I beg your pardon?"

"That is what Irene Adler said upon the stage, when she performed the speech of Shelley's Demogorgon. You are quite correct, Watson – everything she has done has been according to a careful design."

"I am glad that you accept it," I said. "Similarly, take this business of the doll. You would have discounted it as a clue if I had not insisted that we come here."

For the first time, I saw a hint of Holmes's usual character return. In a decidedly more upbeat tone, he said, "Then she has factored your assistance in to the shape of her puzzles."

I paused, then said, "Yes, I suppose that is true."

"Then we both ought to be insulted, ought we not?"

"I see no reason why…" I trailed off, looking down at the child's grave.

I did not raise my head to confirm that Holmes was watching me suffer, though I knew he was relishing my reaction. Worse still, I had no means of refuting his implicit allegation. When Langtry had arrived at 221b Baker Street I would have turned him away, if not for the fact that my wife had insisted that we hear him out – and then, of course, it had been Mary who had discovered the vital clue of the doll placed on this grave at St. Olave's, while I was waylaid by Irene Adler herself. Adler had been playing upon my vulnerabilities and my reliance on others in just the same calculated manner as she had utilised the weaknesses of Sherlock Holmes.

Neither of us spoke as we trudged through the snow to leave the churchyard.

CHAPTER TWENTY-EIGHT

The next day – December 23rd – I arrived at Baker Street at ten o'clock sharp, as we had arranged following our visit to the churchyard. Mrs. Hudson answered the door, carrying the luckless Toby as always, but Holmes hurried down the stairs even as I said my hellos and reluctantly agreed to stroke the dog. I fancied I saw him holding his breath to avoid inhaling the sickly-sweet aromas that came from both the dog and Mrs. Hudson's kitchen, within which Christmas concoctions seemed to be perpetually brewing.

"Are we going out, then?" I asked.

Holmes wound a scarf around his neck and pushed past me into the street, making my question redundant. Before it moved away, he managed to hail the same carriage in which I had arrived.

I followed him and sank back into the same seat I had occupied only a minute before, then pulled on my gloves again.

"I had looked forward to a warming cup of coffee," I confessed.

Holmes regarded me with a level gaze. "Very well. I will buy you coffee in town."

"Really?"

"You seem very surprised, Watson."

"You have never bought me coffee before."

"Then I must rectify that mistake. And I insist that you shall have cake as well. Though you ate breakfast at your usual time of eight o'clock, I observe that you are hungry all the same."

I looked down at myself. "What aspect suggests that?"

"Oh – am I incorrect?"

I blanched. "As it happens, I am a little peckish. At this time of year, little treats and oddments tend to find their way into my diet, with the result that I seem always to be snacking. I blame Mary, who positively encourages such festive temptations – and yet her own figure never seems to be affected. Is it something in my appearance that has betrayed me, Holmes?"

With a smile, Holmes rapped upon the ceiling of the carriage and called for the driver to stop. I looked askance at him, but he held up a finger to bid me keep silent. Now that the trundling of the wheels no longer obscured the sound, I realised that my stomach was emitting a plaintive, high-pitched groan. Holmes called out, "Carry on, please," and sat back, appearing decidedly pleased with himself.

I folded my arms over my stomach and tried not to think about cake.

Presently Holmes had the driver drop us at James Street in Covent Garden, and the emptiness of my stomach began to insinuate itself into my thoughts again. There were a very many good coffeehouses in Covent Garden.

As we entered the market, I said, "You have not explained what we are doing here, Holmes. I cannot believe that we have come here simply to feed me." I looked around at the towering stacks of produce in baskets, the men bustling about with equally precarious stacks of barrels atop their heads, the flower girls bellowing at passers-by and the horses-and-carts somehow navigating these crowds to deliver more supplies. "I don't suppose you're intending to shop for Christmas gifts, or anything of that sort?"

Holmes took my arm and led me expertly through the melee, ducking left and right to avoid the obstacles that appeared in our path. "I said I will buy you coffee and that is precisely what I intend to do. Our destination is on Bow Street, but it is as well to approach from this direction in order to avoid attracting notice."

"Ah – now we get to the matter at hand. Whose notice might we attract?"

Holmes did not reply. Soon I became exasperated at his determination to lead me through the marketplace as if I were a child too young to be trusted not to become lost. I wrenched my arm free and adjusted my skewed jacket – but when I looked up again, Holmes was gone. It took me several minutes of wrong turns, bumping into market barrows and collecting a series of jeers and insults from costermongers before I located him again; he was strolling casually at the far side of the marketplace, as if untouched by the chaos of Covent Garden. I caught up with him, rather out of breath and ever more ready for sustenance.

In answer to my unspoken question, Holmes pointed across the street. The coffeehouse he indicated was rather a fine one, with a neatly painted pale-blue sign and a frontage comprised of a floor-to-ceiling window. Despite my scepticism, my hopes soared. I saw Holmes's eyes narrow as he peered into the interior of the establishment, and then he nodded. Once again he took my arm, but now it was only in a companionable fashion, and I allowed it.

Upon entering the building Holmes did not pause to assess the available seats. Instead, he walked ahead of me to a table a little way from the front window and against a wall littered with photographs of actors in theatrical costumes, many of them appended with scrawled ink signatures, and all garlanded with paper streamers in deference to the Christmas season. I had no time to take in any detail of these portraits, though. My first observation was that the woman sitting alone at the table was evidently expecting somebody to join her, as her head rose and she squinted at Holmes upon his approach – but then her expression turned quickly from expectancy to confusion. My own thoughts followed a similar trajectory when I recognised this woman as Eva Nansen.

"Mrs. Nansen," Holmes said cheerfully. "What a pleasure it is to find you here. May we join you?"

Obeying some ingrained instinct of politeness, Mrs. Nansen gestured at the three unoccupied seats at the round table. "Please do," she said haltingly. Then, after a moment's hesitation, she added, "I am afraid that I expect company at any moment... though I am certain he will be pleased to make your acquaintance."

It was only as I sat at the table alongside this poor woman with cheeks glowing with embarrassment that I realised what situation we had blundered into. I felt a fool for not understanding it sooner, and I silently cursed Holmes for his charade of keeping information to himself at all times, entirely unnecessarily. The newspaper article of the day before had stated that Eva Nansen was to meet the director of the Royal English Opera company, and here we were on Bow Street, the very street upon which the Theatre Royal was situated. Mrs. Nansen wore a suit of finer quality than I had seen her wear before, and on the nearby coat rack was a fur that I presumed was hers. She was clearly determined to impress. Though I knew well that she could not be considered free of suspicion of involvement in the threats made by the 'Greenland spirit', my heart swelled with sympathy for her. In recent years she had lived in the shadow of her husband's fame, despite having established herself independently before their marriage as a fine skier and as a singer of international renown. It seemed perfectly reasonable that she maintained ambitions of furthering her own career.

After the waiter had taken our orders, I made attempts at small talk, but both Mrs. Nansen and Holmes were preoccupied watching people on the street outside. Presently I, too, fell silent, and yet it was only I who appeared to bear the weight of this awkwardness. Each time an unaccompanied man walked along the pavement, I sensed Mrs. Nansen to my right rise slightly from her chair. Conversely, when a woman passed along the front of the coffeehouse, it was Holmes who responded with minute movements signifying his alertness, before he settled again. I was grateful when the waiter supplied my coffee and a bun, giving me something to concentrate upon – though I barely tasted either the drink or the food, so great was my discomfort.

Abruptly, Holmes leapt up from his seat and dashed towards the door. Eva Nansen and I watched in astonishment as he flung it open and strode outside to address a woman who I only now noticed, and who he had almost knocked over with the force of his exit from the building. She had kept to one side of the window, barely looking around the wooden door to peer through the glass. Whoever she was, this was certainly the woman Holmes had been waiting for. She was far shorter than Holmes, and her face and hair were hidden beneath a rough woollen shawl that suggested poverty. I glanced at Mrs. Nansen to see her reaction, but her amazement was equal to my own.

"Is he always like this?" she asked weakly.

"Not always. Only when he is in pursuit of the solution to a mystery."

"And how often is that?"

"Quite often. And when he is not occupied in that way, he tends to remain in his own home."

"Then in future, if I see your friend Sherlock Holmes on the street, I will hurry in the opposite direction. Look, everybody is watching him. I only hope that the person I am here to meet proves to be even later to our rendezvous than he already is, otherwise it will be a task to explain what is happening."

The inaudible discussion between Holmes and the unfortunate woman lasted for half a minute, and then Holmes stood back. Slowly, and with a show of great reluctance, the woman entered the coffeehouse. Her ugly shawl covered her head and most of her body, but beneath it I saw that her clothes were as fine as Eva's own.

As before, I saw a series of expressions pass over Eva Nansen's face, and then she rose and stumbled towards this strange apparition.

"What are you doing here?" she exclaimed. Then, suddenly aware of the surrounding customers who were watching on, she took the woman's hand and drew her to our table.

I half rose and nodded politely at the newcomer, then retook my seat, as did Holmes. The woman's head remained bowed, her pale eyes fixed upon her hands that were clasped upon the table.

"Well, then," Holmes said. "Now that we are all present, we may begin."

Mrs. Nansen stared at him. "All present? I do not understand. I came here to…" Her voice faded away.

"So now you understand," Holmes said with no suggestion of satisfaction.

I looked at each of them in turn. "I am glad that you all see what is going on, but might somebody explain it to me?"

Holmes gestured towards the newcomer. "Very well. Dr. Watson, may I present to you Mrs. Lise Gylling. Mrs. Gylling, I believe you already know Dr. Watson."

I stared in amazement as the woman – Lise Gylling, the wife of Henrik Gylling – met my eyes for the first time and nodded in a wordless greeting.

"But—" I began, but found I could not formulate any sensible question.

Turning to the two women, Holmes said, "I hope you will forgive my theatrical methods, though they rather suit our current environment, do they not? It was I who supplied the information that resulted in the article published yesterday in the *Times*. Mrs. Nansen, I am afraid to say that the director of the Royal English Opera company will not be joining you as you had hoped."

Mrs. Nansen shook her head vociferously. "You are wrong. I received a letter from him personally, asking me to meet him before I leave for Christiania to-morrow—"

"No. That letter, too, was sent by me. You may consider the pretence unforgivable, but the fact that you found it so plausible supports my opinion that it was the appropriate course. I required the creation of some meeting that would take you far from your rented cottage in Child's Hill and which could be made known publicly. As I hoped, when Mrs. Gylling read in the newspaper of your rendezvous, she could not help but come here, too, in the hope of speaking to you directly afterwards."

Lise Gylling still did not speak. Though I had told myself I would hold my tongue, I could not help but say, "I had no idea that you had come to England along with your husband, Mrs. Gylling."

Her already watery eyes filled with tears. "I did not," she said in a hoarse voice.

"But you *are* here!" I said.

"I mean I did not come here with Henrik. I was on the same boat, but he did not know it." Suddenly, she clutched at Eva's hand, gripping it tight. "Eva – I left Marta with her grandparents. I am no kind of mother. I am bad, am I not?"

Mrs. Nansen made soothing noises, then pulled her chair closer to Lise's and allowed her to place her head on her chest. "No, you are not bad. You did something that was wrong, but I understand why."

Holmes and I exchanged glances, but he seemed to have no compulsion to put my mind at ease about what was happening. He waited patiently for Lise Gylling to compose herself. She looked at him, sighed deeply, then nodded to indicate that she was ready to speak.

"There is no use in pretending any more," she began. "It is clear that what you know already is enough to reveal everything that remains hidden. So I will tell you myself, and I hope that you will find in your hearts an understanding that my actions are due to love, not mischief.

"I was responsible for the 'gifts' placed on the doorstep of my friend Eva Nansen." She flashed Mrs. Nansen an apologetic look, but Mrs. Nansen responded only with an expression of the utmost compassion. "I should not have done it. Perhaps the same plan would have worked as well if I had put the raw flesh on the doorstep of our own house... Or rather, perhaps that plan would have failed just as this one has."

I exclaimed, "Then it was you that I saw outside the Nansens' cottage, hunched over and wearing your husband's polar coat!"

"Yes. I did not see you until after I had taken the coat from the wardrobe, by leaning through the window of Henrik's bedroom. You frightened me very much, Dr. Watson."

I began an involuntary apology, then caught myself. "I am bound to tell you that I was much startled by your own appearance as well, Mrs. Gylling. What right have you to go skulking about dressed in such a manner?"

Mrs. Gylling gestured vaguely with a hand. "I was pretending to be the Greenland spirit. Or rather, the Greenland beast – a name invented by my daughter, Marta." In response to my confusion, she turned to Eva Nansen and continued, "When we visited you and Fridtjof in Lysaker, I brought with me a hare, skinned by the butcher. I should not have done it, Eva. I scared you then, and then afterwards, again and again. I am sorry."

Mrs. Nansen shook her head. "You did only what you thought was necessary."

Addressing me again, Mrs. Gylling said, "My hope was that the raw meat would remind Henrik and Fridtjof of their experience in the fjord in Greenland – Ameralikfjord, it is called. When he returned, my husband referred to that event often, as well as the other hardship he endured, though he told me the complete tale of what happened in the fjord only once. The name Ameralikfjord became more like a curse spoken in anger. He believed that it was a spirit who had helped them, but that the gift had carried another message, a threat."

"Then by evoking the memory of the Greenland spirit," I said, "you hoped to dissuade Fridtjof Nansen from returning to that country – or perhaps the polar region in its entirety."

Lise Gylling shook her head. Casting a look of great sadness at her friend, she said, "Fridtjof Nansen's mind will never be changed, and it is not my business to attempt to do so. I only wished for my husband to change his own views. Dr. Watson, he was almost lost to me on that expedition. We have a child. I cannot bear for him to go away for so long again, and an expedition to the North Pole will be ten times as dangerous as the last. From what my husband has told me, he was afraid constantly – afraid of the confusion of the frost-snow, of the plague of mosquitoes, of the hunger and thirst, of the threat of *something* out there beyond their tents – and I know that that fear will cause him to make mistakes." She looked up as a waiter brought a cup of coffee to the table – Holmes must have ordered it surreptitiously – and she sipped it gratefully. "I know that I have played a dangerous, foolish game, making his fear even greater. But it worked, for a time. At times perhaps Henrik did not believe that the threats were made by the same spirit that haunted them at Ameralikfjord, but my actions kept that creature in his thoughts, along with a sense of threat. He began to accept that the spirit had been warning him and Nansen never to return, or worse would befall them. He spoke more enthusiastically about moving out of Christiania, to somewhere more like Lysaker, and building a life for ourselves and for Marta that would suit us. Despite his excursions, Henrik has a strong sense of home."

Once again, she looked at Eva, whose gaze had become more and more blank while her friend had been speaking. I realised that everything that Mrs. Gylling had said about Henrik Gylling was in direct contrast to Fridtjof Nansen: he cared little for his home, and thought nothing of setting off on adventure after adventure. It seemed likely that Eva Nansen would spend much of her married life waiting in an empty home for an absent husband.

"So," Mrs. Gylling continued with a sigh, "on that night in Lysaker I made my first threat. It was very cold, so I took from the rack Fridtjof's large, shapeless coat to keep me warm. In the morning I found that my daughter had not been sleeping, and had seen me outside, and she began telling this story of the Greenland beast. When I saw that my threat had made an impression on Henrik, but not *enough* of an impression to change his mind completely, I resolved to return to Lysaker whenever I could – that is, when my husband was away from our house conducting matters of business – to deliver more gifts of meat. Making the threats against Fridtjof rather than Henrik was intended to keep suspicion from me, and to suggest that if Henrik did not associate himself with the new expedition, he would be free of fear. It was a tiring business despite the journey being only very short, and despite my chore taking only a moment before I could return home – but once I had started I could not allow myself to stop. Then came the announcement of this trip to England. I had to decide: should I stay at home and let Henrik see that the threats were nothing supernatural, or should I come to England to continue making them? Of course, I came here. My hope was that these would be the last threats I would make, and that Henrik would decide not to go with Fridtjof to the pole."

I found myself struggling to take all this in. "But why on earth did you feel the need to take from your husband's bedroom the hooded coat which he had used at the Royal Geographical Society to demonstrate expedition apparel? As far as you were aware, there was nobody to observe you when you placed the raw meat on the doorstep of the cottage at Child's Hill."

Mrs. Gylling shrugged her shoulders. "Perhaps I am as superstitious as my husband. Each other time I had placed raw meat on the doorstep at Lysaker I had worn the same coat – or rather, my husband's coat, which was identical to Fridtjof's coat which I had worn that time in Lysaker. The first two nights I came to the cottage at Child's Hill, I saw the coat lying upon my husband's bed, acting as a second blanket, and I simply reached in and took it. The third night – when you were present, Dr. Watson – it was not upon the bed, and though I told myself it did not matter if I wore it or not, I saw it hanging in the open wardrobe and it seemed a sign – so I climbed halfway onto the bed to take it." She added, "All of it was wrong and unnecessary. Even so, I could not help but look in at Henrik's open window each time I came to the cottage. I never liked him leaving our window open, but now it seemed almost an invitation for me to come close while he was sleeping. I watched him, and then I took the coat, and I brought it back when I had left the meat in its proper place."

I remembered that when I had searched the rooms of the cottage after the events of that night, the contents of Gylling's wardrobe had been scattered on the bed – no doubt due to Lise's hurried return of his coat after she had completed her task.

Another thought occurred to me. "None of this explains who your husband was speaking to in his bedroom that night when I was watching in secret." I turned to Eva. "Was it you, Mrs. Nansen, or your husband? It cannot have been Mrs. Gylling, as she was outside the room, looking in."

It was Holmes who answered my question. "He was addressing nobody at all. He was asleep, or at least partially so."

Mrs. Gylling bowed her head in agreement. "My husband has always been a light sleeper. I took too many chances coming to his window, and an even greater one in climbing over the bed to reach the wardrobe containing the coat. I woke him, or perhaps only half woke him. Maybe he saw my face – I don't know. But he certainly spoke to me, in his confused state. He rose from the bed and continued the discussion we have had so many times, about whether Fridtjof Nansen can be trusted to lead an expedition, about the dangers of trekking to the North Pole. It was awful, seeing him so tortured, but it only made me more resolved to save him from the fate that Fridtjof would lead him towards." She placed her cup on its saucer and put her head in her hands. "And now he will know I have been tricking him, and even if he forgives me, he will leave me and be gone for months, perhaps years."

She began to sob, and Eva Nansen resumed stroking her hair and making soothing sounds.

As if nothing of any consequence had occurred, Holmes said to me, "I would suggest that you finish that bun that you have hardly touched, Watson. It is time for us to reunite this estranged couple."

CHAPTER TWENTY-NINE

Upon our return to Child's Hill we found Nansen and Gylling together in the kitchen of the cottage, poring over maps laid out on the table. Nansen looked up only cursorily as his wife entered the room, but then performed a double-take when he saw that she was accompanied by several others. Gylling, too, staggered away from the table in amazement when he saw his wife. For several seconds he simply stared at her, open-mouthed, and then he rushed to clasp her hands.

"What are you—" he began, but then stopped speaking as his wife pushed herself close to him and pressed her head against his chest. She spoke words that I could not understand, but which I assumed were a repeated apology and a hurried explanation of her actions.

Nansen glared at Holmes. "What is the meaning of this?"

Holmes gestured towards the shuddering woman. "There is your Greenland beast."

Nansen's eyes widened. "Lise was the one who lays those things at our door?" He watched the husband and wife in their embrace, and understanding seemed to dawn upon him. He turned to his own wife. "I suppose that you already know of this before to-day."

Eva Nansen's cheeks glowed. "I knew only these last three days, my love."

I realised that this was a matter that Mrs. Nansen had not made clear. "Then did you see Mrs. Gylling on the very night I was watching the house?"

She nodded. "I went to the front door as soon as I woke, when you began making a disturbance outside. I was there when Lise, in her heavy coat, came to leave the raw meat. We looked at one another for some few seconds but did not speak – there was no need for her to explain, as in an instant I understood everything. Then I closed the door again, to allow her to continue with her task. I went back to my room and only returned to the front door when my husband and Henrik did so, though I ensured I was at the head of the party in case any distraction were required."

It occurred to me that this revelation about Lise Gylling had been the cause of Eva Nansen's abrupt change in attitude about the threats made against her husband, in the days following those alarming events.

Outraged, Nansen said, "Do you keep other secrets like this from me?"

His wife smiled. "There are no more secrets, my love. And this matter concerns Henrik and Lise alone." She pointed at the maps on the table. "I know that even if the threats were made by a true supernatural spirit, they would not be enough to keep you from making your plans to reach the pole."

Abruptly, Nansen beamed. "It is true," he said.

Together, they looked to the Gyllings, who only now parted, holding each other at arm's length and smiling fondly.

"Then you are not angry at me?" Lise Gylling asked.

"How could I be? You did all this to protect me," her husband replied in a cracking voice.

Mrs. Gylling glanced at the maps, which depicted the northern coast of Siberia. "I cannot bear the thought of you being gone so long," she said. "Or rather, I cannot bear the thought of so many months not knowing whether you are alive or dead."

Mrs. Nansen moved forward to take her friend's hand. Of all the people assembled in the room, she was the only other who might understand the woman's plight.

Gylling's head dropped. "I cannot bear the thought either." He did not seem to register Nansen turning sharply to look at him, and continued, "It is not only the thought of leaving you and Marta alone for so long, Lise. I am afraid. I have thought about this a great deal, particularly during our visit to England. I have woken each morning covered in a fine sweat, and I have rehearsed the same arguments – to you, and to Fridtjof. My conclusions have become unvarying. I realise now that what happened in Ameralikfjord… I realise that it hardly matters whether that apparition was real or an illusion, and it hardly matters that its threats were in fact made by you, moving around in the night-time and trying desperately to change my mind. I was afraid in Ameralikfjord, and I am more afraid now, even though the spirit has gone. I have a good life, a good family, and I do not wish to give them up. My thirst for adventure is sated."

For the first time, he looked at Nansen. "Fridtjof – perhaps you already suspected, but now it is time to say it aloud: I will not come with you to the pole."

Nansen strode over to his friend and clasped both of his hands. "You are a great loss to my team. I hope that you help me with the planning of my expedition, all the same?"

"Of course!" Gylling replied in great relief.

Nansen laid a hand on the map. "Then you still come to Lysaker often, and we still talk often." He looked at Lise. "Both of you."

Haltingly, Mrs. Gylling said, "But I have tricked you, again and again."

Nansen seemed to consider this anew. Then, suddenly, he threw his arms around the small woman, all but crushing her in his strong embrace. When he pulled away again, he roared, "And it is a good trick! The Greenland spirit – the beast that makes terror wherever it is seen! Yes, what a trick!"

Holmes cleared his throat. "I think it is only right to say that this deception ought not to be made public, Dr. Nansen."

Both Lise and Henrik Gylling shot him grateful looks.

Nansen bowed his head. "Yes, but it is a great shame. When I one day write of these days, they contain nothing more than *I spoke to old men at a geographical society* and *I met a dull prince*. Nothing about a fearsome beast, nothing about marvellous Lise Gylling, nothing about wily Sherlock Holmes."

"Very good," Holmes replied, "and I will correct the record in the *Times* with a convincing refutation."

Nansen clapped his hands. "Then all is settled, and we all return to Christiania together to-morrow morning – Mr. and Mrs. Nansen and Mr. and Mrs. Gylling. The journey home is like a holiday! The only thing that will make it better is a slight change in direction – perhaps the southern tip of Greenland…" He grinned mischievously in response to the gasps of horror from all around.

Gylling approached Holmes and shook his hand warmly. "I must thank you for your part in bringing my wife and I together again." Then to me he added, "And though I did not appreciate it at the time, Dr. Watson, it was your vigilance that uncovered the secret." He stepped back, and said more thoughtfully, "There is no need for secrets, and everybody would do better to speak their mind freely."

Holmes and I received their repeated thanks in the appropriate fashion, and then made ready to leave. Both men and both women now appeared in high spirits, and I had no doubt that they would succeed in their respective plans for their futures. Just as we were leaving the cottage for the final time, I saw Eva Nansen turn to her husband and I heard her say, "Fridtjof, my love – remember always that I will be coming with you to the North Pole. Otherwise, it'll be all up with me."

As I turned away and proceeded through the orchard to the road, I could not help but smile.

CHAPTER THIRTY

I spent the remainder of that day with my wife, both of us reading contentedly by the fire and my thoughts returning often to an appreciation that our future was likely to involve neither polar exploration nor great secrets between us. The next morning – Christmas Eve – I woke feeling as positive as ever I have been, and I asked Mary, "What shall we do to-day? My practice is closed and there is nothing that must take me away from you."

Mary responded with a warm smile that held only a hint of wistfulness, and said, "We both know the truth of the matter, John. You must go and visit Sherlock Holmes."

I shook my head determinedly. "He is caught up in this challenge of Irene Adler's. It is of no real importance."

"It is important to him. And, in turn, he is important to you."

I frowned. "But he is making no progress whatsoever. The woman has bested Sherlock Holmes, and the sooner he accepts that, the better it will be for him."

My wife responded with a broad smile. "That may be the case – but it would not be good for him to be alone when that realisation dawns upon him. You know how badly he is liable to respond to any failure."

I was forced to accept her wisdom; the thought of Holmes railing about being made the loser in this battle – and at Christmastime, to boot – was too awful to imagine.

"You are kind and wise," I said to Mary, and she nodded curtly as though this were self-evident. "I will return this evening, and nothing will keep me apart from you from then on, until Christmas Day is a distant memory."

She laughed. "I will certainly accept your uninterrupted company to-morrow, John. After that I may tire of you and send you away again."

The moment I entered the rooms on the first floor of 221b Baker Street, I knew I had been right to come. Holmes lay unmoving on the sofa. At first I thought he was unconscious, and then my next assumption was that he had fallen into his habit of consuming narcotics to allay the torturous over-activity of his mind. However, when he finally rolled onto his side I saw that he was wearing the same clothes I had seen him in the day before, and the dark circles beneath his eyes suggested that his ennui was a simple matter of having failed to go to his bed overnight.

"Holmes – you look pitiful," I said bluntly.

My friend groaned. "Perhaps that is the right word to use, in all respects."

I sat in my chair. "Sit up, man."

Holmes did so obediently – another sure sign that he was not his usual self.

"Now listen here," I said. "I have never seen you stoop to self-pity in the past, and I am not prepared to witness it now."

Instantly, something changed in Holmes's manner: his

posture became less stooped, and his eyes no longer dull. I was gratified that I might produce such a change for the better.

"Now," I continued, "imagine that I am not your friend but your doctor, and tell me your trouble."

Holmes stretched his arms and contorted his mouth into a wide ellipse; it was not a yawn but a more practical stretching of muscles, and I heard several clicks as if his limbs were slotting back into their proper places.

"The trouble is obvious, is it not?" he asked.

"It is. You are infatuated with Irene Adler—" When he shot me a warning look, I held up my hand and continued, "You are infatuated with Irene Adler's series of puzzles."

He seemed satisfied enough at this diagnosis. "I have searched every avenue, and nothing has come to light. All that there is, are those four letters – S, O, L, D – and nothing more. I have not only scoured the newspapers, but I have also made extensive enquiries at all of the auction-houses of London, made visits to several dozen jewellers, spoken to property agents… No single sale has appeared more significant than any other."

Despite my determined stance about his attitude, I found myself impressed at the lengths Holmes had gone to in pursuit of this new clue. I myself had barely considered the meaning of the word 'SOLD'.

"Perhaps these are the wrong avenues entirely," I said. It was only when Holmes grunted, perhaps indicating for me to continue, that I recognised that I had spoken aloud. "What I mean is that there is the other matter. The 'thefts without theft'."

Holmes waved a hand dismissively. "I have considered that. I gave particular focus to sales of property connected to criminals from my files, of which there have been a not inconsiderable number. None produced any new leads."

Deflated, I fell silent. Then, once again simply speaking my thoughts aloud, I said, "There have been a great number of these 'thefts without theft'. I am convinced there must be more that we have not identified. Let me see… the statue; the painting; your violin strings; the river. Then there were several which perhaps were not connected with Adler, but which I had on previous occasions added to the tally, when all of these mysteries seemed inextricably linked: the loss of the food rations before Nansen and Gylling arrived at Ameralikfjord; then Lise Gylling's temporary theft of her husband's heavy coat; plus the theft of the corpse from the morgue. More recently, we must add two additional thefts: Edward Langtry referred to his wife as stolen – which can be no coincidence, as his every word was no doubt scripted by Irene Adler herself – and then there is Adler's own pickpocketing of Langtry's calling card from my own jacket. That comes to—" I stopped and began counting silently on my fingers. "Nine instances of 'theft without theft', and—" I broke off with a gasp. "Holmes! How many repetitions of the melody were there in the Adler Variations?"

"Twelve," Holmes replied immediately.

"Then surely there are to be twelve thefts! There are three yet to come!"

"But as you have said yourself," Holmes retorted, "many of those situations had no connection to Irene Adler. You are contorting the facts to match your fanciful notions, Watson."

I laughed hollowly. "Are you prepared to say so with such certainty? Regardless of the fact that the Nansen affair has been tidied away so neatly, I find that I am not able to discount the idea that Adler had some influence over those events, or at the very least that she has been prepared to use them to her advantage in a game with rules that are clearly fluid and liable to change constantly. She said herself that she was opportunistic in her puzzle-making."

For whatever reason, this suggestion seemed to cheer Holmes's spirits. He stood up and said, "You are right, Watson. I must begin afresh, keeping my mind resolutely open. If, as you have argued, she is playing on my worst aspects, then I must prevent myself from falling into traps created by my own characteristics. Here, let us eat breakfast and then set ourselves to—"

He broke off as he turned to face the table, upon which were stacks of books but no food. He seemed unable to account for this, and stood immobile, staring.

"Perhaps you already ate breakfast earlier?" I suggested in a quiet voice.

"I have done nothing of the sort," Holmes snapped. "I can say so with assurance, as I have done nothing at all since dawn, other than to lie on that sofa."

I thought again of the litany of thefts, and my eyes widened. "Holmes – have you seen Mrs. Hudson this morning?"

"I tell you, I have seen nothing whatsoever!" Holmes replied, but then he appeared to understand the point I was making. Without another word, he flung open the door and clattered down the stairs. I followed in his wake, anxious to know that my erstwhile landlady was safe and well. A distinct, powerful smell grew stronger as I descended to the ground floor.

The vision that greeted us in Mrs. Hudson's kitchen was a great shock – though not of the sort I had feared.

Added to the fronds of pine that had been accumulating in the hallway and in Mrs. Hudson's apartment were more wreaths and garlands of holly, ivy and mistletoe, and all of the surfaces at the sides of the room were covered in bowls of fruit and nuts and scattered berries. Pushed into one corner, and far too large for the space, was a large pine tree decorated with ribbons, flags, beads and paper ornaments.

So dizzying was this display of Christmas festivity (and the customary stifling aromas of aniseed and cinnamon) that at first I did not perceive Mrs. Hudson herself; she emerged from behind the tree, wearing a paper crown and the broadest of smiles.

"Mr. Holmes!" she cried. "And Dr. Watson, too! How do you like my decorations?"

Holmes put a hand to his forehead as though the sight caused him physical distress; he had never had any patience for seasonal traditions. I managed a choked, "Delightful, Mrs. Hudson," as I tried to calm my racing heart.

"And what do you think of little Toby's contribution?" the landlady asked.

I looked around the room for the dog, a task made more difficult due to the reams of paper streamers that littered the floor.

"I cannot see him," I said weakly.

Mrs. Hudson turned from the tree and gasped. She darted to the table in the centre of the room and began to push aside the heaps of ribbon and paper strips.

"There!" she said triumphantly.

She had revealed Toby, sitting on the table, his head resting upon his forepaws, his lethargy apparently made no greater or lesser by having been buried under paper. Nevertheless, he was a Toby much changed from his usual appearance. No longer was he plain fawn-coloured; now he was a riot of colour. Around his torso was a vivid green jerkin, and upon his head a red woollen cap with a trailing tip, which was held in place with string.

"What the devil have you done to him?" I blurted.

"I've made him a little Christmas elf!" Mrs. Hudson replied, unconscious of my horror.

I managed to tear my gaze away from this festive abomination to look at Holmes, who was only able to blink in astonishment.

"Well?" Mrs. Hudson prompted.

I swallowed. My throat was very dry, perhaps in part due to the cloying atmosphere within the room. Toby stared up at me, silent and unmoving as though ignoring his plight was his only possible bid for dignity. It is perhaps the case that I have never felt such pity for another living thing – human or animal – as I did at this moment for Toby the dog.

I realised that Mrs. Hudson was still looking at me expectantly.

At last I managed to say, "I am glad that you have found your wool, Mrs. Hudson."

"I beg your pardon?"

I supposed that she would not let me off until I passed judgement on the dog's appearance – but it would have been impossible to approve of what she had done to him.

I waved a hand at the poor creature. "The wool. These are the very colours that you told me that you had mislaid."

The landlady put a hand to her mouth. "My word – you're right! What a coincidence."

At this comment, Holmes seemed to come alive. "Then you did not knit these… items… yourself?"

"No – I only wish I'd thought of it."

"But it is the same wool?" Holmes urged.

"I can't possibly know that." All the same, Mrs. Hudson bent to examine Toby's attire; the dog merely moved his head a fraction to watch her warily. "Though it does look the same. Isn't that strange? A little Christmas miracle."

"Mrs. Hudson – who gave you these items?" Holmes demanded.

"The boy."

"What boy?"

"You know… the boy who deals with Toby."

"A boy from Sherman's?" I asked.

"I suppose so. Didn't you make the arrangements yourself, when Mr. Sherman agreed for Toby to stay here over Christmas?"

"I did no such thing," I said in surprise.

Holmes said, "Mrs. Hudson, do you mean to say that this boy has visited this house recently?"

"This very morning. And yesterday – and every day since Toby's been staying here. The boy brings his food, and always stays to play for a while. A lovely lad, very thoughtful, and not just towards the dog. He brought most of these decorations, piece by piece, and some wonderful sweets and cordials as treats – and the tree this morning, can you believe that? As well as the darling elf costume, of course. Several times I offered a tip, but he refused outright. That's the very definition of the Yuletide spirit people talk about, isn't it?"

I recalled that I, too, had seen this boy, the day that Mary and I had encountered Edward Langtry. The delivery-boy had presented Mrs. Hudson with a holly wreath to replace the sparse one already hanging on the front door, and had made off as we arrived.

Holmes seemed unable to contain his excitement. "Would you describe this boy?"

The landlady shrugged her shoulders. "Perhaps fifteen or sixteen. Lovely skin, bright eyes. Very polite."

"With long hair?"

"Longer than some, I suppose. It sticks out from under his cap. Clean, though."

"And the voice? Higher than you might suppose? Or otherwise very low, almost comically so?"

"Well, both, as it happens. Boys that age do suffer from a changeable tone, you know."

Holmes pinched the bridge of his nose. "You understand that you have been speaking to none other than Irene Adler each morning?"

I gaped at him in amazement. If what he asserted was true, then I, too, had interacted – however briefly – with Irene Adler not once, but twice in recent days.

"Irene who?" the landlady asked innocently.

Holmes eyes became wide.

To avoid him making a scene, I cut him off before he could conjure a retort. "Somebody whose case we are investigating, Mrs. Hudson."

"I don't believe it," she said indignantly. "If that's so, what's she been doing downstairs instead of consulting up there with both of you?"

In a weary tone, I replied, "It's difficult to state the matter in brief."

Mrs. Hudson made a huffing sound and made a show of fussing over Toby's green jerkin. "Well, I don't care who that boy is – or girl, for that matter. I won't have my Christmas fun spoiled."

I nodded at Holmes, attempting to suggest silently that we retreat.

However, Holmes held his ground. "I am sorry, Mrs. Hudson," he said, each word sounding as though it took great effort to articulate, "but I have one more question, if you please."

She turned around, fixing him with a suspicious look. "What is it?"

"This delivery-boy – what food did he bring each morning?"

Mrs. Hudson's features softened. "Toby's favourite, of course. Liver."

Holmes exhaled at length, nodding.

"Is that significant?" I asked.

"Nothing could be more significant." He bent to look under the table. "Where is his bowl, Mrs. Hudson?"

The landlady pointed behind her, to a scullery apart from the main room. Holmes hurried there, then returned with a tin bowl half-filled with meat. He pushed aside the heap of paper strips on the table to make room, deposited the bowl, then promptly thrust his fingers into the mass of raw flesh. I blanched; its appearance was not only distasteful, but the smell of it seemed more powerful than it ought to be, though perhaps that was simply because I could see it. After the events at the Nansens' cottage in Child's Hill, I had no desire to have any dealings with raw meat for some time.

Evidently, Holmes had no such scruples. He raised a chunk of the smooth flesh to his nose and inhaled deeply several times. Then – to cries of disgust from both Mrs. Hudson and I – he put out his tongue and pressed it against the oily surface of the liver.

"Good God, Holmes – have you gone mad?" I asked.

"Aniseed," Holmes said simply.

"Don't be so silly," Mrs. Hudson retorted. "The aniseed is in the sweets that the boy brings."

Holmes shook his head sharply. "It is far more pronounced here in this meat. The other items have been supplied as a means of explaining the presence of the smell."

"What? The meat is flavoured with aniseed?" I asked in astonishment. "I have heard of dogs enjoying the taste, but I have never known it to be fed to them in such a fashion."

"It is not only flavoured, it is laced throughout. And I suspect that it has not been introduced to Toby's diet as any kind of delicacy." He turned to his landlady. "Mrs. Hudson, what are the effects of aniseed upon dogs?"

Mrs. Hudson spread her arms wide. "Oh, they go wild, most of them. They become excitable, playful – for a time, at least."

"And then?"

She looked at Toby slumped on the table. "They're ever so sleepy."

Holmes nodded in satisfaction. "And we can suppose that great amounts of aniseed in food will not only produce such effects in ever-more pronounced fashion, but that also the dog's sense of smell will be much compromised. Clearly, this 'delivery-boy' first approached Toby some time before we had need to ask Sherman for the dog on loan. Do you have the biscuits to hand?"

Mrs. Hudson rooted on the sideboard to locate the paper bag that I had once carried in my own jacket pocket. Holmes took from it a single biscuit and raised it to his nose.

"It is as I suspected," he said. "These, too, are laced with aniseed."

I gasped. "Then Toby's failure to track any scent at the River Lea, and on the night I watched the Nansens' cottage, was no fault of his own – he had been poisoned!"

"With no long-term effects – so long as you vary Toby's diet and now avoid this liver and these biscuits, Mrs. Hudson – but yes. Each time he was fed a biscuit he became greatly excited, followed by a lengthy period of absolute inertia. Irene Adler knew that I would have need of Toby's assistance, and so she rendered him useless."

I thought about this. "Then it is another 'theft without theft'! By feeding the poor beast aniseed each day, Irene Adler robbed him of his sense of smell – and yet the moment she stopped doing so, it would be returned to him, having never truly been stolen." I gestured at the impassive beast. "And then there is this ridiculous costume he has been made to wear!"

Mrs. Hudson interjected. "Dr. Watson – I happen to think it's an absolute delight."

I nodded distractedly. "And Irene Adler knew that it would appeal to you. But Holmes, don't you see that it amounts to another 'theft without theft'? Adler took the skeins of wool some days ago, but now she has returned them in another form, rendering the act no longer a theft at all. So the number of such thefts has now reached eleven. My suggestion of there being twelve in total gathers more support all the time."

"I hardly think that the number is significant, Watson," Holmes said.

"Perhaps not." I tried to put this matter out of mind, reminding myself that some of the items I had counted likely had nothing to do with Irene Adler, and that it was my writer's tendency to link events that suggested a continuous narrative. "Anyway, what concerns me is why she felt the need to *continue* to administer the aniseed while Toby has been here in this house. Did she expect you to make use of Toby again, or is there another reason she wished to keep his plight visible to you?"

Holmes did not reply. He took an intact sheet of newspaper from the pile on the table, spread it out, then proceeded to place upon it each of the pieces of the liver from the tin bowl. Studiously, he sifted through the detritus at the bottom of the bowl, watched on by Toby the dog, who seemed to have no quarrel with somebody rifling through his meal.

Finally, Holmes had cleared the centre of the bowl entirely, and he stood back in triumph.

"What is it?" I asked.

"A dirty table – that's what it is," Mrs. Hudson said in dismay.

Holmes gestured for me to look. I peered into the bowl at the central part that was now clear of meat and juice. A small square of paper was pasted to the interior of the bowl, coated in varnish of some description, and upon it was inscribed a single character: the Greek letter omega.

"Another clue!" I said.

Holmes turned to wash his hands at the sink. When he returned, he was smiling contentedly.

"Thank you both for your great help in this matter," he said. Then he reached out to Toby, laying his hand on the creature's head and then stroking the fur of his neck affectionately. "Thank you, all three."

CHAPTER THIRTY-ONE

I went promptly upstairs after Holmes, but by the time I arrived in his rooms, he had already become a dervish of activity, rooting within the piles of books on the dining-table and muttering to himself.

"What are you searching for?" I asked.

Holmes only pushed me out of the way to move to his chemical bench, upon which were stacked more books. Finally, he exclaimed and held up a thick volume.

"Might that contain a recipe for cooking liver, perhaps?" I asked.

Holmes subjected me to a withering look, then threw the book open upon the bench and began rifling through its pages. I watched impotently, until he jabbed a finger at the open page and exclaimed triumphantly, "There!"

I moved around to look over his shoulder.

"I see nothing of significance," I said, scanning the text. "What is this book – a treatise on mythological characters? Have you suddenly developed an interest in the classics?"

Holmes replied tartly, "I have no interest in such things – as Irene Adler knows very well. You were entirely correct in your assessment of her methods, Watson. She has been intent on playing upon aspects of the world to which I dedicate no part of my mind."

I could not help but smile. "That is a neat way of referring to subjects of which you are ignorant."

Holmes huffed and moved away from the bench. "All the same, I have that knowledge now, and this is what I have been searching for."

"I'm afraid I still don't see it."

"It is directly in front of you – page three hundred and forty-six, beginning at the third paragraph."

I looked down, but nothing in the text announced itself as pertinent. "This is the story of Prometheus. What of it?"

Holmes tutted in exasperation. "You do not remember what play she performed on the stage of the Theatre Royal?"

"Oh! It was *Prometheus Unbound*, was it not?"

"Indeed." Holmes went to the dining-table and took from it a much slimmer book. "I have the playscript here. She recited a section of its epilogue, playing the part of the Demogorgon. The relevance to my own person can hardly be ignored. Here, listen:

"Gentleness, Virtue, Wisdom and Endurance –

These are the seals of that most firm assurance"

He looked further down the page.

"And then later:

Neither to change, nor falter, nor repent;

This, like thy glory, Titan, is to be

Good, great and joyous, beautiful and free;

This is alone Life, Joy, Empire and Victory."

I smiled slyly. "I recall that there was a great deal about love, in addition."

To my satisfaction, I saw Holmes's pale cheeks colour slightly. "That is of no consequence. What is important is that she has cast me as Prometheus. Now, what do we know of him?

That is, other than Shelley's own assessment that Prometheus represents the 'highest perfection of moral and intellectual nature, impelled by the purest and the truest motives to the best and noblest ends'."

His pride at this pronouncement and its relationship to his own character was not lost on me. I was tempted to retort that I presumed that he had never read Shelley of his own volition, and that he had known very little about Prometheus until he had taken it upon himself to gather books related to Greek mythology in response to Adler's challenge. Instead, though, I turned back to the book and began to read the passage relating to the Titan god of fire, Prometheus.

After a minute or so I cried out, "Liver!"

Holmes nodded sagely. "Quite so. As punishment for the theft of fire from the gods, Prometheus was bound to a rock, and an eagle who was a surrogate for Zeus came each day to eat his liver, only for it to grow back overnight ready to be eaten once again."

I grimaced. "How gruesome. I never did understand it."

Airily, Holmes replied, "I believe the liver was thought to be the seat of human emotion."

"You mean you looked it up in this book."

Holmes had the dignity to appear hurt.

Chastened, I added, "So Adler is indeed teasing you. By positing you as Prometheus and then hiding a clue in the dog's meal of liver, I suppose she is suggesting that you lack human emotions, or something in that vein. And she has taunted you day after day, like Zeus's eagle."

"A reasonable conclusion – though it is a joke in poor taste."

"It is strange, though," I went on, "that we have only just concluded another case which related to raw meat, that time used to signify a threat..." I frowned. "Holmes – this is the damnedest thing. That blasted report in the *Times* asserted that the gifts of meat were exclusively liver!"

Holmes did not reply, but simply watched me with interest.

Then realisation struck me. "I am forgetting that it was you who wrote that piece, or at least provided the information to the journalist. But why include it in an article related to Fridtjof Nansen?"

"I am sure that you can work it out, Watson."

I sighed. It was typical of Holmes to demonstrate his mental superiority at a time when he himself was struggling with a problem. In this sense, he had something in common with the playground bully who doles out violence in response to turmoil subjected upon him by another.

"I imagine that you assumed that Adler would read the newspaper article."

"Quite so."

"And when she read the detail about liver, she would appreciate that you understood her taunt about Prometheus."

Holmes nodded.

"And yet," I said, "she had had the same idea, and got there before you." In response to Holmes's raised eyebrow, I continued, "Mrs. Hudson told us that the delivery-boy has been coming here every day since Toby arrived, which was December 18th, and furthermore that he – I mean to say, *she* – brought liver every day. Your own joke was made rather later than that, was it not?"

The change in Holmes's expression was minute, but in the narrowing of his eyes, the tightness at the corners of his mouth, I read a great deal of anguish.

"It seems, then, that I am still only racing after her coat-tails," he said quietly, "and yet so much is now known. Prometheus, the five-letter clue, the—"

"So do you understand the letters?" I asked eagerly.

Holmes waved a hand. "It is all there in the book."

I pushed the volume away from me. "Tell me directly, Holmes. What does the word 'SOLD' mean, plus the Greek letter omega?"

Holmes dropped down into his chair. "The omega is only a signifier. It is the Greek letter sometimes referred to as 'great O' –

which I imagine is another little joke. The final letter, the final clue, and it amounts to nothing at all – a 'great nothing'."

"If it is a signifier... does it signify that the word is a Greek word?"

"Yes. What is more aggravating still is that that word does not even contain a letter omega, and to include it would be a misspelling. Bearing in mind your interpretation of her inspiration for this series of challenges, it is likely that it amuses her to misspell a crucial clue, knowing that I would be minded to dismiss it."

He reached to a side table for a notepad and pencil, and wrote five letters in the centre of the blank page:

Δόλος

I frowned at it for several seconds. "The first letter, delta, is 'D', which corresponds with one of our clues. And then the middle character – is that lambda? – must be 'L'. The second and third are each an 'O' of different appearances, though neither is the 'great O' that you describe. I can only assume that the letter at the end is our 'S'. So the word is 'DOLOS'."

"Very good, Watson."

"But... what does it mean?"

"Put simply, it translates as 'deception'."

I slumped into my own chair. "Oh. Well, that's certainly apt – but it is hardly illuminating, is it?"

"It is not the only significance of the word. The other relates to mythology. It relates to the tale of Prometheus, specifically. Dolos was apprentice to Prometheus himself."

"Ah! Then Adler is positing herself as your follower."

Holmes allowed himself a faint smile. "It seems so. By the way, do you recall the adjective that she used to describe herself when you encountered her at the wintering fairground?"

After a moment's hesitation, I said, "She called herself both cruel and mendacious."

Holmes nodded. "Interestingly enough, the Roman equivalent of Dolos is named 'Mendacius', which is the root of that English word. It seems that she has been broadcasting her intent often, if only we had seen it."

I knew how much this revelation must sting my friend. He was singularly unused to being bettered, and Irene Adler appeared capable of it at every turn.

"This suggestion of your respective roles is a neat counterpoint to her merciless teasing, if she sees herself as your junior," I said. "But I still fail to see where it leaves us now. Simply understanding how Irene Adler views herself in relation to you is hardly the conclusion to this challenge that we might have anticipated. Do you suppose that it truly is the end of it?"

Holmes only glowered at me, but I knew from experience that I might as well have not been present – rather, he was looking through me, sifting through his own thoughts.

Uncomfortable under his gaze, I stood and went to the chemical bench and the open book. I sat in the chair and began reading, and soon became engrossed in the passage about Prometheus and his apprentice.

After some minutes I turned sharply and said, "Here is something that may be significant!"

Holmes did not appear to have heard me. His elbows were upon his knees and his head cupped in his hands. He appeared for all the world like somebody experiencing profound grief.

"Holmes, listen to me, I beg you!" I rose and approached him, brandishing the book like a totem.

Finally, my friend looked up.

"I have it!" I cried.

"*What* do you have?" Holmes asked in a tone of great weariness, as though he were speaking to an over-eager child.

"The next part of the puzzle!" I announced. Turning the book around, I pointed at the passage that had caught my attention. "See here – at one point, Prometheus sculpted a statue, but after being called away he left Dolos to oversee his workshop. Dolos was ambitious, and decided to create a facsimile of the statue. A copy, Holmes – do you see?"

Holmes stared up at me uncomprehendingly.

"Holmes, the statue that Dolos created was of the goddess Aletheia!"

"Aletheia…" Holmes repeated. "Meaning 'truth'."

Rather breathless now, I said, "Yes, and it was your mention of Roman equivalents of Greek mythological figures that has made me think of it… Holmes, this can only refer to the very statue that began this adventure – the statue of Veritas at the British Museum!"

CHAPTER THIRTY-TWO

The doors of the British Museum were shut and bolted, and a notice announced that there would be no public admittance from December 24th to December 26th. Despite this being an entirely reasonable state of affairs, I could not prevent myself from striking the heavy door with my fist in annoyance.

Holmes expended no energy on pointless anguish. He went directly to the western officer's house and rapped on the much smaller door to that building. After several minutes nobody had answered, and I prepared myself for the disappointment of abandoning our quest completely – but Holmes's knocking did not abate, and finally the door opened.

The man who answered was not wearing a uniform, but an open-collared white shirt. With a touch of surprise, I reminded myself that it was the morning of Christmas Eve, and that the great majority of people might be similarly out of their usual routines.

I watched as Holmes spoke to the man at length, inaudible to me. Then he turned and waved me over.

"How did you convince him to allow us inside?" I asked as we followed the man through the same clerks' rooms and studies that we had seen on our previous visit – though now all were unlit, and eerie in their silence.

"Let us say only that the goose on his family's table is likely to be larger than usual to-morrow," Holmes replied gravely.

When we emerged into the unlit museum, we did not turn to the left into the Greco-Roman galleries as I had expected, but instead we passed along the corridors at the front of the building, beyond the unoccupied entrance hall and towards the eastern wing. Before we reached the officer's house which was the twin of the one through which we had entered, our guide stopped and opened a door to a stone stairwell that led downwards into darkness.

"Then the statue of Veritas has been taken into the archives?" I asked.

"The workshop," Holmes replied. "The consensus appears to be that it is salvageable despite the chips to both the removed part and the base."

At the foot of the staircase we came out into a stone cellar with high vaulted ceilings. I shuddered in response to the cold which seemed to come from all directions, and seeped from the flagstones through the very soles of my shoes.

"The craftsman's workshop's this way," our guide said, striding ahead of us.

I followed most carefully to avoid striking my head on the overhanging haunches of the shallow stone arches which seemed designed to make impassable most of the space within the underground area. Even so, I was distracted frequently by the items that surrounded us: framed paintings stacked ten or twenty deep, chests with enormous iron buckles and straps, gleaming silverware abandoned as if worthless – and very many statues, their grasping limbs reaching out from the shadows at every turn. It was with great relief that we arrived at the workshop, where fewer items lay about us – or so I supposed after a first assessment, and yet then I saw that among the stone blocks arranged along one wall were busts and limbless torsos, which elicited more shudders from me.

Holmes was unperturbed by this distinctly Gothic setting. He moved from figure to figure, tutting, until he stopped and announced, "Here she is."

The woman before us was certainly Veritas – that is, it was the same woman with arms raised, and her expression was the same slightly mocking one I had seen before, when she was revealed behind a false wall in the upstairs chamber. Now she leaned back against the stone wall, as though reclining. I glanced down to see that she was still missing her feet, and to my shame my first thought was that this ought to make her less self-satisfied.

"Now," Holmes muttered, "which is the block upon which she stood?"

This second task proved decidedly more difficult; there were many dozens of plinths in the workshop, waiting for occupants, and a great deal of them were hidden beneath sheets or piled one upon the other. Finally, we located the plinth upon which was sculpted foliage and the remains of female feet – but it was placed high upon another block and required a considerable expenditure of energy on behalf of all three of us to bring it down to the floor.

"A chisel," Holmes said, holding out a hand while his gaze remained upon the feet.

"What?" the museum officer barked. "Oh no you don't. You said nothing about tampering with the piece."

"It is already destroyed," Holmes snapped.

"It's nothing of the sort. It's only in two parts. Banging at it with a chisel isn't going to make the sculptor's job any easier, is it?"

"I will pay double the value we agreed upon. Will that do?"

"I—" the man began. Then he seemed to think better of whatever response had first occurred to him, and he fell silent.

Holmes's outstretched hand twitched again. I cast around and located a chisel and mallet upon a counter.

"I don't understand," I said as I handed the items to him. "I thought it was the statue that was significant, not the base."

Without looking up, Holmes said, "You read the passage about the mythological tale, did you not?"

"Yes, but—"

"Then you know about the story of Dolos. In Prometheus's absence, his apprentice sought to make his facsimile of Veritas, or Aletheia, as he called her – but Dolos ran out of clay and could not complete it fully. When Prometheus returned, he was impressed with the work, and decided to claim both statues as his own work. He fired the kiln and baked both statues, then infused them with life. And yet, though the first Aletheia was capable of walking, the second was rendered immobile—"

I interrupted him. "Because Dolos had not completed the feet!"

"Quite so. And as the book states, the forgery was referred to by the name '*mendacium*' – a falsehood, or mendacity. Hence its relevance to our quest."

He placed the tip of the chisel against the heel of the plaster left foot – the foot that was placed flat against the base – then raised the mallet.

"You may wish to look away," I warned the museum officer.

Then Holmes struck.

The foot exploded into a shower of dust and shards of plaster. I had the unfortunate luck to inhale sharply at the same moment, and took in a great lungful of the stuff, and then I was forced to bend double, hacking and gasping for breath.

When I looked up again, Holmes was sifting through the debris. With a flourish, he plucked out a plain white envelope and brushed away the dust from it.

"What… is… it?" I managed to say through my choking.

I watched my friend's face as he examined the contents of the envelope. All the triumph of a few moments ago had been replaced by a tautness that suggested profound disappointment.

"What is it, Holmes?" I said again.

"I was wrong," Holmes said distantly. "I said once that she would never stoop to repeating herself. And yet here we are in the British Museum once again, re-examining the statue of Veritas, and now…" He took several items dully from the envelope and fanned them out for me to see. "It seems that we are expected to attend another performance at the Theatre Royal to-night."

CHAPTER THIRTY-THREE

I find that I never tire of watching my wife watching other people. It is in these moments of voyeurism that I fancy that I see into her mind, into her very thoughts. She is perennially interested in others, and she is rarely more fulfilled than when she is presented with a crowd of people going about their business and she finds herself in a position to simply observe them. Whereas Holmes might exhibit similar behaviour in the same situation, his conclusions would inevitably relate to *purpose*. In Mary's case, the significance of any particular observation of any person is less to do with cause and effect, and the absence of a riddle to solve is no loss at all. She is simply interested in her fellow human beings for its own sake, and her understanding enriches her own life immeasurably. I cannot share her passion. In my case, such an interest in *watching* extends primarily to watching Mary herself, just as I spend a large amount of my time observing Holmes as he observes others. I watch the watchers. What that says about me, I leave to the reader to determine.

Since we had found our seats in the dress circle of the Theatre Royal, Mary had not for a moment settled into hers, so frequently did she turn to look around as our fellow theatregoers hurried along aisles, shuffled sideways into their places and murmured pleasantries and unnecessary apologies at one another. All were in their finest attire as befitted a Christmas Eve performance, with most of the women bedecked in crimson or emerald green and wearing elaborate hats that would no doubt cause great consternation to anybody positioned directly behind.

"The curtain will soon be raised," I said. "Might you put your skills to work and spot Holmes somewhere in the crowd?"

"Are you so sure that he will join us?" Mary asked.

"Of course. There were three tickets. Offering one of them to you was a gesture due to your involvement in the Langtry business."

"And whose gesture was that?"

I blinked. "That is a very good question. I suppose it was Irene Adler's intention all along. But then—"

"Then she anticipated my involvement from the moment she put the envelope in place, when the plaster statue was first created."

"Good lord," I said. "She really has thought of everything."

"Poor Sherlock Holmes," Mary said soothingly.

"Why do you say that?"

"He must be left reeling. Every action he has taken has been foreseen. So what do you suppose was his true response to finding three tickets buried within the feet of the statue?"

I paused, then said, "At the time, I had thought that his assumption was that this performance was his prize. That is, he has completed the challenge and now he will be allowed to see Irene Adler perform again upon the stage. Quite how she has contrived to involve herself in the play, I have no earthly idea."

I looked down at the pamphlet which had been given to me upon entry. The pantomime to be performed was to be *Beauty and the Beast*, and the lurid picture showed a fair, white-gowned woman in the centre of a ring of roses, watched by a grotesque simian creature with its paw clutching its heart. Though it occurred to me that Irene Adler's intention may have been to draw parallels between these titular characters and herself and Holmes, it could hardly be the case that she would appear as Beauty. Much promotional effort had been afforded to the casting of Belle Bilton, the variety-hall singer who had married the Earl of Clancarty, otherwise known as Viscount Dunlo, in a secret ceremony the previous year. No doubt this off-stage narrative was responsible for the great excitement among the waiting audience, and perhaps it also appealed to Irene Adler, whose own romantic affairs had threatened to cause such great scandal.

Putting these thoughts aside, I went on, "They are hardly what you might call friends, Mary, and I suspect that neither one of them desires to spend any time with the other in any fashion that others might call companionable."

I did not voice a thought that had come to my mind several times during our wait for the performance to begin. It related to the Adler Variations, and to the 'thefts without theft'. There had been twelve variations of the melody, and though my tally was admittedly idiosyncratic, relying upon Adler having insight into Fridtjof Nansen's case which we had dispatched at the same time as attempting to solve her series of challenges, I had so far counted only eleven instances of 'theft without theft'.

Mary smiled. "I am sure that you are right. Ah, it appears that our third ticket has not gone to waste."

At this, I looked past her to see in the direction she was facing – but I could not see Holmes. The only people I saw in that direction were a fine-looking couple each removing fine cloaks, and a lone woman who was edging in our direction along the row of seats. So strange were the circumstances that it took me several moments to register that I knew her.

"I don't understand," I said as the woman took her place in the seat at Mary's other side. "What on earth are you doing here this evening, Mrs. Hudson?"

The landlady took off her headscarf primly, making a show of having taken offence. She wore a vivid green blouse that reminded me of Toby's elf costume, and a necklace of pearls.

"I was invited, wasn't I?" she said rather haughtily. "It's not often I'm asked to the theatre nowadays, Dr. Watson. I hope you won't begrudge my accepting the invitation at once."

"Who invited you?" I demanded. Then I winced as Mary struck me sharply in the ribs with her elbow, and in a far softer tone I added, "Have you had some communication from Irene Adler?"

"I still don't know who that might be," Mrs. Hudson replied. "And no. It was Mr. Holmes himself who gave me the ticket, and very grateful I am, too. But if I'd have known I'd have to defend myself just for coming here—"

Mary placed a hand on her arm. "My husband does not mean to be rude, Mrs. Hudson. I'm sure he will apologise for interrogating you."

I grumbled a little, but I knew that there was no use in protesting. "I am very sorry," I said, "and I'm delighted that you have been able to join us. Mary tells me that she has heard great things about this performance, and it is a great pleasure to be able to see it on Christmas Eve, no less, and in such charming company."

Mrs. Hudson appeared placated, and she wriggled into her seat, making herself comfortable as the orchestra began to play and the curtains raised.

Though I began by scouring the stage for any sign of Irene Adler – discounting first Lady Dunlo, then the actors playing Beauty's family, then the members of the chorus at the rear of the stage – I soon lost sight of this purpose, and found myself increasingly absorbed by the performance. At the point that Beauty first encountered the Beast, I realised that my wife's hand gripped mine, and when I looked across at an engrossed Mary I saw that her other hand had been grasped by Mrs. Hudson, whose eyes were equally wide. I smiled with satisfaction, and allowed my attention to return to the stage, and resolved to think no more about anything but the enjoyment of the moment.

CHAPTER THIRTY-FOUR

After the pantomime Mrs. Hudson would not listen to our protestations that we ought to return to our own home. It was past eleven o'clock when our cab pulled to a halt outside 221b Baker Street, and we all seemed to share the same sense of giddiness at the unusual circumstances of arriving at the building together, with Mrs. Hudson unlocking the door and letting us in, as if Sherlock Holmes was no presence at all in our lives. In the entrance hall we shook the snow from our coats and then all looked up at the stairwell in silence.

"I was going to invite you for a drink in the kitchen," Mrs. Hudson said. "But there's no denying that it's a sight more comfortable up there."

I added, "And we ought to see if Holmes is about. It still seems unaccountable that he did not show his face at the theatre, even if on this occasion Irene Adler did not perform as we had anticipated."

Mary chuckled. "Let's dispense of the pretence, shall we? We all want to know what he's been up to, and the reason we're all here is because we're determined to find out."

Without any more discussion, we trooped up the stairs. I went first, and at the door I paused and placed my ear against its surface. I heard the distinct murmur of a voice from within.

"What is it?" Mary, who was directly behind me, asked.

"What's going on in there?" Mrs. Hudson hissed.

I waved a hand in an attempt to quieten them – but perhaps the meaning of my gesture was misunderstood. The next thing I knew, they had both pushed me – only lightly, but enough to tip me off-balance – and in turn my body had pressed against the door, making it spring open. All three of us tumbled into the room, narrowly avoiding falling into a heap on the carpet.

"I'm so very sorry—" I began as I stumbled to rise to my feet. I broke off as I looked up to see Holmes in his usual seat by the fire, and no other person present. "Oh. I thought you had company."

Holmes smiled. "Indeed I do."

I helped up first Mary and then Mrs. Hudson, and we made our way to the fireside. It was only now that I saw who Holmes was referring to – that is, the person who he had been addressing when I had listened at the door. Toby sat on the hearth rug directly before my own chair, gazing up at Holmes. He no longer wore his green woollen jerkin or red cap, and his eyes were bright and alert – in short, he appeared fully restored to his usual character.

At once, Mary and Mrs. Hudson fell upon the creature, stroking and petting him.

Holmes watched them indulgently, then looked up at me and said, "Did you enjoy the performance?"

"Very much," I said. "We all did."

"We missed you, though," Mary added, and I heard an unmistakeable hint of mischief in her voice.

"And you?" I asked him. "I hope your evening has been spent profitably?"

Holmes smiled and nodded. There was a look in his eyes I have rarely seen before; calmness in place of the usual fire.

I hesitated before asking my next question, fearful of breaking the spell. "And what of Irene Adler? She did not appear onstage as we had expected."

"I was correct to say that she would not stoop to repeating herself. The three tickets were an attempt to set me off course. She was once again fulfilling the role of Dolos, or Mendacius the trickster – or, if you like, the role of the conjurer in that remarkable painting that hangs in the British Museum, which seemed to take her fancy."

I nodded slowly. "Then might she have—What I mean to ask is, if she wasn't at the theatre to-night, I wonder if, well…"

Mary stood. She put her hands on her hips and said bluntly, "He's trying to ask if you met Irene Adler this evening."

Holmes's eyes glimmered. "A direct meeting? That does not strike me as consistent with her behaviour at all."

"Holmes," I snapped. "Surely the time for riddles is now over. You have completed her challenge, and let me remind you that all three of us here in this room assisted you in one way or another. I think that you owe us an explanation."

But Holmes only gazed up at me tranquilly, and to my shock I realised that his manner was precisely as unhurried and unoccupied as that of Toby the dog. As if to make this association even more unavoidable, Holmes patted his thighs twice, and Toby bounded up into his lap, writhed happily for a few seconds, then settled himself there contentedly. Holmes bent his head to murmur to the dog in the same soft voice that I had heard from outside the room.

Mrs. Hudson giggled and Mary came to my side, holding my arm, perhaps understanding that this series of events had left me decidedly light-headed.

"How lovely to be all together to-night," Mrs. Hudson said brightly.

To my amazement, Holmes laughed and said, "Indeed, Mrs. Hudson. A very merry Christmas to you."

Mary added, "I should have made the invitation sooner, John and I would be very pleased if you would both join us at our house for Christmas Day."

Mrs. Hudson clapped her hands and gave a squeak of delight, and Holmes nodded his approval far more readily than I might ordinarily have imagined. In response to my raised eyebrow, Mary said, "Do not worry, John. I have ordered a larger turkey than usual. It is not only Irene Adler who is capable of seeing far ahead."

"I think a toast is in order," Holmes said. He ushered Toby from his lap, then went to a cabinet and produced a carafe of brandy and three glasses, and poured one for each of us.

"Will you not have one yourself?" I asked.

Holmes nodded. He moved away and took from the side table beside his chair a glass that already contained a little brandy. To my surprise, I saw beside it another glass – which was empty. Upon the table was also a curled piece of stiff paper.

We received our drinks and raised our glasses in a toast.

"To friends, present and absent," I said.

The spirits went to my head immediately. I found myself laughing. In response to the looks of askance from all about, I said, "I suppose you will say that nobody has been here this evening, Holmes?"

Holmes bowed his head.

"In that case," I went on, "there has been a twelfth theft after all." I went to the side table and pushed at the curled piece of paper, then gestured at the glass. "It appears that somebody has stolen some of your brandy, Holmes – and since you deny anybody has been here, it is surely a 'theft without theft'. Alternatively, is the twelfth theft more related to the bon-bons that are missing from this pulled Christmas cracker? Such things are hardly to your taste, so I will not accept that you have consumed them yourself. Or was something more significant taken from these premises this evening?"

"I rather think you are looking for a strict pattern where none exists," Holmes replied genially. "I would encourage you to accept that not every puzzle requires a neat solution."

I gaped at him in astonishment. Sherlock Holmes was the very last person I might have expected to suggest chaos as an explanation, as opposed to order, and I could not accept that the concept of the twelve thefts of Christmas had been purely my own invention. Then it struck me that perhaps Irene Adler's teasing had affected my friend more profoundly than I had realised, and that, for now, on this rare evening of quiet contentment, he had allowed himself to accept events simply as they appeared.

Holmes picked up the additional glass and put it away. I had the distinct impression that in turning away he was attempting to hide a smile.

I looked at my wife, hoping that at this moment we might perform one of those silent exchanges of information common to married couples of like mind. However, Mary appeared entirely unconcerned by Holmes's unusual behaviour. She strolled to the mantelpiece and took from it a Christmas card – one of only two, the other being the card that I had delivered to Holmes at the beginning of this most recent adventure. She opened the newer card, smirked, and then passed it to me.

At once, I understood that this simple card was Holmes's true prize for completing the devious series of challenges. The picture on the front was a printed engraving of a man clad in a loose garment rather like a Roman toga, standing upon bare rock, his arm outstretched and clutching a flaming torch. He could be none other than Prometheus, delivering fire from the gods to humankind – which was another example of theft, I noted for the first time, though the imparting of wisdom that it represented hardly fit Adler's conception of 'theft without theft'. Beneath the engraving was written in neat typescript – in blue ink which was doubtless an Underwood brand, and the

characters stamped by a Remington No. 5 – the familiar words
from Shelley's play:

"Neither to change, nor falter, nor repent;
This, like thy glory, Titan, is to be
Good, great and joyous, beautiful and free;
This is alone Life, Joy, Empire and Victory."

I stared at the picture for some time, experiencing a vicarious
thrill at Holmes having achieved his goal, and now, on this
convivial Christmas Eve, I finally dispensed of all cynicism about
the lengthy errands that had been required for him to gain it.

Overleaf were written no complete words, only a carefully
inscribed letter 'I' in the lower-right corner. But it was not this
that most startled me. The greater part of the interior of the card
was taken up by another picture – and this one was not printed
but sketched quite skilfully in pencil. It depicted a well-dressed
woman whose pose evoked the version of Veritas that had been
defaced in the British Museum, her arms raised as she reclined
upon a seat. I looked up to determine that it was none other
than Holmes's own chair.

What I could not tell, though, and the question I have
never since found the courage to ask Holmes, is the matter of
the author of this singular image; that is, whether or not it was
drawn by his own hand.

AUTHOR'S NOTE

Much of the detail relating to Fridtjof and Eva Nansen is drawn from two books: Nansen's own *The First Crossing of Greenland* and Roland Huntford's biography *Nansen*. Nansen's account of his expedition inspired other aspects of this novel, too: for instance, though I have no record of his spoken English, I've based his tendency to deploy the present tense on the writing style in his own book.

Nansen did visit London, during which time he met the Prince of Wales and addressed the Royal Geographical Society, though this was in June 1889 rather than December 1890. However, as he became engaged to Eva Sars only in August 1889, she was not actually present during this visit.

Some of the interactions of this husband and wife are also drawn directly from real life. For example, Eva Nansen in February 1892 wrote, *You remember always that I will be coming with you to the North Pole? Otherwise, it'll be all up with me.* By the time Nansen and his new expedition team left Christiania on board the *Fram* on 24th June 1893, he and Eva had had a child and she was forced to remain at home after all.

While many aspects of the Greenland expedition described in this book reflect Nansen's own recollections, all of Nansen's expedition team members that feature in this novel are invented, though their number and some of their roles are consistent with the real team. Henrik and Lise Gylling are entirely fictitious.

The statue of Veritas is not based on any particular statue. There exist five painted versions of Hieronymus Bosch's *The Conjurer* and one engraving, but as far as I know, the British Museum has never exhibited any of them, though there are Bosch sketches of other scenes in its collection.

The first performance at the Theatre Royal is entirely invented, but the theatre did put on a pantomime of *Beauty and the Beast* in 1890, and the details about Belle Bilton and Viscount Dunlo are true.

The characters of Edward and Emilie 'Lillie' Langtry are fictitious, though their names are not: Lillie Langtry was an actress popularly known by the stage name 'The Jersey Lily', who was involved in a series of scandals including an affair with Prince Louis of Battenberg. Holmesian scholars have suggested that she may have been Sir Arthur Conan Doyle's inspiration for Irene Adler.

ACKNOWLEDGEMENTS

This novel was written in a flurry during which time I barely looked up from my work, so my thanks are due to quite a select group of people. Firstly, thanks to Cat Camacho, my editor, who has been the most wonderful collaborator throughout the writing of this novel and my other Sherlock Holmes tales. Secondly, thanks to the wider team at Titan Books, who are all terrific. Finally, thanks as always to my family – Rose, Joe and Arthur – because when I *did* look up from my work, they're the people I was grateful to see.

ABOUT THE AUTHOR

Tim Major lives and writes continually in York. His books include Sherlock Holmes novels *The Defaced Men* and *The Back to Front Murder*, weird science-fiction novels *Hope Island* and *Snakeskins*, short story collection *And the House Lights Dim* and a monograph about the 1915 silent crime film, *Les Vampires*. Tim's short fiction has been selected for *Best of British Science Fiction*, *Best of British Fantasy* and *The Best Horror of the Year*. He blogs at timjmajor.com and tweets @timjmajor.

SHERLOCK HOLMES AND THE THREE WINTER TERRORS

JAMES LOVEGROVE

1889. The First Terror. At a boys' prep school in the Kent marshes, a pupil is found drowned in a pond. Could this be the fulfilment of a witch's curse from over two hundred years earlier?

1890. The Second Terror. A wealthy man dies of a heart attack at his London townhouse. Was he really frightened to death by ghosts?

1894. The Third Terror. A body is discovered in the dark woods near a Surrey country manor, hideously ravaged. Is the culprit a cannibal, as the evidence suggests?

These three chilling and strangely linked crimes test Sherlock Holmes's deductive powers, and his scepticism about the supernatural, to the limit.

"Another Holmes masterpiece" - BookReporter

TITANBOOKS.COM

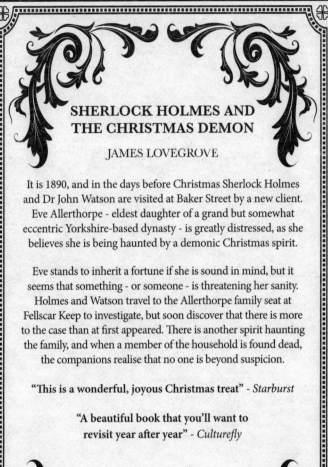

SHERLOCK HOLMES AND THE CHRISTMAS DEMON

JAMES LOVEGROVE

It is 1890, and in the days before Christmas Sherlock Holmes and Dr John Watson are visited at Baker Street by a new client. Eve Allerthorpe - eldest daughter of a grand but somewhat eccentric Yorkshire-based dynasty - is greatly distressed, as she believes she is being haunted by a demonic Christmas spirit.

Eve stands to inherit a fortune if she is sound in mind, but it seems that something - or someone - is threatening her sanity. Holmes and Watson travel to the Allerthorpe family seat at Fellscar Keep to investigate, but soon discover that there is more to the case than at first appeared. There is another spirit haunting the family, and when a member of the household is found dead, the companions realise that no one is beyond suspicion.

"This is a wonderful, joyous Christmas treat" - *Starburst*

"A beautiful book that you'll want to revisit year after year" - *Culturefly*

TITANBOOKS.COM

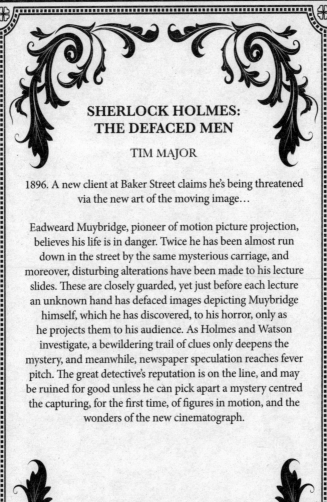

SHERLOCK HOLMES: THE DEFACED MEN

TIM MAJOR

1896. A new client at Baker Street claims he's being threatened via the new art of the moving image…

Eadweard Muybridge, pioneer of motion picture projection, believes his life is in danger. Twice he has been almost run down in the street by the same mysterious carriage, and moreover, disturbing alterations have been made to his lecture slides. These are closely guarded, yet just before each lecture an unknown hand has defaced images depicting Muybridge himself, which he has discovered, to his horror, only as he projects them to his audience. As Holmes and Watson investigate, a bewildering trail of clues only deepens the mystery, and meanwhile, newspaper speculation reaches fever pitch. The great detective's reputation is on the line, and may be ruined for good unless he can pick apart a mystery centred the capturing, for the first time, of figures in motion, and the wonders of the new cinematograph.

TITANBOOKS.COM

SHERLOCK HOLMES:
THE BACK TO
FRONT MURDER

TIM MAJOR

May 1898: Sherlock Holmes investigates a murder stolen from
a writer's research.

Abigail Moone presents an unusual problem at Baker Street.
She is a writer of mystery stories under a male pseudonym,
and gets her ideas following real people and imagining how
she might kill them and get away with it. It's made her very
successful, until her latest "victim" dies, apparently of the
poison method she meticulously planned in her notebook.
Abigail insists she is not responsible, and that someone is trying
to frame her for his death. With the evidence stacking up
against her, she begs Holmes to prove her innocence…

TITANBOOKS.COM

SHERLOCK HOLMES:
A DETECTIVE'S LIFE

EDITED BY MARTIN ROSENSTOCK

A brand-new collection of twelve Sherlock Holmes short stories that spans Holmes's entire career, from the early days in Baker Street to retirement on the South Downs.

Penned by masters of the genre, these Sherlock stories feature a woman haunted by the ghost of a rival actress, Moriarty's son looking for revenge, Oscar Wilde's lost manuscript, a woman framing her husband for murder, Mycroft's encounter with Moriarty and Colonel Moran, and many more!

Featuring stories by:

Peter Swanson
Cara Black
James Lovegrove
Andrew Lane
Philip Purser-Hallard
David Stuart Davies

Eric Brown
Amy Thomas
Derrick Belanger
Cavan Scott
Stuart Douglas
David Marcum

TITANBOOKS.COM

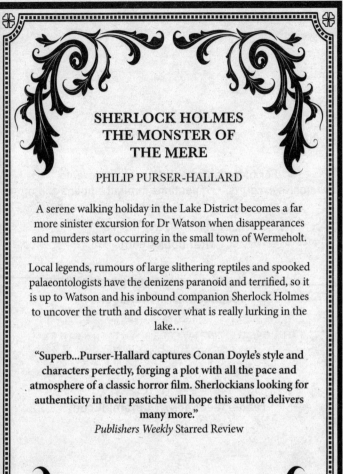

SHERLOCK HOLMES THE MONSTER OF THE MERE

PHILIP PURSER-HALLARD

A serene walking holiday in the Lake District becomes a far more sinister excursion for Dr Watson when disappearances and murders start occurring in the small town of Wermeholt.

Local legends, rumours of large slithering reptiles and spooked palaeontologists have the denizens paranoid and terrified, so it is up to Watson and his inbound companion Sherlock Holmes to uncover the truth and discover what is really lurking in the lake…

"Superb…Purser-Hallard captures Conan Doyle's style and characters perfectly, forging a plot with all the pace and atmosphere of a classic horror film. Sherlockians looking for authenticity in their pastiche will hope this author delivers many more."
Publishers Weekly Starred Review

TITANBOOKS.COM

For more fantastic fiction, author events,
exclusive excerpts, competitions, limited editions and more

VISIT OUR WEBSITE
titanbooks.com

LIKE US ON FACEBOOK
facebook.com/titanbooks

FOLLOW US ON TWITTER AND INSTAGRAM
@TitanBooks

EMAIL US
readerfeedback@titanemail.com